AUG - - 2009

SWAP

Also by John McFetridge

Dirty Sweet

Everybody Knows This Is Nowhere

SWAP

JOHN McFETRIDGE

ECW Press

Copyright © John McFetridge, 2009

Published by ECW PRESS
2120 Queen Street East, Suite 200, Toronto, Ontario, Canada M4E 1E2
416.694.3348 / info@ecwpress.com

LIBRARY AND ARCHIVES CANADA CATALOGUING IN PUBLICATION

McFetridge, John, 1959–
Swap / John McFetridge.

ISBN 978-1-55022-814-4

I. Title.

PS8575.F48S93 2009   C813'.6   C2009-902517-5

Editor for the Press: Michael Holmes
Cover and Text Design: Tania Craan
Cover Image: © Tal Paz-Fridman / Arcangel Images
Typesetting: Mary Bowness
Printing: Friesens   1   2   3   4   5

This book is set in Sabon and Bubba Love, and is printed on paper made of
100% post-consumer waste content.

The publication of *Swap* has been generously supported by the Canada
Council for the Arts, which last year invested $20.1 million in writing and
publishing throughout Canada, by the Ontario Arts Council, by the
Government of Ontario through Ontario Book Publishing Tax Credit, by the
OMDC Book Fund, an initiative of the Ontario Media Development
Corporation, and by the Government of Canada through the Book Publishing
Industry Development Program (BPIDP).

Canada Council   Conseil des Arts
for the Arts   du Canada   Canada   ONTARIO ARTS COUNCIL
                                           CONSEIL DES ARTS DE L'ONTARIO

PRINTED AND BOUND IN CANADA

ECW PRESS
ecwpress.com

For Laurie, Always

CHAPTER ONE

COMING OFF THE AMBASSADOR BRIDGE into Canada, Vernard pulled up to the customs booth, the sign saying it was the longest international suspension bridge in the world. The tunnel would've been faster, but there was no way he was going underground, under*water*, gave him the willies, worse than all those caves in Afghanistan.

The Canadian customs guy looked at him and Vernard nodded, serious, seeing the guy's Glock, thinking, shit, these guys just started carrying guns a couple months ago, probably couldn't get it out of his holster. Fucking Canada.

The guy asked him all the questions, how long he was staying, was he an American citizen, carrying any firearms? Vernard showed him his driver's licence and his Armed Forces ID, blue for retired — honourable discharge, Sergeant Vernard McGetty. Said, "Not any more."

"What's the purpose of your trip?"

Get said it was a vacation. "I'm going to the film festival."

The guy said, oh yeah, and it's not business?

Vernard said, yeah, "I'm Jamie Foxx."

The guy actually laughed and said have a nice trip, waving him through, twenty-eight-year-old black guy from Detroit driving a brand-new Mercedes ML370 SUV, leather interior and twelve-speaker surround on his way to Toronto to meet with some bikers, sell them a truckload of Uncle Sam's guns and set up a pipeline for their coke and weed back to Detroit, stepping up to the big leagues.

Fucking Canada.

Looking back he saw the U.S. customs guys just waving people through, too; cars and vans and campers and trucks. Fucking trucks, must be thousands a day, going back and forth, couldn't check them all. Couldn't check two per cent of them.

Shit, Vernard was thinking, turning up his system loud, Little Walter finding his Key to the Highway, it's easier to cross this border into another country than it is to cross Mack Ave into Grosse Pointe.

Through Windsor it was all Taco Bells and KFC and Burger King, didn't seem like another country at all except for the place selling Cuban coffee, Vernard thinking, right, that's not the only thing from Cuba in there.

Outside of Windsor this part of Canada was flat and bleak, farms, gas stations, fast-food places, and lots of traffic. Vernard was surprised there could be this much open space so close to Detroit, a foreign goddamn country, and you'd never know it was there.

Four-hour drive, Detroit to Toronto, six lanes of steady traffic going in both directions.

An hour in Vernard pulled into a gas station. Filled up and parked in the back behind the Wendy's with all the trucks, shit, looked like hundreds of them all lined up. He went inside and saw the guy he wanted sitting there eating a cheeseburger and drinking a shake.

"You keep this up, you might get fat."

The guy, three hundred pounds at least, his whole face smiled, shaking his big bald black head, standing up and saying, "Fucking Get, man, they let you in this motherfucking country?" They hugged, backslapping, and sat down across from each other in the little plastic seats.

"Saw your cousin on the news, man."

The big guy, once Corporal Duane Thomkins, now just Tommy K, looked off into the distance. "She so fine, all the reporters want to talk to her, all dressed up in her fatigues."

Vernard, sliding easy now back to being just Get, said, "They knew what she was sending home, man, blow they muthafucking minds."

"You know it." Tommy laughed out loud. Then he said, "Eat up, man, next stop is all Mickey Dees."

3

"I'll wait till I get there."

They walked out back to the truck lot behind the restaurant, stopping to look at Get's new car, Tommy saying, "Motherfucking German-ass piece of shit, man. Drive American."

"What do you drive?"

"Fucking Peterbilt, man, 370, air ride, MP3, DVD, got a satellite map, goddamn double bed. Look at these sorry-ass motherfuckers; Volvos, Swedish fucking bullshit, Hino, what the fuck kind of rice paddy piece of shit is Hino?"

Get said, "You're loyal, Tommy, patriotic. That's cool."

They got to Tommy's red Peterbilt hooked to a fifty-three-foot trailer and he opened the door, saying, "Fucking right I'm patriotic, man. Where'd we be without Uncle Sam?" Climbed into the sleeper and came out with a dark green duffle bag.

Get didn't even look in the bag, he just hucked it over his shoulder feeling the weight, nodding, yeah. "We'd be some sorry-ass niggers."

Tommy said, "No hassle at the border?"

"Guy was happy to see me," Get said. "But you never know, next time they could tear my car apart."

"Shine that fucking Maglite up your ass."

Get said, oh man, don't even joke.

Tommy smiled again, that full of life-is-good enthusiasm, and said, "Don't sweat it, a million trucks a day, they can't look at every one. You got somebody crosses here every week," and winked. Then he said, "There's only one can."

"Yeah?" Anybody else Get would have given a hard time, matter of respect, but not Tommy. Get was the boss, but Tommy would never really be an employee. "Guess I just have to shoot the motherfuckers one at a time."

Tommy said, yeah, make every shot count.

Get said, "You going to Toronto?"

"The Big Smoke?"

"What?"

Tommy laughed. "Assholes call it that, looking for a name, be cool, play with the big boys."

Get hefted the bag, said, they playing with the big boys now.

"They don't even know it. Naw, man, I'm going to Montreal. Some fine French chicks there. And the food, shit, food alone's worth the drive. You should come."

"Maybe next time."

"You say that, man, but you all business, never take a break. You still that skinny-ass nigger on the bike."

"Yeah, but the Army made a man out of me."

Tommy laughed and gave him a hug, saying, "You

fucking funny, you know it. Shit. Your mama be proud."

"Thanks man."

"Don't have to thank me," Tommy said. "You paying me."

Get said, yeah, but you're worth it.

Tommy got into his rig and started it up, saying, "Every penny." He blew the air horn on his way out, and Get walked back to his car, his German-ass SUV.

Three hours to Toronto, see what it's like, this Big Smoke, wants to play with the big boys. Meet with these bikers think they're running the show, sell them this weaponry, see if they really can deliver the meth and X and coke and the tons of weed they say they can.

Get felt good, ready to really step up, make some changes in the Motor City, make his mama proud.

● ● ●

5

They walked into McVeigh's, Andre Price the only black guy in the place, thinking every black guy who ever came in was carrying a badge and gun.

At least a gun.

He said to McKeon, "Good thing I have my Irish escort."

She sat down with her back to the wall under two rows of black-and-white pictures of men's faces, looked like blown-up mug shots to Price, and said, "I'm the wrong kind of Irish."

He said, shit, it was just too complicated.

A young guy maybe twenty-five, tattoos on both fore-arms, came over to the table and asked them if they wanted to see menus and Price said, no, just something to drink. "Guinness, I guess, that's the one, right?"

McKeon asked for a cup of coffee and when the young guy left Price said, wouldn't that keep her up all night, and McKeon said, "It's not even midnight yet, you think we'll be going home anytime soon?"

"If we don't catch something, we'll punch out." Price looked around the bar, first time he'd ever been in and that surprised him, here it was right downtown, corner of Richmond and Church, but it was real Irish, not tourist, not a Ye Olde pub. The walls were covered with those pictures that looked like mug shots and a framed newspaper page that said "Provisional Government of the Irish Republic to the People of Ireland" across the top and was filled with text.

McKeon said, "Here she is," and Price turned to see an East Indian woman in her twenties wearing jeans and a grey hoodie coming towards them. She got to the table at the same time as the waiter and they smiled at each other. She ordered a half of Smithwicks and sat down.

She said, "Thanks for meeting me here, detective," looking at McKeon and then at Price, saying, "detective," again.

"Call me Maureen, okay? Muneera, right?"

"Yes."

Price watched the two women, wondering how this would work, all these relationships. He and McKeon were partners, but McKeon and this Constable Muneera Anjilvel were both women cops; he and Anjilvel were both black, or at least brown, faces in the very Irish bar, but McKeon said she was the wrong kind of Irish.

The waiter came back with Anjilvel's half pint, a lot lighter colour than Price's Guinness, he didn't know if Smithwicks was Irish beer or not, and the look between the waiter and Anjilvel, both in their twenties, seemed like the start of a connection.

Shit, it was too complicated. Price figured he'd just sit back and watch.

Anjilvel was looking around, nervous, so McKeon skipped the small talk and got right to it, asking her why the secret meeting.

"All the shit that's happened," Anjilvel said. "Crazy."

Price watched her looking nervous, conflicted, but he didn't think she really was. The Toronto police were in the middle of a huge internal investigation, eight of their own guys arrested by the Mounties and everybody else under suspicion. But still, his read was that Anjilvel wasn't sneaking around because she didn't know what to do. He thought she was really sure about something. A lot of things.

She said, "I really appreciate this," and McKeon nodded, looking right at her.

"Okay. Here's the thing. Remember last week, that guy died at the hotel?"

"Dealer from Buffalo, got shot five times?"

"No, the other one."

McKeon said, "Guy his girlfriend killed, stabbed him?"

Anjilvel said, no, the car salesman. "Up by the airport. Drug overdose."

McKeon said, no, they didn't really know about that one. "Wasn't a homicide."

Price watched Anjilvel nod to herself, that look like she knows something you don't. Or maybe that she knows something she wishes she didn't. She said, okay. Drank some beer, put the glass down and said, "It's probably nothing."

McKeon said, "Start at the beginning," like she was talking to a witness.

7

Price thinking, first witness, first suspect.

"Okay. I'm riding with Brewski, right?"

"We're all sorry about that," McKeon said.

"Right. So, we get the call, guy's drunk or stoned or something. He's walking around the hotel smashing stuff. Those lights on the walls, the emergency exit lights, anything that'll smash. So we get there and we stop him."

"You and Brewski?"

Anjilvel looked at McKeon like it was a joke, but no one was laughing or smiling. "Me and Brewski. He actually got out of the car, came into the hotel, they got a bar in the lobby. So, I get the guy under control, you know. Once he's cuffed he calms down. He's crying and his feet are bleeding but he's not in bad shape. Tells me he's in trouble, deep shit, he doesn't know what to do."

Price said, "But he's stoned, right?"

"Oh yeah, he's dazed and confused. But he's scared. Oh, and he's naked, did I say that?"

McKeon, drinking her coffee, said, no, you didn't mention that.

"Well, he was. And one of the drugs he took was Viagra."

Price said, "Uh-huh."

"Yeah. It's not really relevant, though. I mean, it didn't come into play."

McKeon said, "In a manner of speaking," and Anjilvel looked up like maybe it was a joke she was supposed to laugh at.

She didn't, she just said, "Anyway, once he's calmed down, Brewski comes out of the bar and we take the guy up to his room. I figure we'll let him get dressed, take him to the hospital. The guy was looking okay, he took a cold shower."

8

"He was okay?"

"He was calmed down, his breathing was good, steady, he was coherent."

"You take him to the hospital?"

She shook her head. Drank some more beer.

Price leaned back in his chair holding his pint of Guinness. He liked it, nice and dark and cold. He thought it was supposed to be warm, room temperature or something, but maybe that was English beers. He was only starting to figure out the difference.

Anjilvel said, "Then the detectives got there."

"Who?"

Anjilvel looked like she didn't want to say. She drank some beer and nodded, then said, "Okay. Detective Roxon and Detective Keirans."

"Who called them?"

"I don't know."

Price said, okay, so?

"So, they said we could leave, they'd take it from there."

McKeon said, "Yeah, and?"

"And we left. Next day I hear the guy was DOA at Humber General. Overdose."

Price looked at McKeon, drank some of the Guinness, and said, "Well, a drug overdose."

Anjilvel said, "I just thought, you know, I should tell someone."

"No, that was the right thing to do," McKeon said. "It's the right thing."

"It's probably nothing."

Price thought, yeah, right, nothing. Or it could be exactly what it looked like. He said, "Did the guy know them?"

"Called them by name."

McKeon said, "Okay, the thing now is, sit tight. Let us look into this."

Price's phone beeped and he answered it.

Anjilvel looked at McKeon like they were the only two people in the place and said, "You'll keep me out of it."

"You don't say another word to anyone."

Anjilvel said, okay, good. "I haven't even said anything to Brewski, I don't think he even knows the guy died."

Price hung up and said, "We have to go." He finished off his beer, stood up, and dropped a twenty on the table.

Anjilvel stayed put, said she was working midnight to eight, maybe she'd get something to eat before she punched in, and Price noticed the waiter bringing over a menu as they left, wondered if he'd flirt so much, he knew she was a cop.

10

• • •

The on-ramp to the Gardiner Expressway was closed; a fire truck, an ambulance, and a cop car blocking the way, and uniformed men and women from all of them standing around smoking.

McKeon popped the siren a couple times and flashed the headlights to clear a path in the traffic and pulled right up to the ramp on Lake Shore, under the expressway.

One of the uniformed cops, a guy in his fifties, said, "McKeon, you're going to love this."

She was already out of the car walking towards the scene saying, "I am?"

The uniform, Dixon, said oh yeah, this is a good one. "Guy was driving up the ramp, see?" The car, a brand-new Dodge 300 with the big front grille and the little windows making it look like a thirties gangster car, had gotten halfway up the ramp, stopped, and rolled back, turning sharply so its back end was against the left side and its front end against the right, blocking the road.

Dixon said, "And pow, somebody shoots him in the head."

Closer now, McKeon and Price could see the passenger window covered in blood splatter and the driver's head flopped onto the steering wheel.

McKeon saw the woman's body, waist up on the passenger seat, the rest of her on the floor, like she was kneeling and slid off, as Dixon was saying, "Then they popped the chick."

Price said, "Holy shit."

Dixon was laughing. "You know it, detective."

McKeon walked around to where the driver's side door was open and said, "His pants are down."

"And," Dixon said, "get a load of her outfit, love the fishnets. Getting a little road head, eh, couldn't wait to get to the room."

Another uniform cop standing beside the car, younger than Dixon but otherwise looked just the same, said, "Or getting his money's worth on the way."

McKeon said to Price, "Great." She looked at the uniforms. "What's the ID say?"

"No idea."

"You sure they're dead?"

"VSA, detective, that's what the pros tell us." He pointed to the firemen and ambulance guys leaning against their rigs drinking coffee. Vital Signs Absent.

McKeon said, You're really working hard tonight, and the younger uniform said, Hey, it's a crime scene, detective.

"Once they said they were dead we didn't want to disturb anything."

McKeon said, "Right," and leaned into the car. She didn't see a gun anywhere, but thought, you never know. She picked up the woman's white leather purse from the floor of the car, had to pull it out from under the woman's butt, miniskirt slid up, nothing on underneath but a garter belt. Close up like this McKeon saw the woman was older than she thought, had to be mid to late forties, in good shape, showing off a very nice body in her miniskirt and expensive silk top, push-up bra, little leather boots, at least five-inch spike heels.

McKeon stood up, opened the purse, and said, "Jesus Christ."

Price, walking back from checking the computer in the unmarked, looked over her shoulder and said, "Yeah, that's it, registered to a Michael Lowrie, Mississauga."

McKeon, looking at the driver's licence from the purse, said, "Sandra Lowrie. Wife?"

"Looks like it. Guy's got no record, nothing outstanding, not even a parking ticket."

"Shit."

The tech guys arrived and went right to work. McKeon — it was her turn, she was the lead, what they called the major case manager, trying to make it sound like a normal day at the office — watched them get started. She said, Hey, to Cruickshank, the senior guy, and let him do his job.

Then she flipped through the wallet. Credit cards, video store card, library card, pictures of the kids. McKeon said, "Oh shit." Two kids, teenagers, a boy and a girl, and another girl, maybe six. Pictures taken on a beach somewhere, the five of them. Then a couple more pictures on a ski hill.

McKeon said, "Domestic? Murder-suicide? Kills her, then himself?"

Price said, "No man would kill his wife while she's doing that."

"Yeah." McKeon looked around at the line of cars inching along Lake Shore, looking for the next on-ramp, all the people straining to see the crime scene. "And I don't see a gun."

Cruickshank, the tech guy, said, "Sorry to disappoint, detectives, but the shots were fired from outside the car."

Price said, Come on now, Shanks, "You know we can make the evidence say anything we want."

Cruickshank kept taking pictures, walking around the car, saying, "Right, forgot about that, detective."

Price walked up and down the ramp, the few feet from the car with the victims in it to the police car. He stopped and said, "So they come up the ramp here, heading out for the suburbs, someone comes alongside and pops them. Why?"

McKeon asked Dixon and the other uniform about witnesses, and they both shrugged.

Dixon said, "Kids called it in," pointing to an SUV at the bottom of the ramp. "Said it was like this when they got here."

Price said, "This is one of the busiest streets in the city, ramp to one of the busiest expressways. No one saw it happen?"

"No one who stuck around. We got here like a minute after they called it in."

"You were so close? I don't see a Tim Hortons around here."

"What can I say, we're good."

McKeon said, "Look, people live under this express-

13

way, someone must have seen something."

Dixon said, "Nada, detective."

McKeon said, "Ask again."

When he was gone McKeon said, "Road rage?"

"There's some traffic cameras around here, we'll see what we can find." Price shook his head. "But it doesn't look like there's any damage other than hitting the wall after the shooting."

"So," McKeon said, "guy's driving home, the wife's going down on him, and somebody kills them?"

"Maybe it's personal, affair or something."

"Happened pretty fast, guy knew what he was doing. Doesn't look like he wasted any shots."

"How do we know it's a guy?"

McKeon said, "Shit, the kids. I'd like to keep the details out of it."

Price said, Yeah? "What are the chances?" He motioned to where Dixon was standing beside a van with a TV station logo all over it, some kind of Action News.

"Great."

Price said, okay, first thing, get the scene cleared up. "And we better go see the kids."

McKeon said yeah. Then she said, "What about Anjilvel's thing?"

"What about it?"

"You want to do anything about it?"

Price had the passenger door to their car open and he said, Slow down. "Let's just have one big giant crappy thing on our plates at a time."

McKeon said, "Okay, sure. If that's all you want."

● ● ●

Boner couldn't fucking believe it.

He figured by the time he got to the club it would be a funny story, ha ha, but he was going to look bad, no doubt.

He picked up the guy fine, coming out of the condo building at the bottom of Yonge Street right by the lake — had that thing in front was supposed to be art, looked like a twenty-five-foot-high egg beater — and watched him cross the street to the parking lot and get into a brand-new Dodge 300, just like J.T. said, silver with the little windows. Boner liked the car, it looked like Al Capone's shit or something.

The parking lot was big, right next to a huge boat been turned into a restaurant, Captain John's, and there were a lot of cars coming out at the same time, and Boner lost him.

But only for a couple of seconds, then he picked him up again a block away on Lake Shore, that road under the expressway. The guy was heading for the on-ramp, which Boner figured was perfect, catch him there, do it, and just keep going. And it went perfect, he pulled right up beside the guy and shot him in the head, easy. The MK9, Army-issue Colt J.T. got from his buddy, the black guy he brought up from Detroit, with the silencer on it — what the guy called a can — made hardly any sound at all and no flash.

But then as he was pulling away, she sat up.

Some chick in the car, and Boner knew that was wrong because J.T. said he was leaving the hooker's condo, and Boner saw the guy walk to the parking lot and get into his car alone.

Boner shot her, too, a couple of times and then stepped on it. In the rear-view he saw the Dodge roll back and block the ramp. Perfect. Would have been perfect if it had been the right fucking guy.

15

He was past Jameson heading west out of town before he started to laugh, realizing he shot the guy because she was going down on him, Boner didn't know the chick was in the car. The wrong fucking car. If she'd been sitting up he'd have known.

It actually was funny.

He got off the expressway and back onto Lake Shore heading east into town, to the clubhouse, thinking now he'd still have to find the guy and do him, tell J.T. it still wasn't done. Still be a prospect for another month.

Getting to be a full patch with these guys not as easy as it looked.

CHAPTER TWO

NUGS SAID, "OKAY BOYS, LET'S GO. These crimes don't
commit themselves," and the guys laughed, walking out
the door. Some of them said they were going to Jackie's
and Get didn't know who that was till J.T. said it was a
tittie bar a few blocks away.

Get was still trying to see who was who here.

He'd met J.T. in Afghanistan, the guy was with the
Canadian forces but he seemed more like a freelancer,
setting up deals and talking to all the private-company
security he could. At first Get thought he was just another
clueless Canadian, but then he saw the guy could really
deliver, get rid of the middleman, set him up with some
guys out in the mountains could ship more dope in a day
than he could sell in a month. Something happened, J.T.'s
cousin got killed or something, and the next thing, they
were shipping J.T. home.

But he'd made a couple of good connections for Get,
and they stayed in touch.

Now here he was practically running this chapter of the bikers in Toronto.

Get wasn't surprised, this J.T. could think on his feet, but these bikers he didn't understand at all. For one thing, they didn't have any bikes. They were driving SUVs and minivans. Hell, the guy with the French accent, sat around and didn't say much, was driving an Audi convertible and wearing a golf shirt and Dockers.

There was even a black guy in the club, guy they called OJ. Get thought he had an accent, maybe Jamaican, but he sure didn't look like any of the Rastas back in Detroit, he was casual, like the token buddy in a sitcom.

J.T. was saying, "I got to meet a chick, you might like her."

Get said, oh yeah, and J.T. said, yeah. Get had no idea what the fuck was going on. It wasn't anything like he expected. The guy he gave the guns to, called him Danny Mac, J.T. introduced as the sergeant-at-arms, like they were back in the fucking Army, and then that guy had him show some kid they called Boner how to screw on the can. J.T. said the kid was a prospect — like he was trying out for the team — and then he came back and said he'd fucked it up, hit the wrong guy. J.T. said, the wrong guy? And the kid told it like a funny story. Then he said he'd get him tomorrow, go up to Woodbridge and shoot the motherfucker at his social club, and J.T. said to hold on, wait a while, he'd let him know, and the kid went to Jackie's tittie bar with the rest of them.

Now J.T. was saying to Get, "Part of it was letting the man's people know we knew where he spent his off time," and Get said he heard that. Half of doing a hit was the message it sent. Get had met J.T. in a parking garage out by the airport and when he handed over the guns he'd got from Tommy, J.T.'d said come on back to the clubhouse, actually said that, the fucking clubhouse, like they were kids. When they got there Get saw it was more like a fort right in the city, had big cement pillars out front and cameras all over it, a reinforced steel door and no windows, like a stash house back home, but it was just in a row with other houses and it had a fucking sign on the front said, "Saints of Hell," so they weren't keeping it a secret.

These guys talked like old-time bikers but they acted like businessmen.

Now J.T. was saying, yeah, this chick. "She used to work the massage parlours, gave the best hand jobs, fucking incredible. Her hand jobs were better than any other chick's blow job."

Get said, what's her blow job like, and J.T. said, "Never could find out."

"No?"

"You do, let me know."

Get said he'd be sure and do that.

J.T. said hang on a minute and went to talk to the French dude.

There was another guy there, Nugs, was the actual national president, also didn't look like a fat biker, he was in shape, had short hair and a clipped goatee. There were some young guys there, older than the corner boys Get used back home, maybe early twenties, getting food and cleaning up. J.T. told him they were hangarounds, what they call the guys do the dirty work before they get to be prospects, which also basically do the dirty work but get a bigger piece for themselves, before they become full patch members, which Get figured was like a made guy in the Mob.

Get had to admit, he was impressed with the organization, not what he expected at all. It was kind of like the

19

Mob, but more equal opportunity. No way a guy like OJ could ever be made.

Like the way they brought Get, paying cash for all that firepower, J.T. offering to show him their operation, see they could be his biggest supplier, help him to really step up back home, take him to a new level. Something Get's mom was really pushing for.

J.T. came back and said, "Okay, let's go."

"Meet the hand job chick?"

"Sunitha, yeah. She's got a new thing."

Get said, okay sure, wondering what the hand job chick's new thing could be.

●　●　●

20 Sunitha Suraiya was thinking she actually could use a day at the spa, would be good, a real massage, a pedicure, manicure, the full wax treatment, then go downtown, hit some clubs and get laid. Maybe one of the Raptors. She wasn't sure the basketball season had started yet, she saw something about hockey on TV but hockey players were such chumps, farm boys and Russians, so tight with their cash.

She was in the passenger seat of the car, a five-year-old BMW M3, parked by the subway station at Yonge and York Mills, Lydia behind the wheel smoking a joint, talking about last night, laughing, saying the guy with the dickdo thought he had a chance.

Sunitha lit a cigarette and said, The what?

"The dickdo. You know, had a belly sticks out more than his dick do."

Sunitha said, "Thought he was going to get with you?"

"Me or White Girl, or both." She inhaled deep, let it

out slow. Lydia was dark, dark-skinned, her long black hair hanging past her shoulders in tight braids.

"Wasn't the problem he had a dick?"

"White Girl still do that sometimes. She's confused."

Sunitha said, Why do you put up with her, and Lydia said, Why do you?

"I'm not fucking her."

"Maybe not that way."

Sunitha was going to say something, what you mean by that, but her phone beeped and she answered it, saying, yeah? She said uh-huh a few times and then, okay, flipping the phone shut. She said, "Okay, she says it's just like the virtual tour on the website, no security for shit."

Lydia had the car started and pulled away.

Sunitha opened the bag at her feet, saying, "They got a room right behind the reception desk they use for lock-up, only the queen bitch gets in."

Two minutes later they were at the front door of the building, looked like an old brick house a block away from Bayview, very upscale. Sunitha had her long black hair pulled back in a tight ponytail and she wrapped it up under a toque and put on sunglasses.

Lydia put on sunglasses.

They got out of the car carrying gym bags and Sunitha said, "That's all?"

"We all look the same to them."

They walked in the front door of the spa, a black woman almost six feet tall and an East Indian woman maybe five-five.

The queen bitch just about shit her nice white dress even before Sunitha pointed the gun at her and told her to be fucking quiet and open the door.

She got it together, saying, you don't want to do this,

21

some kind of European accent Sunitha would bet a hundred was fake, but she unlocked the door. Then she stood there, looking pissed off and holier than shit.

Sunitha said, "What're you waiting for, bitch, get inside," and shoved her in.

The reception area was all white: carpet, walls, desk. There were a few glass shelves with a couple of bottles on them and a few pictures in black frames. The queen bitch matched it perfectly. The locked room was white, too, but there was a desk and a chair, a bunch of shelves and some lockers without any locks.

Lydia said, "That your fucking security?"

Sunitha was tossing purses and wallets into her gym bag, saying, "They're only worried about the staff."

Lydia said, "Cunt."

Sunitha said, "Okay, the cash."

"We don't have any cash, I don't know what you think this place is."

Sunitha put the barrel of the gun on the bare skin between the queen bitch's tits and said, "We know exactly what kind of place this is. Give me the cash."

"In the desk."

Sunitha opened the drawer and took out a black bag not much bigger than the wad of cash inside it and said, "Okay, go."

They dropped the gym bags on the desk and walked down the hall, the receptionist leading the way.

A woman stepped out of the lounge wearing a white robe, almost as white as her skin, and said, "What the hell?"

"Take your rings off."

She got that look like she was talking to a maid and said, "I don't think so," and Lydia punched her in the face, saying, "Don't think, bitch, do it."

The all-white woman screamed and started shaking, her whole skinny body, and Sunitha shoved her down the hall.

A man stepped out of a room, also wearing the white robe over his fake tan, and some kind of rubber hat, looked like a condom, with hair sticking through it.

Sunitha pointed the gun in his face and said, "Be a hero."

He looked like he was going to cry.

They got his rings and a nice gold chain he had around his neck, and they got more jewellery off the rest of the people in the spa. There weren't many, maybe a half a dozen and that included White Girl Brenda, but they took a ring off her too, make it look good.

Sunitha and Lydia were back in the car, in and out in less than ten minutes and gone, east on York Mills and north on the Don Valley Parkway.

Lydia, looking deadly serious, said, "Bitch, that is better than sex."

"Fucking A."

They both laughed.

Lydia said, "Where you get that 'Be a hero' shit?"

"It felt like a movie, didn't it. Like it wasn't real."

"That's cause you stoned."

"Maybe."

"That shit is better than dope. I'm so fucking high, look at me, I'm shaking." She took her hand off the wheel and she really was shaking, driving 120, weaving through the traffic heading out of town.

Sunitha said, "You need a day at the spa, calm yourself," and they started laughing again.

They had it together by the time they got to the condo, Sunitha making them drinks, CC and gingers, and waiting for White Girl Brenda who got there, like, a half hour later, saying the cops acted just like the bitches working there, all sucking up and trying to be nice to the customers.

Lydia said, "Fucking cops."

Brenda, a big-boned girl almost as tall as Lydia, said they should have waited till she had her massage and facial. "And the Brazilian, that chick was smoking hot."

Lydia said, "You two-timing bitch."

"Hey, if they're hot, I'll fuck 'em."

"Glad I'm hot."

They laid out the jewellery and cash. There was almost six grand in the black bag and another three grand from the purses and wallets. The jewellery looked even better.

Sunitha said, "Okay, I'll take this to J.T., see what we can get. You want to come?"

Lydia said, no, that's okay. "We got stuff to do," and she laughed, and White Girl Brenda kissed her hard on the mouth.

• • •

What Big Pete Zichello wanted to know was, who knew he was at Becca's and who wanted to kill him?

He knew plenty of guys wanted to kill him. These bikers, these fucking Saints, taking over everything for starters, or his boss, Angelo Colucci, had a deal with the assholes Big Pete made no secret of hating, and after those city cops killed the car salesman shylock, Kichens, when he offered to wear a wire — it could even be them. But who knew he was at Becca's?

As soon as he saw the thing on the news about the suburban couple shot in their car going up the ramp onto the Gardiner, at the same time he was there, and he saw they were driving the same silver Dodge 300 he was, and nobody had any idea why anyone would kill them, he knew what it meant.

Somebody was trying to kill him.

Problem was, it could be so many people.

So now he was standing in his brother-in-law's car lot on Highway 7 trying to decide what to get. He didn't really need a new car, whoever wanted him would know what he was driving, it's just now the thing was full of bad luck.

Ernie'd showed him a couple of suvs and the new Cadillac and said maybe he'd want to try something Japanese, but Big Pete didn't think so.

Now Ernie came back out saying, "What about a ragtop?" and Big Pete said, no, he didn't like them, too much noise.

"Come on, Ernie, I need a car."

Ernie, as usual, making like it was great he came by, great to see him, but really not wanting him there, trying to get rid of him and dump some piece-of-shit five-year-old BMW.

Since that fucking biker came in from Montreal, French asshole but you could hardly tell, fucking Audi and golf shirts, taking over the whole goddamn country, Colucci looked so old. He was only sixty-something, shit, Big Pete knew guys in their eighties with more balls. This Toronto bullshit, they never really stepped up.

So when the bikers came sniffing around for a deal it was Big Pete told them to shove it up their fucking tailpipes.

Then that fucked-up hit, totally botched, killed some guy taking his kids home from soccer instead of the asshole Eddie Nollo they were after, and Colucci started to talk like it was over, like the bikers had all the muscle and it was time to move on.

Maybe it was time for fucking Colucci to move on, is what Big Pete thought, but he never said anything to anybody. He didn't know what the other captains would do, and the truth was, they didn't have that many soldiers. Big Pete had to take care of Nollo himself, which he did, thank you very much, without a word to anybody. Shit, he was thinking, maybe *he* should make a deal with these bikers.

Looking around the lot, he said to Ernie, "What about that one, the Lexus," and Ernie said he thought he didn't want any Japanese.

"Lexus is Japanese?"

"It's a Toyota, Pete, for Christ's sake."

"I like it."

"It's only six months old."

"I don't care."

"It's only got twenty-five hundred clicks on it, I can't take it on a straight trade."

"What else you need?"

"What do you mean, what else? I need at least ten grand."

Pete said, "I'll give you five, and a week at the spa."

"Janie working?"

"Take your chances."

Ernie said, okay, sure, like Big Pete knew he would. Just another jerk thinking with his dick.

Not like Pete, spending all his time downtown with Becca. When he met her at a party after a Raptors game, she was a Raptor Pack Dancer, she seemed like a fun girl, sexy, and not much bullshit.

So he made a date, made a rare trip downtown to see her. She was smart, she knew right away what he really did, what he was into, and she didn't mind. She was Portuguese, grew up at Dundas and Keele and knew the business. Called herself an actress, too, and she'd been in a couple of commercials, but he figured she still turned a few tricks. He didn't care about that, in fact he liked it when she had her friend over, Stacy, a real pro, a real PSE, Porn Star Experience, and they double-teamed him. He could tell it wasn't the first time they'd done it. But still, Becca's was where he was set up, he'd have to take care of her.

Ernie got a kid to bring the Lexus around, and Big Pete gave him the keys to the Dodge.

Somebody figured out something, and they went after him when he left Becca's place, so that's where he was going to have to start.

Drive all the way downtown, this time in his six-month-old Lexus, only has twenty-five hundred clicks on it.

●　●　●

Get said, the fuck, man. "Take me out here, look at some desperate housewife shit."

They were in J.T.'s Avenger, driving slow through the burb, so quiet at night, and he said, "Don't worry man, these people're so worried about not being American they wouldn't call the cops if you were coming out of the house carrying the flat screen."

Get said, yeah? "Have to take your word for that."

"It's why we're here, nobody ever says anything," and he pulled into a driveway, looked like every other driveway, a minivan parked in front of the garage.

They walked in through the front door, didn't knock or anything.

Get said, "Nice, man, very nice."

27

There were three women sitting in the living room, smoking cigarettes and flipping through magazines. They were all Asian, very good-looking, wearing miniskirts and halter tops, hair all done up, long colourful fingernails and shiny lipstick.

One of the women said, "Hi Mr. J.T., you want fuck?"

Get said, "Yeah, nice."

Now J.T. was saying, which one you want, man, and Get said he didn't know, they all looked so fine. "Any speak English?"

On the way out to the burb J.T. said it was a surprise and Get thought it would be a grow house, these guys doing so much of that now, Get wishing he could do that back home but there was no way his boys could set up in some fucking bungalow in Pontiac, they just drive by the house people start calling the cops.

And a whorehouse? Come on.

J.T. said, "Last year it was massage parlours, we had over a hundred of them, but the fucking cops wanted too much to leave them alone."

"So now this? Who knows it's here?"

"Let them know online. We've got over twenty of these houses up so far. They're really easy for the customers, too, guys are usually right around the corner, you know."

Get said, yeah, easy.

The three Asian chicks were looking at them smiling, no rush. They were in the living room, looked like any suburban living room, a couple of couches facing each other, a fireplace, bay window to the street, curtains closed. Past the living room was a dining room but it had a desk in it instead of a table and chairs, and then the kitchen. The place was clean, smelled nice, MuchMusic on the big screen.

J.T. said, "Hey Belinda, come on, show my friend a good time."

One of the women got up, smiling as she walked towards them, took Get by the hand, leading him upstairs and saying, "You want hot tub?" and Get said, yeah, sure.

"I been on the road."

J.T. said, "Have a good time, my man, enjoy."

Get followed Belinda up the stairs thinking he liked this Toronto, this Big Smoke, he could get used to it.

• • •

Richard Tremblay was pleased the way things were going. In the last year, since they'd won that fucking war in Quebec, wiped out every other biker gang and stepped up against the Italians, made their deal with those Irish bastards at the port and he watched his mentor and number-one guy in the Saints of Hell, Mario "Mon Oncle" Bouchard, get arrested in Montreal along with five other top guys and a whole bunch of crooked cops, they were doing great. The cops who took them all down, a task force made up of Mounties, Toronto and Montreal city cops, and two provincial police forces, were still celebrating.

What they didn't know, the whole thing was put together by Richard, a Mountie, and a couple of Toronto city cops.

Now his whole plan was coming together — exactly the way he'd hoped it would — but he could feel something not right.

He'd rented a condo and was living pretty much full-time in Toronto and not hating it as much as everybody else who moved from Montreal said he would. Place was full of Chinks and Pakis and niggers, that was for damned

29

sure, but they all wanted to do business and he really didn't give a shit where they came from.

Kristina, his movie-producer girlfriend, was still a lot of fun and didn't bitch too much about him spending so much time in Costa Rica. He was going to have to tell her the resort he was running was really a tourist brothel, though, and he wasn't sure what she'd say. She was hard to figure.

And best of all, business was good. There were some stragglers, some deals had to be firmed up and some guys brought into line — this Toronto really did have a hundred operations from all over the world, fucking Triads, Jamaican posses, Russians, assholes speaking every language there was, but they could do it, they had the manpower, they had the flex.

But there was something.

Nugs, who'd been president of the Rebels in Toronto and become national president after they patched over to the Saints, was finally stepping up. Maybe too much, like he wasn't just president in name only, out there for the cops and other gangs to key on, the way Richard planned it. No, the guy was stepping up like he might want to start calling some shots.

Like he was wondering why he needed Richard.

When the rest of the guys were gone, Richard said to Nugs, "Big Pete, eh?"

"Got a horseshoe up his fat fucking ass."

"You know what happened?"

Nugs said, yeah. "One of the prospects, Boner, kid looks ready to step up so he got it, lost the car for, like, a second on Lake Shore and when he gets it again he pops him, but it's not Big Pete, it's some guy with a chick in the car."

Richard said, "Kid didn't see her?"

"She was blowing the guy, she sits up, he pops her, too."

"Least the guy went out with a bang."

Nugs said, "So to speak."

Richard shook his head, neither of them laughing or even smiling, but they both did think it was funny. Richard said, so, "You giving it to someone else?"

"It'll get taken care of."

Richard wanted to say, it fucking better, but he didn't, he just looked at Nugs, thinking, this it, this where you start to make a stand, start acting like you're really in charge? Then he said, "It's our end of the deal."

Nugs said, yeah, well, but didn't look too worried, and Richard was thinking he didn't want to push it too hard now, but knew it would come to that.

He said, we have a good deal here, a good arrangement, and Nugs said, "I don't know about that," and Richard said, what?

Nugs said, "We're splitting a lot of territory with a lot of people."

"There's enough to go around."

"Yeah?" Nugs was looking at him. "We been talking about the Gunmen for a long time."

"Bunch of assholes," Richard said, "not worth worrying about."

"Looks bad. We're supposed to be the only ones here, and there they are, still riding."

Richard was thinking, shit, now's not the time. He said, "You sure you have the flex," saying it clear, saying *you have*, and Nugs just said, "We're gonna find out."

And Richard said, yeah, "I guess we are," feeling Nugs starting to step up, starting to be the man in charge.

Then Nugs was saying, "The black guy who was here,

31

J.T.'s old Army buddy, brought some impressive weaponry up from Detroit."

"Steady supply?"

"Looks like it. He's talking about being a big customer, too, weed, coke, X, and maybe meth. His uncle and his mom are some kind of dealers in the Motor City looking to go big there."

Richard said, good, that'd be good.

"Yeah, J.T.'s showing him around town."

Richard said, "Maybe give them Big Pete," and Nugs said it wasn't really a priority and Richard was thinking, oh no? Maybe not for you, but it was a big deal for Richard. The deal with the Italians only worked because Richard said he could deliver Nugs and the Saints, he could sell them the deal, but now he wasn't so sure. Colucci could make it work on his end, but the deal was they had to take out Big Pete, settle everybody else down, knowing if they didn't do that this shit would boil over into a war. Looking at Nugs, Richard was starting to see how he might want that. These Toronto guys, this whole Ontario, they sat on the sidelines, waited to see who came out on top in Montreal, waited for them to join everybody up coast to coast, and only then they started listening. He could see them, Nugs and his boys, thinking they missed out on something, wanting to have their own war. Shit.

Going after these Lone Gunmen, stupidest name Richard ever heard of for a dozen guys, the one biker gang in the province hadn't patched over. The deal was international, worked out at the meet in Amsterdam. The Saints got Canada and gave up Texas and Arizona. They closed two decent clubs, a real money-maker in Austin, but these Lone Gunmen fuckheads were still affiliated with Los Gusanos in Texas and wouldn't shut down. Still selling their shitty watered-down coke and weak-ass homegrown all over the province and shipping to the states. Selling it way too cheap but not moving much volume, not really a threat, just looked bad.

Richard said, "You really think we have the soldiers?"

Nugs said, "Oh yeah. We're done talking." He sat down on the couch in the lounge, what was once the living room of the house. Now it had a pool table and a bar in the corner and still looked like it did when the place was really a clubhouse for bikers. It was still convenient, close to downtown and the expressways so guys could get to it from their homes in the burbs and beyond, and it was still fortified and secured, even electronically. "More than done."

They could talk in the clubhouse.

Richard said it was too bad. "Mad Mike didn't used to be such an asshole."

"Bosco was a good kid," Nugs said, "but the game's changed."

"Yeah," Richard said. "Moved on, left them behind. They've got nothing, no flex, no new blood, no prospects worth shit." Thinking, not like us, so many guys do anything to join us, join the winning team, do anything we say. Just have to get them to shoot the right fucking guy.

Nugs said, "Yeah, well, that's the idea."

"Okay, you going to talk to Oakland about it?"

"Let them know."

Richard said, "You're going to take out a whole fucking chapter, what, ten guys, but one fuck-up and you're leaving Big Pete alone?"

Nugs said, for now, and Richard said, yeah, okay, seeing that one deal slipping away, knowing if it did the rest would collapse. The whole thing was a fucking house of cards, held up because they gave their word, he gave

33

his word, and people agreed, one relationship built on another. Something like this, something like Nugs not following through on what they're supposed to do, it wouldn't just change the one deal, the whole thing would fall apart.

Then Richard said, "So, how's everything on the boat?" and Nugs said, great, the boat was really working out. They'd made a deal a few months earlier to buy a laker freighter from a guy, said he had it fitted out as a giant grow op. Asshole hadn't really done anything, grew a few plants in the pilothouse, but he'd made up some decent plans to turn it into an op.

They blew the guy up in a sailboat they'd traded as part of the deal.

Now Nugs said the crop was coming along okay, smaller than they thought, "But the meth, man, the lab is fantastic and we deliver both sides of the border."

Richard said, good. "And the gold?"

"Got a couple guys laid off from Stelco, steel workers, but they know their shit. Set up the kiln, hooked it up to propane tanks, like welding equipment? Melting it down as we speak."

Richard said good. "Make Moctezuma happy."

"Fucking gold," Nugs said. "Guys say they don't lose anything melting down the bars into new bars, it's all 995/996 fineness."

"Twenty-four karat," Richard said, like he knew what he was talking about, having just found out the difference between diamond carat and gold karat. "But the new bars have no markings, no stamps."

"Like the man wanted, can't be traced. We're also buying up all we can, melting that down. Take it anywhere in the world, same value, nobody asks any questions."

Richard was thinking, no, they don't, they just take the gold.

"It is pretty cool," Nugs said, "where we are, how far we've come. Twenty-five years ago, kids selling hash in high-school hallways."

"Smuggling cigarettes."

"Now we're doing multi-million-dollar buys, using gold bars, like James fucking Bond."

"If this anti-terrorism shit didn't make it such a pain to transfer money."

"If the American dollar wasn't worth shit."

"If these fucking Colombians weren't so paranoid."

Nugs said, "So, when are you meeting him?"

"Moctezuma? We have enough bars, need over five mil for him to deal. Next week?"

"At almost six-fifty an ounce? Easy. It just keeps going up. You meeting in Venezuela, what's it called, Martini Island?"

"Margarita," Richard said. Then he was going to tell Nugs, no, they were meeting in Costa Rica at Richard's resort just down the coast from Jaco, the little place with the Russian hookers he opened last year, was going so well he was looking around for another hundred acres, maybe open another one. But then he thought Nugs was asking too many questions, trying too hard to look casual, Richard watching him shrug it off, but seeing it. Seeing Nugs think about it, shit.

Moctezuma was Richard's contact from way back, one of the best, steadiest, suppliers of raw coke there was, no matter how much you needed, fucking Rafael de la Calleja Moctezuma could deliver, fucking tons of it. Richard watched Nugs sitting there not saying anything, but thinking, he could tell, how hard would it be to set up

35

his own connection. Richard wanted to tell him, fucking hard, Nugs, takes years to build up this kind of trust.

But he just said, "It was a lot easier, we used to meet in Florida."

Nugs said, "There's always new challenges, we'll always find a way."

And Richard thought, yeah, always new challenges till you *are* the new challenge.

Made Richard think it might be getting time for him to have a look at those gold bars himself, maybe time to get out, maybe look at Honduras or Belize.

● ● ●

Get came down the stairs thinking this nice suburban house, was this what his mom was talking about, this the way she wanted to live? Pushing him and his Uncle Main, her little brother, into stepping up, bringing in their own supply, cutting out MuMu and his New York, New York fucking attitude. Movin' on up, like the song says, not to a deluxe apartment in the sky but a big house in Grosse Pointe, six bedrooms, a fucking library and a Sub-Zero on the patio in the backyard.

Could be all right. Have to get a chick speaks English, though. The Asian chick was good, but she went through everything like it was laid out in a menu.

He nodded at the two women still sitting in the living room and then saw J.T. at the desk in the dining room talking to a dark-skinned woman. Not as dark as Get, more what his uncle would call a half-assed nigger, but fine, fine looking.

J.T. said, "Hey Get, my man, this is Sunitha," and Get thought, oh yeah, the hand job chick. He held out his hand and they shook and he thought, yeah, smooth hands, nice long fingers and a firm shake. He almost laughed.

Sunitha said, "What's so funny?"

"Nothing."

But he did like the way she didn't take any shit.

There was a pile of jewellery and credit cards on the desk and J.T. said Sunitha and her crew just hit a spa.

Get said, "A spa?"

Sunitha said, "They're all the rage with the fat, rich, and lazy."

Get said, yeah, I heard. He was trying to place this Sunitha, she sounded like she might be educated, maybe middle class from a suburb just like this one. He liked the way she didn't try to sound all street and ghetto like she saw on TV.

J.T. was saying, "They send in White Girl Brenda, makes an appointment and goes in, then she calls Sunitha and Lydia when it's clear."

"Nice."

"Most of the time they've already taken off the jewellery."

J.T. said, "Lydia is, like, this six-foot black chick."

There was a scream from upstairs, a woman yelling, and J.T. said, "Where's Leo?"

The two Asian chicks were already standing up and one of them said he was at the Greek's, getting takeout. "Is only Mr. Miyaki."

J.T. went up the stairs fast.

Sunitha looked at Get and didn't say anything so he said, "Why you call her that?"

"Brenda? Because it's her name."

"White girl."

"Because that's what she is."

"You brown girl?"

She took her cigarettes out of the purse on the desk beside the credit cards and the jewellery and said, no, it's from a movie. "The one with J-Lo and George Clooney, they rob a rich guy Clooney met in jail."

Get said, oh yeah. "That's going back, that one. Was in Detroit, that's where I'm from."

She looked at him and nodded. Then she said, "There's a guy in the movie, White Boy Bob."

Get said, "Yeah, he works for Don Cheadle, nigger should have been the star."

He looked at Sunitha. Man, this chick, he couldn't get a read on her at all. Usually, chick like this, seeing his thousand-dollar sweater, his five-hundred-dollar shoes, his fine physique if he do say so hisself, usually a chick like this would see right away the potential and be trying to get with him. But this Sunitha, she was just standing there, smoking, looking at him.

Get said, "Was based on a book."

"What?"

"That movie, J-Lo and Clooney. It was based on a book. Man writes them in Detroit. Old white dude, like eighty years old, you'd never guess that."

Sunitha said, yeah? "Who the fuck reads books?"

And Get thought, shit, this chick. What is it about her? Hot body, great rack, great ass, nice face, and attitude. Shit, trouble. And not the good kind.

Then J.T. was coming down the stairs with a little guy, almost pushing him, but the guy was keeping his balance, holding his clothes in a bundle, and J.T. was saying, "Okay, okay, just sit the fuck down."

Sunitha walked into the living room to see what was going on.

38

And Get was thinking about that day in front of 1300
Beaubien, Gizzer in there all night, the cops working him
over because he finally turned eighteen. Get and Nodie
going to meet him and some guy sitting on a ratty blanket
on the sidewalk, books spread out all over it, held one up,
said here you go young bucks, just for you. Get looking
down at the guy, saying, oh yeah? The guy, not a Muslim
but wearing the white knit cap, had a scraggly beard,
saying some of this book takes place right here in this
building right here, some of it in the Frank Murphy Hall
of Justice, you be there soon enough. Nodie said fuck you
and the guy said, some of it's in the morgue, you be there
soon enough, too. Get grabbed the book out of the clown's
hand, saying, fuck you too, walking away. Later, though,
waiting for the bus, he started to read it. Had a number in
the title, *Man #89*, or some shit. He'd never read a book
in Detroit, never read a book all the way through, but this
one had streets he knew, guys he knew, black guys
committing crimes right there in Detroit, just like the
cripple on the blanket said. It was the seventies in the
book, man, niggers in maroon suits and floppy hats, but
Get knew guys like that now. Just different clothes.

Later Get went to John King Books, big old five storey
warehouse on Lafayette, stole every one they had by the
old white dude. Some of them were fucking *westerns*.

In the living room the Asian chicks were helping the
little guy get dressed and J.T. was telling him he could not
use vibrators on the girls without condoms. The guy had
a Ziploc bag and was saying something about wanting to
take it home wet and Get just shook his head, man, guys
thinking with their dicks.

Then Get saw something in Sunitha's purse, right there
where she got her smokes.

A book. One of those big paperbacks, something about the inheritance of something. Of loss. Look at that. Who the fuck reads books.

Now she was coming back, taking a drag off the cigarette and blowing out smoke, saying to J.T., how much?

J.T. counted out five grand and said, "Split it up how you like."

"Come on J.T., that shit's got to be worth twenty grand. Do you know the price of gold today?"

"Do you?"

She didn't say anything but Get got the feeling she did.

J.T. was still holding the money. "You want it or not?"

Get watched her put the cash in her purse and he just knew White Girl Brenda wasn't getting an even cut.

Have to find out more about this Sunitha.

CHAPTER THREE

PRICE SAID, "NONE OF THE PAPERS said anything about the blow job."

"So far."

"It's old news now. There'll be something more fucked up today, take the headlines."

McKeon said, "We can only hope."

She looked up and saw Detective Levine coming in, his tie loose, sport coat wrinkled, guy probably weighed all of a hundred and forty pounds. He ordered a double-double — the most popular coffee Tim Hortons sells, a little coffee and two heaping spoonfuls of sugar and two servings of eighteen per cent cream — a jelly glazed and another coffee, black.

"Where's O'Brien?"

Levine sat down and said, "I won't let her smoke in the car," and took a big, dribbly bite of the doughnut. "Those things'll kill her."

McKeon saw Detective Louise O'Brien holding the

door for a couple of guys coming out, taking a last drag off her cigarette, tossing it into the parking lot and coming in.

She sat down at the table and said to Levine, you having any coffee with that cream and sugar, and he said, you're welcome, pointing to the other coffee.

O'Brien drank some and said, "How can you eat that?"

"They've got more."

O'Brien rolled her eyes.

McKeon wished she could look so put together, though, like that nice tweed blazer and the matching pants, some kind of V-neck argyle sweater, and hell, even some makeup. The brown hair falling around her shoulders could even be its natural colour.

McKeon had her hair tied back and she was happy enough that her dress pants and her jacket were close to the same shade of blue.

Well, O'Brien's kids were older, they weren't going through the terrible twos.

Price was saying, "So, it's all quiet on the western front."

"Not a word." Levine drank some more coffee and said, "Sweet." Then he said, "Open and shut, as they say. Guy died of an overdose."

McKeon said, "And his past dealings with the police aren't raising any flags?"

"He was a drug addict, Maureen. They usually have dealings with the police."

"And businesses? Partnerships?"

Levine nodded, I know, I know. "What I'm saying is, whatever happened, happened. It's over."

"This guy was likely supplying VIN numbers, and cars, to all kinds of cops."

"Not all kinds," Levine said. "Just to one, who is awaiting his day in court."

McKeon said, right. "One that we know of."

Levine said, "Look, this guy was an accident waiting to happen. He was a car salesman."

"So, he liked cars."

"Guys don't become car salesmen because they love cars, they become car salesmen because they're lazy and they love money. He really loved money, he was a coke-head, he spent a thousand bucks a week on hookers."

"And now would not have been a good time for him to turn his life around and start doing the right thing, what with that day in court coming up."

"Oy vey, you."

Price said, "Meet the new boss, the same as the old boss."

McKeon nodded, knowing they were all thinking the same thing, how with so many cops arrested, the mess spreading everywhere, it was enough to just try and contain it, keep it in-house as much as possible.

Make it something that was, something that's been taken care of.

Not something that's still going on.

O'Brien said, "What about your horny suburb couple? What's going on there?"

McKeon thought, yeah, back to business. But now that they were talking about it, this other thing wouldn't just go away.

"Painful," Price said. "It's awful, those kids."

"How they doing?" Levine finished off his doughnut, drummed his fingers on the table, and looked around like he might want another one.

"The wife had a sister in Oakville, they're with her.

Their minister's with them."

O'Brien said, "Minister? Like in a church?"

"Yeah, they went to church," McKeon said.

Price said, what? "It's not so weird."

Both women looked at him and he said, "Okay, a little weird in the car maybe, but you know, they're husband and wife."

O'Brien said, "Makes it weirder."

McKeon said, "Not something you're ever going to get," and Price said, you never know.

Levine said, "We can dream," and O'Brien said, please.

"Okay, no," Price said. "It's not that far out. Last year, Cassie and me, on that flight to London, it was long, you know."

McKeon said, "Yeah, and?"

"Well, it was dark, we had a blanket."

O'Brien said, "First of all, you weren't in a car on the Gardiner, and second of all, no one wants to hear this."

Levine said, don't say no one.

"Okay," Price said, "it wasn't the same. But if the flight was any longer."

McKeon said, "What's weird is, we can't find out where they were."

"They told their kids they were going out," Price said. "They do it once in a while. The daughter, seventeen, very put together by the way, honour student, part-time job, volleyball team. She said they do it about once a month, like a date."

"Keep the relationship fresh," Levine said. "Sounds good."

McKeon said, "Yeah. Really fresh."

Price drank some coffee and said, "But nothing on the credit cards that night, nothing on calendars, no friends or relatives had plans with them."

"Well they went somewhere," O'Brien said. "They make any phone calls?"

"Couple hours earlier they called the daughter, see how she was. She was fine, home with the youngest. Other kid was at a friend's house."

"And there's nothing looks out of place? They're not living past their means, way in debt, anything?"

"Not yet."

"Hey," O'Brien said, "anything else happen near there, they might have seen something, be witnesses?"

"To what?"

"I don't know, something."

Levine said, "You're going to find a boyfriend or a girl-friend. Someone was supposed to be leaving the marriage by now."

"I don't know," McKeon said. "We walked around their house, it seemed happy enough."

"And it's not like they were pissed off at each other on the way home."

"They were," Price said, "I'd like to get Cassie that pissed at me."

O'Brien said maybe they went to a movie.

"Or the film festival's on now, right?" Levine was still looking at the fresh doughnuts on the trays behind the counter.

Price said, yeah, "You see Sean Penn smoking in the hotel. He's a bad boy."

O'Brien said she'd like to smoke in the hotel.

"You become a big movie star, Louise," Price said, "we'll all suck up to you, too."

Levine said, "Not even that big."

O'Brien said, "This damned town."

45

For a moment no one said anything and then McKeon looked at Levine and said, "You sure about the car salesman?"

"Sure? No, I'm not sure. I thought we just closed this can of worms."

Price said, "Once it gets opened . . ."

"I know." Levine tapped his knuckles on the little plastic table between them and said, "I'm not going to look too hard."

McKeon said, good enough.

Knowing he'd look hard enough.

● ● ●

Richard said, sure, he'd thought about it a lot, he was investing a lot of money, and Kristina said, no, not like that, like what it means, and Richard said, what?

"What it means," Kristina said, "to men and women, to their futures together."

Richard said, oh right, yeah sure, of course. "They don't have any future."

Kristina said, "I'm sure you're joking, but please go on," and Richard watched her get up out of the bed and walk naked to the dresser and get her smokes. She stood there with her back to him, her head tilted to one side, her hair falling that way off her tanned shoulder and lit her cigarette, waiting for him to say something. They'd been talking about his Costa Rica resort, the Gladiator Club, the sex tourism place. They'd been together a year now and were getting used to each other, not many surprises, and Richard was thinking she liked sex with him, which he couldn't have said about many of the chicks since Sylvie, all those young girls, the strippers and escorts do anything he wanted but no ideas of their own, going through the motions, doing it all on autopilot, but when the clock radio came on and he woke up ready to go, she wanted to talk. She'd been awake for a while, he could tell, thinking about something and when he said, What, she said, Why would a guy go on vacation for a week and get a hooker?

Richard had said, "Escort," and she'd said, "Oh well, that makes all the difference." Richard had thought about blowing her off, just saying how the fuck would I know why some pathetic shit wants to blow three grand a week to bang a Romanian hooker, but he looked at her, she was looking up at him and she was curious, she wanted to know what he thought, maybe just to get it, not to get all pissy about it, but he wasn't sure, so he'd said, "This for a movie?" and she'd said, "Maybe."

All the talking, he wasn't ready to go anymore, so he told her, a guy works his ass off all year, bosses giving him shit, he's got no time to think, to relax, he sure doesn't have time for all the bullshit dating, all those fucking rules, he finally gets a week off he wants a sure thing. He doesn't want to go to some resort, spend five days buying drinks for chicks so he *might* get laid the last night while they're both too drunk to remember. He wants to have a real vacation, a good time, he wants to get laid in the morning, he wants a little something before dinner in case he has too much fun at karaoke, drinks too much and passes out. Then he comes back to his job all relaxed and ready to go for another year.

Kristina'd sat up then and said, you think that's okay, and Richard said sure, and she said, but what'll that do to the future of dating, of men and women? Now he was thinking maybe she was getting pissy, going to get her

47

smokes. She was turning around now, looking at him and blowing out smoke, leaning her nice naked butt on the dresser and saying, "But what about the women?"

"The hookers? Believe me, they get well paid."

"No," Kristina said, "I mean the women back home? What are they supposed to do?"

Richard watched her take a drag, let the smoke out in a slow steady stream looking right at him, and he thought maybe she wasn't pissed off, maybe she just wanted to figure this out, maybe it *was* for a movie. Man, he couldn't figure her and he wasn't sure if he liked that or not.

He said, "The women back home have what they want. They have spa days and girly weekends and shit."

"So this is like a spa for guys?"

"It sure is. We get the laws changed, we can do it here. Have to make it look like something else, golf weekend, or something. Guys here would probably even play a round. We got a deal with golf courses there, too, sailboat rentals, scuba diving, all that."

"A real vacation."

"You know it."

"And they get the same girl for the week?"

Richard said, you saw the web page. "The way it works, you get a room and a girl. A little extra cash, you get two girls one night."

"Every man's fantasy."

She took another drag and he said, "You going to give me one of those?"

She picked up the smokes and walked back to the bed. Richard was pretty sure she was showing off her slim body, smooth, no hair anywhere, she had some spa days, got herself pampered. He was pretty sure she'd had some work done on her tits, maybe her nose, but it was quality.

She dropped the pack beside him and sat on the edge of the bed.

"I guess I can see it."

"Here's the thing," Richard said. "Men were never these powerful guys in charge of anything. Every guy I ever knew, they were afraid of their boss and afraid of their wives or their mothers. And some of these looked like tough guys." He looked at her, she was looking right back at him, interested. "They're working all the time, never getting anything they really want. Truth is, it's hard to find a woman gives a shit if the men in her life are happy."

"Oh really?"

"They always give you what makes them happy and you're supposed to like it. And all we hear about is her needs, what she wants, what makes her happy, what doesn't make her fucking happy, what's wrong with us. Every time I turn on the TV it's some stupid guy, his wife making fun of him, or it's what he's supposed to do for her."

49

"But poor baby never gets what he wants?"

"You see all those guys killing themselves in traffic every morning, going to work it's dark, coming home it's dark, living like vampires, you know what they want?"

"A long hot bath with scented candles, dark chocolate?"

"They want a blow job in the morning before they go to work. They get that, they can take on the world."

Kristina said, I'll keep that in mind, and Richard said, you do that, and she slapped his thigh, playful, but enough that he felt it.

She said, "You don't want a woman who's your equal?" and it made him think of Sylvie again. Every time he thought he was getting over her, he was right back, looking around the room to talk to her, looking at his phone, hoping it would ring. If she hadn't died, would he have ever made his move, taken out Mon Oncle and be sitting here now?

He said, "Why can't she give him something he wants, still be equal?"

"What does she get out of a blow job?"

"See, that's the thing," Richard said. "Sex is like keeping score now, orgasms don't just feel good, they're points. You get a point, I get a point. You don't get a point, shit, I hear about it."

"Not from me."

Richard said, yeah, it's true, you're okay, and she said, gee thanks.

But now he was thinking about Sylvie, shit, she had that Québécois temper on her, and a mouth. The time she told Mon Oncle to fuck off, standing there naked on the stage, hands on her hips, they might have gone at it right then, he hadn't laughed. Richard knew she was his equal, hell, more than that. Told her all his secrets, all his plans, shit, half of them were hers, he'd never have done anything on his own. Like he was doing now.

He said, "It's just, there aren't many women like you."

She still had her hand on his thigh from her playful slap and now she started moving it up and down, coming close to his balls but not touching them, saying, "So, all you need is a little sex in the morning?"

"Doesn't sound like much when you say it."

She stubbed out her smoke in the ashtray on the night table and then kissed his stomach, moved down and took him in her mouth.

Richard leaned his head back on the pillow thinking,

yeah, he needed someone to talk to, tell his secrets, work out his plans, but he knew there'd never be another Sylvie in his life.

When he finished, Kristina smiled at him and went into the bathroom. He heard the water running and she stuck her head out the door, brushing her teeth and saying she was going to take a shower and then she had a meeting. Then she said to him, "You ready to take on the world?" and he said, yeah, I am.

Feeling like maybe he was.

• • •

Jessica, the receptionist in the homicide office, said she had someone who wanted to tell the detectives where the Lowries were on Saturday night.

Andre Price said, Who? and Jessica said she didn't know.

"No, I mean who are the Lowries?"

"Your homicide? Guy getting a blow job in the car? From his wife?"

Price said, "Not everything's a question."

Jessica said, "She wants to talk to Detective McKeon."

"She said that, she used my name?"

"She just said the woman detective."

McKeon looked at Price and shrugged.

Jessica said, "Line three," and McKeon picked up the phone.

Price leaned back in his chair, rubbed his eyes from staring at the computer monitor all morning, getting nowhere, and then watched Jessica walk back to the reception desk. She was maybe thirty but dressed young, plaid miniskirt, white blouse and boots almost up to her knees. Price wondered about her, what she thought about all this, she almost never said anything.

Then he saw Levine and O'Brien getting off the elevator and coming into the pit, the big open area with the detectives' desks, not even any wall dividers, Levine saying, "All I'm saying, Louise."

Price said, "What's he saying?"

O'Brien looked at Levine like she wanted it to be a private matter and Levine said, "Come on, everybody's going to know."

Price looked at O'Brien and she said, "Okay, maybe a man's opinion would be good."

Levine rolled his eyes.

O'Brien said, "So, I called Bill this morning."

"Yeah?"

"He's in San Diego for a conference. So I call him and a half asleep Spanish woman answered the phone in his room."

Price said, "You sure it was his room?"

Levine said, "You see."

O'Brien said, that's what Teddy here said. "But come on."

Price said, "And the chick, she says she doesn't know anybody by that name and you must have the wrong room."

"Yeah. So I call back and Bill answers, like I woke him up."

"'Cause you did," Price said. "You were at that meeting with Nichols at eight, don't know what his problem is, so you called Bill at eight-thirty, which is five-thirty in the morning in San Diego, right?"

O'Brien said, oh yeah, forgot about that.

"Right. And the clerk, when you talked to him, was probably all the way asleep, coming through an eleven to seven shift, pushes the wrong button."

Levine said, "This is what I've been saying."

O'Brien looked right at Price and said, "You really think so?" and he said, Louise, come on.

"I know Bill. I know how he feels about you," Price said. "Shit, he tells everybody how you fuck him non-stop, every room in the house."

O'Brien was walking away then, saying, all right, all right, and Levine said, "And not just the house, he told everybody about last winter at Blue Mountain, you know how easy he could get frostbite doing that on a ski hill?"

She was almost out of the pit, her back to them, both hands in the air, middle fingers raised, saying, "Enough, already," and Price said, "You know what he risks for you?"

McKeon hung up and said, "You're going to love this."

53

Price watched O'Brien walk away and said, I am?

"They were on one of those dinner cruises in the harbour."

"Yeah, so?"

"The Club 4420 cruise."

Price said, okay.

"It's an adult lifestyles club."

"An adult what?"

McKeon said, "I had to ask, too. It's for couples and select singles."

Price said, "Shit."

"Yes, Andre, it's a wife swapper's club."

"Fuck."

"That's what they do, they meet people who want to add a little spice to their lives. Says so right here."

Levine said, please tell me this is your blow job in the

car, and McKeon said, "No, Teddy, it's the newest thing in gangbangers, key parties all the rage at Jane and Finch."

The web page was up on McKeon's monitor, Club 4420 across the top and a picture of a good-looking woman in her forties with blonde streaks in her hair. The headline said "For People Who Want to Add a Little Spice to Their Lives," but Spice had a line through it and above that it said "Sex" in a font that looked like it was hand-written with red lipstick.

Price said, "I knew I should have taken a sick day."

"This is Millie Green, she owns the club with her husband, Mark. They usually have dances every Friday and Saturday night at Sweet Dreamz, a bar out on Dixon, near the airport. Saturday they had the harbour cruise."

"How many?"

"Funny you should ask. Seventy-five couples."

"Shit."

"And twenty select singles. Fifteen men and five women."

Levine said, "Five single women went?"

"A hundred and seventy people."

Levine said, hey look, Andre. "Last Thursday of the month is bisexual males night, you might want to check that out."

Price said, shit.

A couple of other detectives had walked into the pit and one of them, Armstrong, tall, wide-shouldered native guy wearing a suit just as expensive and stylish as Price's, said, "The what now?"

Levine said to the guy with Armstrong, "Hey Bergeron, you still work here?"

Bergeron, a little shorter than Armstrong, said what's that supposed to mean, and Levine said, "You moved in with Harvey Goldbach's ex, the settlement she got."

Bergeron said, "I haven't moved in with her," and it could have been the beginning of something between him and Levine, something that could get ugly, but he said, "Yet." Then he said, "We just got back from Italy. She loves the food."

"Shit."

They'd all been talking about how Bergeron was dating Ruth Goldbach, who'd kicked her big-time real estate lawyer husband Harvey out and then taken a settlement instead of going to court. Rumour was she got the big house and a bigger pile of cash.

Now Armstrong said, "This your couple in the car?" and Price said, yeah.

Levine said, "Guy getting blown by wife gets blown up."

"Keep working it, Teddy, you'll get something."

O'Brien came back, the only other cop dressed as well as Price or Armstrong, McKeon thinking it looked like she shopped at Holt Renfrew, but how could she on her salary? And she always managed to have some little feminine thing on, some pink brooch or hair clip or little scarf, something to take the edge off. Today it was a grey and purple knitted flap over the holster on her hip, making it look like the softer, more ladylike Glock. She said, "You still talking about my sex life?"

McKeon said, "You work these shifts and you have a sex life?"

Armstrong said, "They were swingers?"

McKeon said, well, they went on the cruise anyway.

Price said, "I know those, the booze cruises, Cassie's office went on one last summer. There's a few all leave at the same time, must be four or five boats. Everyone uses the same parking lot."

"Hey, that's good," McKeon said, "I hadn't even thought

of that. Something could have happened in the parking lot. Now we're looking at maybe five hundred people. Thanks a fucking lot."

"I was thinking witnesses, Maureen, maybe the parking guy saw something."

Levine said, "All those swingers getting off the boat, I bet he saw something."

O'Brien said, "You mean like wife swappers?"

McKeon stood up and said, "They call it 'lifestyle,' now. Come on, let's go," and Price said, where?

"We're going to go talk to Millie and Mark Green."

Levine said, "Have fun."

But then he followed them towards the elevator and said, hang on.

McKeon and Price stopped by the elevator and looked at him.

Levine said, "That car salesman thing?"

"Yeah?"

"Yeah." Levine looked around making sure no one was listening and no one was, but it still took him a few seconds. "Yeah, look, he was telling people he knew a lot more than he said he did."

"Yeah?"

"I'm not saying it's anything."

"No," McKeon said. "But it could be."

"It could be."

"Shit."

Levine said, yeah. Then he said, "A couple things I'm following up. Guy was maybe a go-between, putting people together."

McKeon said, "And he was in business with cops? I thought this shit was over with."

Price said, "You wished it was."

Levine said, "We all did."

Yeah.

"I have to talk to someone on the task force. They keep telling us a major war is coming."

"It's in all the papers," Price said.

"Stuff like this, getting rid of guys like the car sales- man," Levine said, "either calms people down or gets them wound up."

"If they want a war," McKeon said, "they're going to have one."

"I'll let you know," Levine said, "if I hear anything," and walked back to the pit, and McKeon and Price got on the elevator.

●　●　●

57

Two guys pulled up to the curb at the Black Bull riding Harleys, big ones, loud. They got off slow, long legs covered in leather stretching over the bikes, taking off their helmets and looking around, knowing everyone on the patio was looking at them.

Nugs said to Danny Mac, "Don't fuck with them," and Danny said, shit no, they might screw up your port- folio, and the two real bikers, short hair, neat goatees, chinos, and golf shirts drank their beers and blended into the crowd.

It was a beautiful sunny day, mid-September, late after- noon. The trendy Queen West patio was packed, the bankers on wheels were standing in line now, waiting their turn like everybody else.

Nugs said, "You remember when having a beer on a patio was radical in this town?"

"Nothing open on Sunday."

"Everything closed up tight at one."

"Only tittie bar was the old Le Chic, remember, on Dundas?"

"That fucking Greek," Nugs said. "Law said no nude dancers, he had them go topless, then they put on those little tees, remember, his wife got them all those Blue Jays tees, all torn, their tits coming through? And took off their G strings."

"Hey, they were never totally nude."

Nugs said, yeah, thinking back to those days, not even that long ago, late seventies, early eighties. They were teenagers looking at their first tits, those stoned chicks with hairy bushes. Then it was like overnight, things just changed. Sleepy old Toronto didn't know what hit it. Far as Nugs could tell, it still didn't have a clue.

The waitress came to the table with two more beers, put them on the table and stood with her hand on her hip, saying, "Can I get you anything else?"

Nugs looked at her thinking she might be twenty, tattoos on both arms, around her cute little belly button, tramp stamp on her back sticking out of her shorts, and pierced all over: eyebrow, nose, three rings through her bottom lip, and rings all the way around her ears. He was thinking she was cute, in a little-girl way, take away all the makeup and the add-ons she wasn't far at all from her suburban high school. Like she was playing dress-up.

He said, no, that's fine thanks, and she nodded and turned to some other customers.

Danny Mac said, "Things change."

"They sure do."

"And sometimes," Danny said, "we make them change."

Nugs said, yeah, thinking they were getting to it now, what they wanted to talk about.

Danny saying, "We've been over it."

"Yeah," Nugs said. "We're ready."

"We are."

They were talking about it a lot lately, about stepping up, being the real power, coast to coast. It was like they'd avoided it all these years. Just like Toronto, Nugs thought, pushed into being the big time when Quebec started talking about dumping Canada and all that money ran out of Montreal as fast as it could. Ran all the way down the 401 to Toronto and hit it in the face. Back then Toronto was like the world's biggest hick town, like a kid brother always looking up to Chicago and L.A. and New York. Took a while for the place to get back on its feet, but that's what it felt like now, like it was finally starting to flex.

And that's what it felt like for Nugs and the boys. They'd been in the game a long time, but small-time, local, never looking beyond. Nugs and Danny Mac, Spaz, Alex, Ozzie, they were the original outlaw bikers in Toronto, the Rebels. Danny Mac was the first one with a motorcycle, his older brother, Hank, one of the Yorkville hippies in the sixties — the seventies in Toronto, everything came a little later — but the only thing Hank really liked about it was the drugs. He went from being one of the original hippies to being one of the original homeless and Danny took his bike.

They were at Central Tech then, Danny and Nugs, sixteen years old selling hash and Thai stick they got from Hank's dealer, another hippie called himself Keet, and they worked on the bike in the school shop. Made enough for Nugs to get his own bike in grade eleven, an old Triumph he bought off a little British guy lived on Clinton Street. Halfway through that year Keet got picked up.

Cops even came to the school and talked to them but Nugs and Danny Mac kept their mouths shut. The one cop, looked like the picture on an old football card, brush cut on his square head, finished threatening them and trying to scare them and said to the other cop, looked just the same, they don't know shit, they're too stupid. Nugs and Danny Mac stood there by the back door of the school, all the other smokers looking at them, and they just shrugged and didn't say a word.

A couple weeks later a guy parked a van in front of Harbord Fish and Chips when school was letting out and when Nugs and Danny Mac walked by he waved them over. The guy seemed cool, he had long hair, but not like a hippie, it was parted on the side, just covered his ears and he had long sideburns and a moustache, wore a dark purple suit. There was a woman with him, really skinny with long, long blonde hair and she had a leather jacket on over a tight minidress. Not tie-dyed, it was one solid colour, all orange.

The guy said that was his name, Guy, said he heard the cops came and talked to them. Nugs, he was just starting to be called Nugs then, a lot of people still called him Frank or even Frantisek, but he always had a nugget of hash, he looked at the guy and said, "What the fuck is it to you?"

Guy laughed, said, yeah, you're the ones I'm looking for. He told them Keet and a couple of his dealers got picked up, left a big hole in his operation and did they want to take over, sell bigger amounts to other dealers in this school and Harbord Collegiate and to the Catholic high school on Dufferin. Danny Mac started to say yes right away, but Nugs stopped him, said, how do we know you're not a cop? The guy said, do I look like a cop, and

Nugs said, how do I know? "She could be the fucking mod squad."

Guy said, "You got some balls, kid, I'll give you that." He was enjoying himself, but it was also his business. He got serious and said, "Okay, how about Marcie here gives you blow jobs? No cop would do that."

Nugs, climbing in the back of the van, said, "I wouldn't want one from a cop."

Danny waited on the sidewalk talking to Guy about how much they thought they could move and Guy asking him if they knew anybody went to Northern Heights or Jarvis Collegiate.

They started making some pretty good money right away and by the time they stopped going to school a couple years later they each had new bikes and Spaz and Ozzie had joined. Guy was a good supplier into the eighties, until he was just high all the time, became unreliable, started calling himself the Cocaine King, telling people to fuck off or he'd sic his bikers on them.

That was the first time they'd had one of these talks, deciding what to do even though they all knew. By then they knew Guy was getting the coke from Angelo Colucci and the hash from the Point Boys in Montreal, so they stayed an extra day at a party at Guy's family cottage. Killed him in front of the fireplace, strangled him, packed him into a sleeping bag with a hundred pounds of rocks, tied an anchor to it, and threw him off his own boat a mile out in Georgian Bay.

Now here they were, twenty years later, talking about getting rid of someone else. Lots of someone elses.

"Could be a real war," Nugs said and Danny said, yeah, it could.

Nugs said, "We've got the manpower?"

"More every day."

"You're sure?"

"I'll make fucking sure."

"What about cops?"

Danny said they'd lost a few good contacts when Richard arrived, when Mon Oncle got busted and half Toronto's narco department got busted by the Mounties. "But," he said, "we're rebuilding. We're doing all right."

Nugs said, okay, you're right, knowing he was. When the Saints finished their war in Quebec, took on everybody from the cops to the other bikers to the Mafia and established solid chapters in every other province, the only game in town, they started moving on Toronto, everybody knowing it was the real prize, biggest market in the country, last place to get organized. Always seven or eight different biker gangs and they pretty much lived in peace, everybody had their territory, the Rebels no more than anyone else, they were just downtown. Then, after 9/11, everything changed in the import business and Mon Oncle and his boys started showing up at parties more, giving more free samples — they had some decent coke in those days and very good supplies of meth and weed — and they had the capital and the swagger. Nugs knew right away, so did Danny and the rest of the Rebels. They'd been telling those French assholes to fuck off for years, but everybody knew it was different, it was a new era.

So they hopped on their bikes, rode to La Prairie just south of Montreal and they patched over. They all did, the Death Riders, the Wild Hogs, everybody. Except those fucking Lone Gunmen. Everybody else sewed those two-hundred-and-twenty-five-dollar colours imported all the way from Austria on their vests themselves. Nugs remembered laughing at the cops, shocked it happened so fast, not knowing the deals they'd worked out, the negotiations that had been going on for years. It was the old Five Families in New York, but modern-day Toronto, so it was more like a corporate merger. They walked out of that clubhouse with their Saints colours and showed them off to the cops taking pictures. Fucking Spaz saying to the cops, "We came, we saw, we conquered, eh?"

It wasn't all smooth in Toronto right away, though. All over Ontario it looked like it might fall apart, turn into another war, they could have spent years killing each other. A few guys were killed, a couple of frogs, Claude and Denis, shot out at the airport, and a couple of the Lone Gunmen disappeared, only Nugs and Danny Mac knew how far out into Lake Ontario those bodies had been dropped. But then Richard showed up, started getting everybody on the same page, and back in Montreal Mon Oncle and a bunch of his best guys got picked up. Made for some openings at the top.

Next thing, Nugs is national president, the money's flowing, and everybody's calmed down.

"First the Lone Assholes," Danny Mac said. "Then another shot at the fat man."

Nugs said the Assholes for sure, but, "The other guy? I don't know," and Danny said, no?

"How many fronts you want to fight a war on at once?"

Danny said, yeah, sure, "But that's the deal."

"What I'm thinking," Nugs said, "is that's not really our deal."

"Not ours?"

"Not yours and mine, you know?"

Danny said, yeah, he knew, but it was the deal that was made, and Nugs said, yeah, sure, but not by us. He could see Danny knew what he meant, not by us, the old Rebels, the Toronto guys. It was Richard's deal, came in with the Saints.

Nugs said, "I'm thinking maybe we don't have to do anything about that right now."

"No reason to rush it," Danny said.

Nugs said, right. He was thinking Big Pete had no idea it was coming, maybe this fuck-up could work for them. Richard's deal with the Italians included getting rid of Big Pete, because Pete didn't like the deal, made sure everybody knew that. Maybe if they didn't take him out, the Italians'd have their own war, Big Pete starting a mutiny, taking out a lot of guys. Then Nugs and the boys could clean up what was left, be a lot easier.

Danny said, "It gets complicated."

"It does," Nugs said. The waitress came to the table, gave them a couple more beers and while she was putting them down Nugs said, "It's like that Italian guy, what's his name, Marconi."

Danny said, guy invented radio?

"No, the other one, guy made all the deals, ran the place from behind the scenes."

The waitress said, "Machiavelli. Wrote a book called *The Prince*."

"Yeah, him."

The waitress said, "Explained to the prince how to keep himself in power."

Nugs leaned back in the plastic chair and looked up at her, saying, "Good book?"

"All right." Then she said, "Bismarck made a lot of deals, too, kept most of Europe in line for a long time."

"Yeah, what happened?"

"Usual, somebody got strong enough, big enough,

didn't think he had to take orders from anyone else." She looked at Nugs and said, "It's what guys do, right," and Nugs said, "Sometimes it can't be helped," and she said, "That's what they all say," winking and walking away.

Danny Mac said, shit, and Nugs said, no, she's right. "It's what we do."

The two guys who'd shown up on the loud bikes finally got a table on the patio. They were wearing leather jackets and they made a big deal about taking them off and putting them over the backs of their chairs. They ordered Stella Artois beers from the cute little tattooed waitress and said to make sure it was cold.

Danny Mac said, "I don't fucking believe it."

One of the guys was turning around in his seat, looking over the whole patio like he owned the place, and Danny was looking at his T-shirt. It was black and didn't have any sleeves, frayed where he'd tried to make it look like they were torn off to show the big muscles in his arms, looked like the guy lifted some serious weights. But what Danny was looking at was the fucking Saints of Hell logo on the front, the red skull with the devil horns and the flames.

Nugs said, "Holy shit."

Danny finished his beer, stood up and said, "Come on." Nugs followed him, walking between the plastic patio chairs to the table the guy with the Saints shirt was sitting at, and Danny said, "Where'd you get that?"

The guy said, "Why, *you* want one?" He looked at his friend, shook his head and said, "You can't buy them in stores."

Danny said, "Oh yeah?" Then he said it again, "Where'd you get the fucking shirt?" And the guy, getting pissed off now, said, "What's it to you?"

65

Danny said, "Take it off."

The guy leaned back in his chair, looking up at these two guys, not very big, dressed like maybe they were managers at the Gap across Queen Street and said, "What?"

Danny said it slow, like he was talking to a kid. Or an idiot. "Take the fucking T-shirt off."

The guy looked at his friend like it was funny, he looked around the patio, a lot of people looking now, and then he looked at Danny and said, "Why? You want to see my manly chest?"

Nugs hit him the face with a beer bottle and the guy screamed, both hands over his bleeding nose.

Danny grabbed the shirt and pulled, ripped it right up the front, the guy yelling to fuck off, my wife made this for me, and Danny wrapped the two ends around the guy's neck and started pulling hard.

The other guy started to stand up but Nugs still had the broken bottle and he said sit still and the guy stayed sitting. Everybody else on the patio moved out of the way.

Danny choked the guy with the shirt, held on till he was out of his chair, turning all kinds of red, and then he let go enough for the guy to fall to the cement, saying, "You do not wear these fucking colours," waving the T-shirt and walking away with it.

Nugs looked at all the faces on the patio staring at him and he said, "It's copyrighted material," and followed Danny, thinking, yeah it's what we do and we're ready, time to step it up, make a statement.

CHAPTER
FOUR

J.T. WAS DRIVING WEST ON THE 401, Get looking out the
window of the brand-new minivan they'd picked up at a
car rental place J.T. said was owned by the sergeant-at-
arms, Danny Mac, but really run by his wife, Gayle, and
the way he smiled when he said it, Get was thinking there
might be something going on there. J.T. said a lot of the
legit businesses were turning pretty good profits these days.
"And this way the van never gets listed as rented out."

Get said that was a sweet deal, looking into the back,
the seat folded down and the hockey bag filled with MP5
pistols, a couple of M14 rifles and a couple of grenade
launchers Tommy had thrown in, said might be fun. Get
was liking the set-up these bikers had in Canada more
and more and he asked what a patch was.

J.T. smiled and shook his head, said, "It's a fucking
patch, a piece of cloth, like a Boy Scout badge."

Get said, yeah, he was never in the Boy Scouts.

"No, eh," J.T. said. "Well, this is the big patch. Send

them over from Italy or Austria or Belgium, something like that."

Get said he thought this whole thing was from California.

"Back in the day," J.T. said. "Where it started, I guess, but it's all over the world now. Used to be there were maybe ten, twelve full-patch members in the whole country. Everybody else was a wannabe, a hangaround or what they call a prospect."

"That like you?"

"Yeah, for now. And they have other gangs, you know, they have their own names, their own colours, but they're puppets, call them associates, they do what they're told."

There were eight lanes of traffic, steady in both directions. They'd passed the airport, the highway lined with warehouses and industrial malls, all looking pretty close to brand new. Get saw a lot of signs for housing developments, "double-wide lots" and three-thousand-square-foot houses selling for three-fifty, four hundred grand. It seemed to him like this whole area was full of money being spent.

J.T. was saying, "Used to be, you had to spend years working your way up, but a couple of years ago, these guys, the Saints, they took over the whole country. They started out about thirty years ago in Quebec, around Montreal, where all the mobsters start in Canada — well, used to, there's a lot of Asian stuff out in B.C., Chinks and Pakis — but the Saints got big. They fought a fucking war with other bikers in Quebec, took out like two hundred guys, it was wild, like the old west, man, fucking shootouts in parking lots, bombs going off all over the place. Then they took over the whole country."

"Yeah, I heard, they said guys patched over?"

J.T. cut across three lanes of traffic to the 410, heading north. "That's what the cops call it, we don't say that." He smiled at Get, made him wonder who the "we" he was talking about was. "They had a fucking ceremony, actually brought in sewing machines."

Get was starting to notice a lot of the traffic was black guys. Not black, like American black, but dark, dark-skinned Pakis. Or something. He said, "Sewing machines?"

"Like my mom used to use."

Get said his mother wasn't much on sewing.

"And they actually took over all these other clubs, sewed Saints colours onto their jackets."

"You have a jacket?"

J.T. said, oh yeah. "But I can't wear it yet, till I get my patch. If I get voted in."

Get said, if.

"And boots and leather pants, man. And a bike. Shit, when I got back from Afghan and I called up Chuckie — this was right after the big takeover when these guys were starting to look like they knew what they were doing — he brings me to a clubhouse, shows me around, says what kind of bike you ride?" J.T. was smiling at the memory. "I said, you know, a Harley, what else. I was driving the new Charger then, before the new Avenger came out."

"You like Dodge?"

"I like horsepower."

"But you didn't have a bike?"

"I went and picked one up," J.T. said, "after I saw the way they worked and saw some future in it. It's too fucking loud and you can't carry shit."

Get was laughing. "Some fucking biker you are."

J.T. was laughing, too, saying he was the new breed. Then he said, "You know, they got a lot of crap in with the new patches, but some decent money-makers, too. But then, what really happened, this guy Richard Tremblay, the French guy you saw at the clubhouse, he came down to Toronto and like a week later the top guy in Montreal, guy they called Mon Oncle 'cause he was like everybody's favourite uncle, gets picked up. Right now he's the only guy in a women's prison, they built him a special wing."

"Because the Saints are so big, they might break him out?"

"Truth is, man, the Saints don't give a shit about him. He's gonna rot. They're just about done this reorganizing, getting back to only a couple dozen full patches, settling things down."

"Yeah, they giving out retirement plans?"

"Only one way to lose a patch."

Get said, yeah, like these guys we're going to see.

"We finish this," J.T. said, "that'll be about everybody. Then we deal with the Italians, get them in line."

Get thought, shit, that's ambition. He was supposed to get a real feel for these guys, see the operation and tell his mom and Uncle Main if they could be counted on, if they could be steady suppliers. Main always going on and on about how it's all about uninterrupted supply, they could get that, they could live their dream of running all of Detroit, maybe all of Michigan, themselves. At least that was his mom and Main's dream, Get thinking now it was looking like he could make it happen. If that was what he wanted.

J.T. said the Italians were having troubles of their own. "They're not all one big happy family, you know? For years Toronto was run out of Montreal, even though Toronto got bigger, because Montreal had the connections with New York, called it the Sixth Family. You ever hear that?"

Get said he didn't follow it much. "But my mom, and my Uncle Main? They're all over this mobster shit, think it's a way to get their black ass out the ghetto."

"Worked for the Italians."

"That's what they say, I don't know. You not American up here in Canada," Get said, "but you got to be close enough to see things in black and white."

"I thought Americans only see green."

Get said, yeah, "That's what we say," but he wasn't so sure. The street, the Army, everywhere he'd been, fucking Iraq, people saw things black and white. His mom, his uncle, a few of the others, they were always looking for ways to go big, thinking money talked loudest, but Get, the more he saw the world, the more he saw ways to get screwed. Banks, big companies, all those guys supplying the Army with all their shit — they were just playing the same game on a bigger field.

J.T. said, "Anyway, we're supposed to have a deal with the Italians, was part of the patch-over."

"But it isn't working?"

"I don't know, when Boner botched that fucking hit," J.T. said, "which was kind of funny, hitting that guy, his wife going down on him."

"Yeah," Get said, "funny."

"I thought we'd send him right away again, go finish it off, maybe even give it to me."

"Do the job right."

"I know Richard really wanted it done, but now Nugs says it it's not a priority."

"Shit," Get said. "Can only be but the one boss."

"Yeah," J.T. said, "but which one, right? Richard, the boys in Montreal, they united all the other bikers, coast to coast, they got all the big Colombian connections, they set up all the shit with the Italians for everything through Europe."

Get said, Europe, and J.T. said, yeah, heroin. "You remember all that French Connection shit?"

"Old movie with Gene Hackman? Car chases?"

"That's the one. That shit was real, came in through Montreal down to New York."

Get was thinking, yeah, his cousin Obie loved the movies, showed them that *French Connection* on one of his movie nights, all the kids laughing at the scene in the bar, those two white cops coming off so tough, all the brothers in their Hollywood pimp get-ups lined up and taking it. Get thinking he knew a few bars now, he'd like to see two white cops all by theyselves . . .

J.T. was saying back then the bikers were street dealers and muscle. "Or hijacking trucks, or busting up warehouses, enforcers, you know? But mainly drugs. They bought wholesale from the Italians and they sold in every bar, every corner. You wanted to sell in Montreal, you worked for them."

"The way it is," Get said.

"Yeah, right, except they got so big. Once they got rid of all the other bikers, all the other dealers, this Mon Oncle, one day he says, why the fuck we taking orders from these Italian assholes, and he gets on a plane to Caracas, drives into Colombia, starts bringing back his own coke."

"Yeah," Get said, "because they already the muscle."

"Damn right. Starts small, but over the years, works his way up. Italians so fucking full of themselves, watching too many movies, believing all that shit. Didn't wake up till it was too late."

"And this Uncle guy, he didn't see Richard coming?"

J.T. said, yeah, I don't know about that. "There's a lot of rumours, Richard keeps to himself."

Get could see it, though. Guys work their way up together, make it bigger than they ever thought they could, find themselves in charge, nobody left to take on. Start looking at each other. That was about where his mom and Uncle Main were, ready to make a move, Get thinking since he got out of the Army he wasn't that skinny nigger on the bike anymore, wondering how strong they'd let him get.

Wondering, how strong did he want to be.

These guys, the bikers driving fancy European cars, they seemed to have some good ideas. He said, "But your man, Nugs, he's the president?"

"National president, yeah. Richard, he's the last of the Brothers."

Get said, "Brothers?"

"They're from Quebec, you know, French and Catholic, get a lot of their names and shit from that. When they were all these independent chapters all over the country Richard and this Mon Oncle and a few other guys get the idea to join them all up, a real coast-to-coast operation, you know? But the way it worked, every guy joined a chapter, not a national organization."

"Like a cell," Get said.

"Yeah, or a particular family, like the Mob, a crew."

"Posse, gang, it's all the same."

"Then these guys form something they call the Brothers, like monks, you know? And they don't have a chapter, a city, anything like that, they're nomads, they go all over. What they did," J.T. said, "was they talked to all the motorcycle clubs in the country, convinced them to join up."

73

"Shit," Get said, "like that movies about the gangs in New York."

"*Gangs of New York*," J.T. said, "that was shit."

Get was thinking of another one Obie showed on movie night. "No, man," he said. "All the gangs join up, but the big man doing it gets killed, the Staten Island guys get jacked up for it, have to make it back home?"

"Don't know it, but basically, yeah, that's it, that's what these guys did. Thing is," J.T. said, "it's done now."

"No more need for the Brothers."

"And only the one left." J.T. looked at Get, said, "He's still got all the contacts in Colombia, though, especially for the big-time shipments."

Get said, yeah, knowing all about that, lessons he learned from his mom, the Importance of Supply, lose it for a day — you lose your customers. MuMu in New York also playing it close to his chest, these Colombian connections not that easy to come by. After a minute he said, "Which way we going now?"

J.T. said they were going north. Northwest a little. Get was lost. They'd left the big highway and were going through a suburb.

And Get was surprised the suburb was mostly black people, or at least that dark-skinned brown. Like that Sunitha chick he was thinking about so much, thinking how that could only be bad. He said he didn't think Canada had so much colour and J.T. said it was just in the cities.

"We turn onto Highway 10, pass through Orangeville, you seen your last brother."

"What about Indians?"

"Pakis? Running the general store, maybe."

Get said, no, "I mean like Tonto and shit."

J.T. laughed. "You serious?"

"Yeah."

"Actually, you know, I think there is a reservation up here, probably pretty small. We do deal with the Mohawks out by Cornwall, they have a sweet deal, reservation is over the border, half in Canada, half in New York State."

"Just walk the shit across."

"Yeah, but those fucking Warriors, they always want such a big cut."

Get said greed was a real problem. "Hard to find a man do an honest day's work for an honest day's pay."

J.T. said, you get that from your old man, and Get said my uncle. "He was with Young Boys, back in the day."

J.T. said, "So they were really all kids?"

"Started way back before we were born," Get said, "like in the seventies, some shit like that. Couple of guys, dealers, you know, small time, Eastside, my neighbourhood. Working that corner across from Birney Elementary, looking at all those kids in the playground, got to thinking."

"'Cause the kids don't go to jail. We have that young offenders law here, too."

"That's part of it. But the other thing is, cops can't try to turn a twelve-year-old informant. Can't pay them off, you know, wire them up. Social workers all over it." Get was thinking about his own social workers, do-gooder chicks from community colleges.

J.T. said cool.

"But they got too big, man, Fabulous Frank and the Gee Man. In the eighties it went from heroin to coke, it was all over town, in the downtown offices and out in all the suburbs and they were moving it all. My uncle said it

75

was like a drive-through, kids set up like lemonade stands."

J.T. said, "It got too public."

"They were famous, Fabulous Frank and his gold-plated Glock. They went down around the time I was born, eighty-two, eighty-three. My uncle was like sixteen, getting ready to move up anyway. Had to regroup."

"Probably didn't take long."

They were through Brampton by then, driving on a two-lane highway that was straight as a ruler, you could see for miles, up and down over hills, farms on both sides.

Get said, "When the demand's that heavy, there's always someone trying to supply. Wilma kept things going, she's Fabulous Frank's wife, visiting him in Jackson, and a lot of people say she was really running things. She moved out to New Mexico, or Nevada, some shit like that, came back for business." What his mom wanted to do.

J.T. said it was a lot like these bikers. "These guys we have now, Richard and Danny Mac and OJ, maybe they used to ride bikes all the time and shit, but now it's a real business."

Get said, yeah, OJ, he didn't know the Saints had any colour. "Thought that was against their rules."

J.T. nodded, said it was. "Maybe it still is in the States. They have it right there in the charter, no niggers. No cops or ex-cops."

"Shit."

J.T. said, yeah, but in Canada it was different, even in the beginning. "It said, no members of African descent. You know, polite fucking Canadian gangsters."

Get laughed.

"But they've always been a little separate, you know?

Shit, they had ex-cops right away in Montreal and the whole black-white thing is different. It's just business with these guys."

Get said by the time he came along it was still the Young Boys model but they called them different things, Pony Down, The Threes, other things, and there was no famous leaders or anything. "It's like working at McDonald's, you know? Ronald fucked off somewhere and you just worry about your franchise." Except if your franchise is losing market share and someone else is moving in, it doesn't get settled at head office. Get was looking at the trees going by, every once in a while a house with a pickup out front and sometimes a mountain bike and almost always a Ski-Doo, thinking how he was getting so tired of it and he wasn't even thirty. It was all so different after being in Iraq. Coming home, it seemed so small, everything the same. Whatever you did last week you just know you're doing next week. His mom's big-time plan, make the move, go big or go home, Get was thinking, was he not sure about it because he didn't think it would work or because he wasn't sure he wanted it even if it did? Thinking he wasn't about to tell J.T. any of that.

J.T. said, "There's a place up here, has pretty good burgers, you hungry?" and Get said sure.

The place was like a fast-food restaurant, but part of it was an old Toronto streetcar with tables you could sit at.

They got cheeseburgers and fries and onion rings and Cokes and sat out in the streetcar. The place was empty and Get asked how they could make a living.

"Cottage country." J.T. took a huge bite of the burger and said, "People are lined up out the door on Saturdays all summer, going up to their cottages. Friday nights, too."

Get said he heard of some guys had fishing boats or

77

maybe went hunting in northern Michigan, up in the Thumb, they called the peninsula. "But not many from my neighbourhood, you know."

J.T. said in Canada cottages used to be a middle-class thing; typical family, house in the burbs and a shack on the lake but that was all changing. "You got million-dollar places in Muskoka now, movie stars flying up."

"That where we going?"

"No," J.T. said, "that's the other side of Georgian Bay. We're going up to a place called Owen Sound. I guess way back when, it used to be something, big port or something."

"And that's where the Gunmen are?"

J.T. said, "They got two shitty-ass clubs. London and Sarnia. They deal with the Rebels in Detroit."

"Got a place on Eight Mile."

"You know them?"

"They still have that no-nigger rule."

"Such assholes. Bosco calls himself vice-president. Vice-president of fuck all. The prez is up here, Murdoch, got himself a farm. They're with Los Gusanos in Texas. They were supposed to patch over to us, or get the fuck out of the way, but they're too stupid."

Get finished off his cheeseburger and sucked Coke through the straw. He said, "Some guys believe all that shit about being independent, renegades, all that."

J.T. said, yeah. "And some people think that shit in Afghanistan we were in was something to do with liberating people."

Get nodded, said, "Liberated something."

"Yeah, you and me. Come on." J.T. piled all the wrappers on his tray and dumped them in the garbage can on his way out.

Get followed him to the minivan thinking how he'd like to get liberated some day.

•   •   •

Sunitha said Brampton was Desi, not black, and Get said, "What's that?"

"Indian. India Indian."

"Like Pakis?"

She looked up at him, shaking her head, saying, "It means 'motherland,' anyone with roots there. But we only say it to each other."

Get said, "Like nigger. White boys so pissed off there's a word they not allowed to use."

He liked the way she never stopped her rhythm, both hands, up and down on his dick. She really did give a hand job as good as any blow job, and she didn't get distracted.

She said, "Yeah, we have to keep something for ourselves. Or we used to, people're using it all over now, magazines, TV shows, we gave it up too easy."

"I saw some Negroes, too, what were they? Rastas and shit?"

She still didn't miss a beat, up and down, squeezing and easing off, squeezing and easing off, and looking him in the eye. She said, "How come you Americans can live right next door and not know a fucking thing about Canada?"

Get said, because. "Who gives a shit about Canada."

She shrugged a little, playful, looking away, saying, "It's got some things you like," looking back at him with those big brown eyes.

Get laughed and said, "Bitch."

79

She had a lot of that lotion smelled like kiwi on her hands and she slipped her fingers around his balls, soft like, barely touching him, then she squeezed a little, finger on his taint, her other hand still tight on his dick.

Get said, "That is good. Come on, let's fuck," and he started to sit up.

She said, "Oh, I don't know," and he said, it's easy, I'll show you how, and she laughed and said, "I don't know if I want to," and Get said, sure you do.

She looked at him and he knew she was a little scared, she was smart enough to figure that out when they hooked up downstairs, but he didn't think he wanted her to be. Realized that this was the first time he felt that way since Lisa in Bahgdad.

He said, "What?"

She started stroking him again, licking her lips and saying, "I like the taste of kiwi," and Get said, no wait, hold up, "What's the matter?"

She said, "Nothing, you're a nice guy."

"Yeah?"

"You're really going to like this."

He said, yeah, that's good, thinking anybody else he would have just said let's fuck and they'd have fucked and also knowing that if he'd say it serious enough she'd do it, too, but he wanted to know why she didn't want to.

She licked the kiwi lotion off her finger and he said, "Okay, wait a minute," but she didn't stop. She was good.

Get pulled away a little and said, "Hold up, now, stop."

She said, "What the fuck?"

"How come you don't want to?"

She shrugged. "Time of the month?"

"Be serious."

"Okay, you know why?"

"No, I don't."

She looked away and said, "Because I like you."

"So that's why you don't want to fuck me?"

"Not now, not like this."

Get looked around the room, decent place, nice suburb house, and he said, "What?"

She looked at him and she said, "This is a whorehouse."

"So, you not a whore."

"I feel like it, okay? If you were just some fucking sad john, I'd give you a rub and get out."

He looked at her looking at him, trying to figure this chick. She was probably as old as he was, mos def past twenty-five, got her own thing going with the robberies, okay with the fucking if it didn't mean anything. Yeah, he thought, okay. He said, "But I'm not."

She said, "No, you're not."

"Okay." He sat all the way up, leaned back against the headboard on the bed and reached for his jacket to get his smokes. He took one out and offered her the pack and Sunitha said, yeah, okay, just a sec.

She stretched out face down on the bed, reaching over the edge for her purse and Get couldn't help thinking, what great legs, what a fantastic ass, her skin so smooth and brown against the tighty whities, only thing she had on, her big tits flattened out on the mattress.

He was staring at her with that look on his face when she sat up with some baby wipes in her hands saying, "What're you looking at?" and he said, what do you think?

She finished wiping her hands and reached out for the smokes, long thin fingers, looked like she got a few manicures before she robbed the spas. He handed her the pack

81

of Camels and she took one out, took the lighter from him and fired it up.

He watched her blow the smoke at the ceiling, lean back on an elbow and look up at him. He said, "Okay, what you want to know?"

He watched her take her time, smoke, think about it. He was glad she didn't play some stupid game, ask him what he meant. She didn't want to fuck him like a whore, she wanted to get to know him, see if they liked each other.

But then she said, "What's the point, you finish here whatever you've got going with J.T., you head right back to Chicago."

He said, "Detroit," realizing he hadn't even been thinking about going back. Not even thinking of it as home anymore.

"Hell, I don't you know, you married, girlfriend, anything?"

"No."

She looked at him sideways, didn't believe him, and he looked right back at her, said, "What else?"

She smoked, letting it out slow, then said, "Okay, baby-daddy, how many kids you got?"

"Shit, more'n I can count."

She said, shit, you see, and Get said, "I'm kidding, I don't have any."

She put the cigarette in her mouth, staring at him through the rising smoke. He waited while she inhaled and blew the smoke out and then she said, "Why not?"

"'Cause I didn't want any."

"You always get what you want?"

"Yeah."

They stared at each other.

She said, "You always know what you want?"

And he thought, yeah, that's it right there. Might be something they have in common. Not what he expected her to ask about, though. When him and J.T. got back from up north, back from that fucking bloodbath with the Gunmen, shit, eight guys, did each one when he pulled into the lot behind the Harley dealership — coming up to see the prez, big emergency meeting — stuffed into whatever piece of shit car they drove, or tow truck, Get couldn't believe it, fucking tow truck drivers, bouncers at shitty-ass clubs, guys working in body shops, these the badasses won't patch over? Him and J.T. working serious, saying it was just like being back in Afghan, smoke a big joint and lay in the weeds, wait. Whole thing took less than a few hours and they were back in Toronto, the clubs were still open, but they were antsy, needed to settle down. J.T. said maybe they shouldn't go out, running into some asshole could get ugly, they should just stay in.

Then when Sunitha got there with some more jewellery and credit cards — this time from a massage parlour she said mostly served dykes — Get was way more interested in her than in any of the little Asian chicks didn't speak English.

Now he was looking at her thinking, no, he didn't always know what he wanted. He never really thought about what he wanted, everybody else always seemed to have it planned for him. His mother, not even twenty-five when he was ten, getting him his first corner, he was a natural, worked his way up, still working his way up, his mom always finding another level they could get to. He said, "What do you want?"

She said, "We're talking about you."

"I'm the one wants to fuck, what do you want?"

83

He watched her pick at the waistband of her panties, not look him in the eye, say, "I want to get out of here."

"You can go anytime."

She reached way over to the night table and flicked ash into the empty beer bottle. Then she said, "I want to go rich."

Get smoked and looked at her. She still wasn't looking at him. He said, "You got some idea?"

She waited a bit, then she looked up at him, those big brown eyes again, said, "Why, what's it to you?"

"Everybody like to be rich," Get said. "You don't get that way robbing old ladies getting they pussies waxed, you must have some other idea," and he waited while she thought about telling him her plan, made up her mind she didn't want to, then wasn't sure.

84

She said, "I've got an idea."

"I know you do. You been working it out, but you can't do it yourself and it's too big for Lydia and the white girl."

Sunitha laughed and said, "But you're just the guy to help?"

"I might be, I knew what it is."

She took another drag on the cigarette, blew a few rings and then blew them away with a long stream of smoke. "I have to work out some more details."

Get looked right at her. He did like her, no doubt. And he wanted her to like him. He never thought like that — till the Army. Tommy K'd been telling them for years what a great scam the Army was, but nobody believed him. Then when Get's mother saw that picture in the paper, building in downtown Bahgdad tagged Chicago Mob Boys, she started to see it was true, punks going to Iraq and shipping home guns and bombs and the purest dope they'd ever seen, she wanted in on it. Uncle Sam was going to make it available, they wanted their share, and Get was the best bet. Army looking for bodies so bad they were changing the rules all over the place. All kinds of guys getting in never finished high school, had done juvie time, were known affiliates.

And, truth told, Get liked the Army right away. Did his infantry training at Fort Benning, Georgia — hotter than Tommy put up with at Camp Leonard Wood in Missouri learning to drive a truck — and the next thing he knew, seemed like the next goddamned day, he was in Baghdad. Asshole sergeant trying to scare them, first day, take them out to work a roadblock, street didn't look that different from back home, shit it was nicer, cars going by, buses, Get thinking who the fuck's riding a bus to work in Baghdad the middle of a war? Then somebody starts firing at them, just popping off a few rounds, no big deal, but the rest of the new guys, shit, falling to the ground, pissing themselves, yelling.

Except for Get and a white boy with a shaved head and a tattoo on his neck, they took up positions, returned fire. Asshole sergeant took them back to the base, said to the white boy, you Aryan Nation? White boy says, no, White Rule. Okay. Sergeant looks at Get, says, "Whatever you are, over here we're all in the same gang, you got to leave that shit in America. We're here to kill the ragheads, not each other." Fair enough, man, no one saying anything about giving it up for good.

But the time he spent there, Get started to see things different. The months he was in and out of that juvie jail behind 1300 Beaubien, right next to the big boys in the Wayne County Jail — all that fucking razor wire around it — he was never away from anything long enough to

85

think about it. Never away from the people he knew. Shit, he realized, his whole life till then he'd never been twenty blocks from all the same people, half of them family, cousins and aunts and uncles. But in Iraq and then Afghanistan, when he got promoted and got more freedom, he started to see things.

He started to see himself. See what he could do if he ever got away.

Sunitha was sitting up now, dropping her cigarette in the empty beer bottle, saying, "You hungry?"

So, she didn't want to tell him her big plan yet. She was starting to think about it, think about him like that. Like someone she could talk to. And he was starting to think about her as someone he could talk to.

See if maybe her plan could get them both away.

He said, "Yeah, I bet J.T. ordered Chinese," and they got dressed and went downstairs.

● ● ●

Angelo Colucci was watching the TV mounted on the wall behind the counter, couldn't take his eyes off it, saying, "Eight fucking guys, what are they, animals?"

But he was impressed, Big Pete could tell.

There were six or seven guys sitting in the restaurant, the pizza place with the wood-burning oven, watching the scene on TV. Cops everywhere, mostly OPP from Owen Sound, but a couple of cops from Sarnia and even Toronto, gone up to identify bodies and help with the investigation.

Rocco, the guy they had actually running the restaurant, watched the TV reporter talking about the dead bodies all stuffed in the trunks of cars and said, "Looks like she's about to come."

"Best fucking thing ever happened to her."

The eight bodies — early reports had said as many as twelve, the reporters seemed disappointed now — were most of the Lone Gunmen motorcycle gang from Sarnia and Windsor. They'd all been shot and dumped on a piece of land owned by the gang president, Mad Mike Murdoch, just outside Owen Sound. He was in custody and the rest of the gang was missing.

Big Pete knew this meant they were next. Really, *he* was next.

The only guys not watching TV in the place were three truck drivers eating calzones, two of them brothers, telling the other guy he should always gas up at the Shell on Rutherford Road and collect the points, the other guy was saying all those points are bullshit, you can never cash them in for anything, and one of the brothers said, no, last year they got enough, they bought their father a snow blower.

Big Pete had seen the three cement trucks when he'd arrived a half hour ago. Now the drivers had finished eating and were drinking espressos. Made Big Pete wonder if the straight life was a good idea, could he haul cement all over town, buy his old man a snow blower? A little late for that now.

That was their biggest problem now, too many guys looking for something else, not enough ready to step up when they need to.

Colucci motioned him over and they went in the back room.

"So that's it," Colucci said when he closed the door, "all the other bikers gone."

Big Pete said, yeah, that's it. "These Saints, they're the only ones."

87

"Fucking animals."

Big Pete didn't say anything. Eight guys in one night, it was a lot but it wasn't a record in their business and he knew Angelo knew it. Shit, everybody knew about Angelo and the guys from Montreal went down to New York in '81, took out three captains in one night, really made them something. Now Big Pete was thinking maybe they'd been riding that too long.

Colucci said, "So these Saints of Hell, these assholes on wheels, they think they run the place now?"

"They don't really ride bikes much anymore," Big Pete said. "Not the top guys. And they have a lot of soldiers."

Colucci was sitting on the edge of the big table, the back room more a private office than a storeroom, his arms crossed over his chest, and he said, "I fucking know that."

Pete waited, a good idea what was coming.

Colucci said, "So, what do you think we should do?" and Pete said, you know.

"Why don't you tell me."

Big Pete was looking right at him, thinking, was it you tried to kill me? Stand here and talk to me like nothing happened, maybe try it again tomorrow? "I think we should pop these motherfuckers, take them all out like they did those assholes," pointing his thumb back to the restaurant, the TV.

Then Big Pete watched while Colucci thought about it, he could feel him going over everything in his head, trying to decide what was best for him — and only him, Colucci only ever thinking of himself.

Colucci said, "There's a lot more than eight of them."

"Yeah, there is."

Probably too many to take out, Big Pete knew that, but

he wanted to find out which way Colucci would go. Couldn't just roll over and take it up the ass, had to do something.

"We have a deal," Colucci said. "We have a truce, it's working. Nobody wants a war."

No, Big Pete, thought, you don't want a war, do anything to avoid it. Then he thought, maybe taking out Big Pete was the anything. He was the only guy, didn't like the deal they made, let everybody know, didn't like where it was going, these asshole bikers bringing in all their own coke and now their own heroin, the whole Afghanistan fuck-up changing everything.

"Really," Pete said. "It's working so good?"

"It's working."

Pete said, come on. "They're doing whatever the fuck they want. They took over all the downtown clubs."

"Not all."

"They've got all their own supply, all the coke, all the meth, we don't even know where they're cooking it. Now they're putting money out on the streets all over, they got massage parlours on every fucking corner, they don't give a shit about this fucking truce, this fucking bullshit deal."

Colucci shrugged like, what're you gonna do. "We didn't take them serious enough."

"They're not serious, they're fucking assholes, punks."

Colucci wouldn't look at Big Pete, saying, "Every time we turn around they're there. They got deals with everybody in town, all the Chinks, the Pakis, fucking Irish assholes."

"Even us."

Colucci said, "Yeah, even us," and looked at Big Pete like maybe it was time. Maybe they weren't just going to roll over.

89

Big Pete said, okay, good. "We shouldn't do anything right now. It'll look like we saw this shit on TV and got scared."

Colucci was nodding, at least he agreed with that, and Big Pete thought yeah, okay, he needed the time, too.

See which way this shit was really going to go, who was trying to kill him and who he should make his deal with.

He needed to see what he could get out of that hooker, Becca, find out who she was talking to.

"We can take out a couple of the top guys," Big Pete said, "and give something to the cops, that fucking task force supposed to be in our pocket, let them take some out."

"Do their fucking jobs," Colucci said.

Big Pete said, right, thinking, give him time to do his.

90

• • •

Millie was saying how getting together with other couples, having sex with each other's spouses, that's what really kept the marriages together and McKeon said, "Yeah, keeps that spark?"

And Millie said, yeah, it sure does. She said, "Look, detective, as far as I know, you only get one life, right? And it's short. But it's long enough to get bored."

"Bored?"

Millie said maybe that wasn't the right word. "Crushes. You remember when you were a teenager, detective, and you got crushes on people? Now, maybe sometimes you still do, but it makes you feel bad because you're married."

Price was thinking this wasn't getting them to their

murder, so he said, "That what was going on with the Lowries?"

Millie looked right at him and smiled. She kept looking at him, like now he was the only one in the room, the same way she'd been looking at McKeon, and Price had to give her credit, she was good. She was saying she didn't know anything about the personal lives of Michael and Sandra. "I can only speak for myself, detective."

McKeon said, and you still get crushes, and Millie kept right on smiling at Price and said, certainly I do. And then like she was tearing her eyes away, but it was hard, she looked back at McKeon and said, "But Mark is the love of my life. He's the man I want to grow old with."

"It's just in the meantime."

She smiled at McKeon and said, "In the meantime. You know, detective, it's what ruins perfectly good relationships. Perfectly normal feelings come up, we try and drive them out of our heads but they keep coming, they're natural, and we're so conflicted. Most people start lying and cheating and hurting each other."

"Or," Mark said, the first thing he'd said since hello, "they become real assholes."

McKeon said, well then, a lot of people must go through this, the amount of assholes we see.

Millie said, "Everyone goes through it."

Price said, yeah, well, "Last Saturday, did anyone turn into an asshole on the cruise? Anything happen with the Lowries?"

Mark said, "I don't think we have to tell you."

"You don't have to, but it would sure be decent of you."

"Really, nothing happened on the cruise."

Millie smiled like a teenager and said, "Well, I wouldn't

say nothing," and Price figured you give this woman a straight line, she's going to take it.

He said, "But no fights, nobody got drunk, nobody got pissed off."

"There were over a hundred people," Mark said. "Someone must have gotten pissed off."

Price was actually starting to like this guy. Sitting in the living room of their condo, a few miles from downtown, too close to the burbs to be really trendy, but still very nice, fifteen floors up and looking out over Lake Ontario to New York State, the guy and his wife really seemed relaxed. Like they had it together. The guy was probably ten years older than his wife, he'd said he was retired from Bay Street and if he was sixty he was in good shape. Bald, but so was Price.

The wife looked a little older than the picture on the website, she was probably in her fifties but, man, Price thought, she takes care of herself. Still, he was pretty sure, you pissed her off she'd let you know right away.

"Okay," McKeon said, "maybe we can start with a list of who else was on that cruise."

Price liked the way she said it, so casual, no biggie, but he had a hard time not smiling.

Millie smiled. She said, "Not a chance."

Mark said, "We have over thirty-five hundred members in our club and many of them are lawyers. Probably even lawyers you've heard of."

"Nothing happened with Mike and Sandra," Millie said. "They're like a lot of couples, they come to the club for the atmosphere, they flirt, they feel sexy but that's about as far as they take it."

McKeon said, "So not everyone ends up with another partner?"

Millie said, "No, detective."

"We're an off-premises club," Mark said. "There's never any actual sex at our club, certainly not on the cruise." He looked at Price and said, "But it would be legal, the Supreme Court said so."

Price said the Supreme Court says a lot of things. He was seeing they weren't going to get anything useful here but McKeon didn't want to let it go.

She said, "So, the Lowries, how long were they members?"

Mark said they weren't going to give them any more information. Something passed between him and his wife, Price could tell they hadn't agreed on this idea of calling the cops. He figured they'd expected it would come out and they just wanted to get out ahead of it.

Millie said, "We're not ashamed of anything we do, we use our real names and we've been in the newspapers and on TV a number of times."

McKeon said, "But."

"But, not everyone feels this way. Mark almost never sees his grandchildren, his children don't approve. Some of my family won't speak to me. Many of our members feel they have to hide and sneak around."

"But there's a new club in Parkdale," McKeon said. "Very public, people line up on Queen Street to get in."

Price noticed Millie shrug it off but he saw it was a sore point for Mark. He said, "New competition?"

"Not new. They used to work for us. Josie and his pussycat."

Millie, right away trying to make nice, said, "His name is Jocelyn, he's European."

"By way of Chicoutimi."

"And his wife is American, Katherine, Kat."

93

Mark said, "Club Spice they call it, took it right off our slogan."

Price said, "They taking many members?" and Mark said no, at the same time his wife said some people join both clubs.

"Membership isn't expensive."

Mark said, "They're trying to be downtown and hip and young, so that's where you've got the drunks and drugs and the problems."

"But you don't?"

Mark was getting pissed off, and Price was thinking, good, but the guy was smart enough to take a break and let his wife be nice.

She said, "You should come to one of our dances, see how it works, I think you'd be pleasantly surprised. Most of the people know each other, it's very laid back, fun. We have host couples to make introductions for newcomers. You never feel left out."

Mark said, look. "What ever happened to the Lowries had nothing to do with our club, it was just unfortunate timing. Like Millie said, we don't really know that much about their personal lives. Maybe they had debts, or shady business dealings."

Price said, "Shady business dealings?"

Mark said, "I'm sorry detective, I'm a little out of my league here."

McKeon said, sure, we understand, no problem and Price looked at her sideways, thinking good cop was one thing, but it was like she was trying to help these people stay out of it.

Then she stood up and started thanking them for calling, telling them how much they appreciated it and Price thought maybe she had something in mind so he stood up, too.

They were out the door a minute later, Millie saying to them, "Stay happy," and riding down in the elevator when Price asked, what the hell?

"They weren't going to tell us anything."

"We could have pushed them a little harder."

"Wouldn't have done any good."

They walked through the lobby of the condo building to their car, parked right in front of the doors. There was a yellow ticket on the windshield from the condo company, looked just like the real thing. Price took it off and dropped on the floor of the passenger seat, getting in.

McKeon got in behind the wheel and started the car.

She said, "You heard him, how many lawyers are members, they know their rights."

"They also know something happened on that cruise, know some names."

"You think some swingers from the suburbs pulled up beside the car, popped two people and drove away like nothing happened? You think this was an amateur?"

"Well, they didn't seem to be into anything, piss off any pros."

McKeon looked at him and said, "Maybe we should go to one of their dances, ask around."

Price started laughing and said, "Oh shit, Maureen, you looking to add some spice?"

"That woman liked you."

"Yeah, I'll bring it up with Cassie, hey hon, you want to go to a wife-swappers club? I'll be the one, come in tomorrow carrying my balls in Tupperware."

"Don't know till you ask. She made some good points."

Price said, "Yeah, maybe not."

But he looked at McKeon different, wondering what was up with his partner.

•   •   •

Gayle looked over the minivan and said it looked good, clean, and J.T. said, "We aim to please."

She was still leaning in the side door, flipping the seat back up, and J.T. leaned in close beside her and said, "We really do," and she looked at him like, are you crazy? Here? But that was one of the things she liked about him.

The good-looking black guy was there, too, looking at the new Camaro and the Nitro and Gayle didn't think he had any idea about her and J.T. Who'd think that, a woman in her late forties and this guy, not even thirty.

That, and she was married to Danny Mac, sergeant-at-arms and a full patch for almost twenty years, and this kid was getting voted on in a couple of days.

Still leaning inside the van, J.T. said he had a couple things to do, but he'd be home around seven and Gayle said, so, what's it to me, and J.T. said, nothing, not a thing.

Gayle said, "You are so bad."

"Bottle of wine, some sushi from that place you like, the spicy salmon."

She knew from outside the van it looked funny, their two asses sticking out, taking way longer than it should to check over the interior but she didn't want to say good-bye yet. She looked at him sideways, Jesus, he was good-looking, like that fucking Brad Pitt in *Thelma and Louise*. And she was Susan Sarandon, the cool older chick. When she first saw J.T., when she snuck him into the garage, that night at the barbecue at OJ's, said she knew what he was looking at, she was amazed he didn't shrivel up and die right there. She thought, God, he must be a fucking psychopath, one of these guy's wives coming on to him and he doesn't freak out. No, he just said, yeah, I'm looking at it, looks good. Made her feel seventeen years old again, she pushed him up against the beer fridge, kissed him right there. Next day went to his place, woke him up and screwed him all day.

Now he was standing up saying, "Here's something weird," and she pulled herself out of the van, looking around, seeing the black guy sitting in the Avenger, waiting, and she said, yeah, what?

J.T. leaned back against the van and said, "I was talking to my lawyer, that Chinese chick, Rachel Chin."

"Yeah." Gayle saw them together, the two kids, twenty-somethings, having drinks in some trendy bar, chocolate martinis or vodka shots in glasses made out of ice, talking about what they have in common. She said, "So?"

"She tells me she heard Sherry talked to a divorce lawyer downtown."

"Sherry, Spaz's wife?" It made Gayle think, no way, he's not thinking about that. She looked at him, not caring now who was watching or what it looked like, thinking he's got to know this is just fun, just a little living on the edge, for the rush, it isn't real. She said, "That's crazy."

He said, "Yeah, I know, but what I heard, she offered this lawyer a lot of money, a very big piece of a big settlement. Said something about knowing where the real money was."

Gayle said, "Holy shit. I knew Sherry was dumb, I didn't think that dumb."

"I thought you'd want to know."

"You tell anyone else?"

J.T. said, "You think I'm that dumb? Tell you the truth, I wish I didn't know."

97

Gayle said, yeah, I know what you mean, and looked at him again, smiling this time and he was smiling back. Good, she was thinking, good. He knows the score, the real score.

She said, "Thanks. I'll straighten this out, don't mention it to anybody."

"Don't worry," he said, "I'm good with secrets," and he winked at her as he walked away.

She watched him go all the way to the Avenger, get in, say something to the black guy and drive away. Then she laughed, thinking fucking kid has balls of steel.

Too bad she was going to have to end it soon. Plant some money on him, say he stole it. 'Cause she sure as shit wasn't going to end up driving off a cliff.

CHAPTER FIVE

DANNY MAC LIT ANOTHER SMOKE and turned the stereo down in the car, his brand-new Toyota FJ, the new Land Cruiser series, came in bright colours, yellow or blue or red with the white roof and built-in rack. Danny's was black, black roof, tinted windows. Nice interior. He said to the hangaround, Mick, skinny kid with a lot of tats, that it was basically just fraud.

"Just forgery. The papers call it identity theft, or some crap, but what happens is, you forge somebody's name on a mortgage, pay it off, gets discharged they call it. Then you sell the house to someone else."

Mick said, "This what happened to your mom?"

"My aunt. The thing is, she owed like one more year, less than ten grand. She's sitting there one day, guy knocks on the door says he bought the house, she's got to go."

They were parked behind a strip mall in the west end of town, north Etobicoke, what used to be a working-class neighbourhood now falling to shit.

Mick said, "The fuck she does."

Danny took a drag on his smoke, rolled the window down a crack, and said, "Damn right. But she can't get the fucking deed back. The bank says the mortgage has been discharged and the house sold. Got a new mortgage on it now."

"But it's a forgery."

"So my aunt starts calling people. She calls the cops, they can't do shit because the new sale is legal. She calls a lawyer, she can't do shit because my aunt's got no money, and then she calls the bank and they say there's nothing they can do because they're the victims of a crime here, too."

"Weren't they supposed to make sure the signature was legit?"

Mick was tapping his hands on his knees like a drummer.

Danny looked at him, all wound up, and thought, yeah, we'll see about this kid. About all the kids. Nugs getting ready to really be the national president, Danny pushing him into it — though it wasn't hard, he could tell Nugs wanted it — just have to make sure they really have the manpower, the soldiers. Lots of these guys think they want to be bad boys, push comes to shove, how many really do? That's what they've got to find out.

Danny said, "Fucking banks. They're blaming it on a crooked lawyer, say the deed was registered properly so the fucking lawyer is crooked — which I'm sure as shit the fucker is, we'll deal with him later — but this banker asshole was in on it."

"Yeah, you sure?"

"He knows the paperwork, he knows who's so close to paying it off, who looks like a little old lady can't do anything."

Mick drummed faster, saying, well, he got that wrong.

"Plus, he had the buyer lined up, guy pays almost nothing for it, some fucking asshole thinks he's a developer stealing old ladies' houses, getting them tossed out, then he puts up a monster house, twenty-five Pakis living in it. Or, he sells it again, just flips it. My aunt went to see this banker asshole, she's in fucking tears, he kicked her out. I went to see him yesterday, told him to tear up that paperwork, my aunt's not going anywhere, steal the money from some other account. Guy says there's nothing he can do."

"Nothing?"

"That's what I said, I said there was plenty he could do, he knew what was good for him. Asshole looks at me, says, 'You threatening me?' What the fuck did he think I was doing?"

"You losing your touch?" Mick was smiling when he said it but Danny Mac wasn't, so he said he was only kidding and Danny said, yeah, okay, I get it. He was happy to get his aunt out of a jam, his mom could be a hero to her big sis, but he also wanted to see about these kids, see what they could really do, if they had any flex.

"Still," Mick said, "it's a good scam, maybe we should get in on it."

Danny said, yeah, it is. "But where we going to find a crooked lawyer?"

Mick was laughing and Danny said, "Here he comes, the fucker. Go talk," and Mick was out of the car and walking to where the bank manager was getting to his car.

The manager, still in his thirties, Danny'd figured he must be ambitious, slowed down when he got to his orange Nissan Murano, supposed to look like gold or some shit. Danny watched him, thinking, yeah, what's that? Somebody keyed your new fucking car, put a scrape all the way down the side. Watched him follow it, looking surprised, right to the back end when he finally saw Mick standing there.

Danny thought he'd say something first, but the kid just slammed the tire iron into the guy's stomach, a good shot, and the guy bent over, then the kid smacked him in the side of the head, knocked him down to his knees. Then the kid slammed him on the back a few times and when the guy curled up in a ball he let him have a couple more on his arms he had wrapped around his head, Danny thinking, shit, that's got to hurt.

Then Mick walked back to the FJ and got in, still pumped, saying. "Fucking asshole."

Danny said, "You tell him?"

"What?"

"My aunt's house? You tell him to fix that fucking paperwork?"

Mick said, oh shit, and got out of the car, walked back to the guy, up on one knee now, holding onto the bumper of his Murano.

Danny thought, fucking kids, still have a way to go. Watched the kid smack the bank manager in the head a couple of times, put him right down. Then the kid knelt down and dragged the guy out from under the car by his hair, said something to him, dropped his head to the pavement and walked back to the car.

This time Mick got in saying, "Fucker knows what to do," and Danny pulled out of the lot.

They were driving away, south on Albion, and Mick said, asshole. "Says he knows people. I fucking him told, yeah, and they know us, don't fuck with us. Asshole."

Danny said, good, he got the message.

"He got the message."

And Danny thought, good. Whoever he thinks he knows isn't good enough anymore. Now it's us, the old Rebels taking over.

And with an army of these hangarounds, these guys like Mick and Boner, they can really make shit happen.

•   •   •

Coming out of the jewellery store and walking fast down the sidewalk, Lydia couldn't see out of the screen in her burka and tripped over the little fence around the parking lot, falling on her ass. Sunitha walked right past her and opened the car door, saying, "The fuck you laughing at?" and White Girl behind the wheel said, "Oh, come on, look at you."

In the back seat Sunitha wanted to look in the bag, the dark blue purse she got to match the burka, but she knew better. It was heavy. It was good. She pulled the burka over her head.

Lydia said the guy never suspected and White Girl said, "I didn't know how you did it, you couldn't distract him with your tits."

Lydia was pulling at the burka saying, "Oh he was looking, he knew where they was," and trying to get the thing off, but there wasn't enough room in the front seat of the Beamer and Sunitha said, watch it, you'll tear the damned thing, we're going to use it again, so Lydia sat there wearing it. She said, "Where'd you get these?" and Sunitha said, "eBay."

White Girl said, fucking A.

"That plastic thing you used to tie his hands," Sunitha said. "Where'd you get that?"

"Tie wrap. Home Depot, baby. Taught me that at

Western Tech, shop class, use it to tie up all the wires."

White Girl said, "You could be an electrician you know," and Lydia said, yeah, I know. She said she was taking the whole course, she liked it, but when they started running wires and they brought out the knees pads for them to wear, she said fuck that.

"All those boys, looking at me wearing fucking *knee pads*? I don't think so."

Sunitha said it was good, it went clean. She looked out the window at Brampton passing by, the suburb. She didn't want to come back, too close to where she grew up, but White Girl was right, the jewellery store was used to chicks coming in wearing burkas, head scarves, all kinds of shit. Lots of jewellery stores out here were, they could do this a lot more.

And J.T. would take all the gold and silver and diamonds they could bring him, he just paid so crappy.

Turning onto Highway 10, White Girl asked if they wanted to stop at Tim Hortons but Sunitha said no, she wanted to get home, thinking this place'll never be home again.

Then White Girl said it was good they were so sexy in those tents, he never looked down, and Lydia said, what do you mean, and White Girl said she didn't think many burka-wearing chicks wore the Adidas Ali Boot Hi Special Edition. She looked over her shoulder at Sunitha and said, "What did you pay for those, two hundred?"

"You think I shop at fucking BOGO Paymore?" Sunitha put her feet up on the back seat, right on top of the balled-up burka.

Lydia said, "Float like a butterfly, sting like a bee."

Sunitha was looking at the boots, like a boxer's boots, white, with black writing all over them, quotes from Ali.

She liked, *It's not bragging if you can back it up.* She said, come on, "Those people love Muhammad."

"Different Muhammad."

Yeah well, Lydia said, he never looked down. He buzzed them in, there was no one else in the place, and the guy came around from behind the counter, all sleazy and dripping with greed, saying how could he help the fine ladies and Lydia pulled that Glock out from under the burka and said you can fill the bags, asshole. Guy seemed to be more pissed off at being called names by a chick, he didn't even move so she smacked him hard, knocked him off his feet and got the tie wraps out. Did his hands and feet, shoved one of those red velvet rugs from under the jewellery in his mouth while Sunitha cleared out the whole display case. The drawers underneath were locked, and the guy wouldn't tell them where the keys were right away. Lydia pulled the velvet thing out of his mouth and said, "I'm only going to ask you once," and the guy said, "Nigger bitch," and Sunitha was surprised Lydia didn't shoot him in the head.

The way she stomped on his balls, though, Sunitha knew it would be a long time before he was back at a rub and tug looking for a sixty-dollar blow job. Gave up the keys, though.

They took the 427 south off the 401 and headed towards downtown.

White Girl smoked and offered the cigarette to Lydia who took it and then couldn't get it into her mouth through the screen in the burka. She said, shit, and White Girl said, don't worry, girl, "You be smoking soon enough."

Sunitha thought about saying something sarcastic, you two are so cute, all flirty like that, but she let it go. Good for them, they found each other. She remembered working in the massage parlour, Lydia coming in, still in high school, tall skinny black girl with those big lips, said she was tired of giving it away for free. Really, though, Sunitha could see her looking at the little Thai chicks like a man would, seeing why she was really there. Staying in school so she could be on the basketball team, was supposed to get a scholarship to some big American college but she punched out the prick in town set up all the recruiting camps, guy asked for a blow job, Lydia saying, "I told the mother-fucker it was sixty dollars."

Still, at the summer camp for underprivileged kids she met White Girl there doing community service — White Girl's father using his money to keep her out of jail and trying to teach her about life, how hard it would be if he ever cut her off.

Didn't know his little girl could be so resourceful.

Lydia said, "How much you think we get?" and Sunitha said ten thousand anyway, and Lydia let out a holler, whoo-hoo, girl! But Sunitha knew it was a quarter what it was worth. A tenth.

She knew J.T. and Nugs had something going, they were stealing and buying up all kinds of gold and silver, melting it down and using it to buy coke in South America, heroin, all kinds of shit. Hell, she was buying up gold online herself, it was still going up. Every time some-body said it had topped out, the gold bugs watched it go up again. Six hundred, six-fifty an ounce. Sunitha thought it could be seven-fifty this time next year, some guys online said a thousand.

What she really wanted to do was find J.T.'s stash. Now that would be a score.

Lydia said, "We drop you at your place, okay? Start planning the next one."

Sunitha said, okay sure, knowing that meeting with J.T. would get rid of any idea of going after what he's got. His way of dealing with that shit was worse than the gold miners in South Africa.

Unless she knew a guy could help. Maybe some guy from Detroit.

• • •

Kristina Northup said, "Are you telling me there's never been a major inquiry or a Royal Commission or anything like that into organized crime in this city?" and Garry looked at her and said, "Are you kidding, in Toronto?"

"And no big investigation into police corruption?"

"Again I say, in Toronto?"

"Well, there must be plenty of crime."

"But if it's as hard to organize," Garry said, "as a decent catered lunch is this town, there's nothing to worry about."

They were walking around back of a five-million-dollar house in Rosedale. Used to be two old Tudor houses on the lot but they'd been knocked down and this huge house put up, all modern clean lines, concrete and steel, big windows and a huge deck looking out over the tennis courts in the backyard and the woods of the ravine. Kristina was thinking if you sat on the deck and didn't look up too high you could think you were way out in the country, not almost in the middle of a huge North American city. Then she thought, shit, why would you ever want to be way out in the country?

The location manager, Abigail, had gone inside to talk to the maid, and the scout, Kristina couldn't remember his name, guy looked like a teenager with a fake beard, was wandering around with his camera shooting everything in sight.

Kristina said, "It just seems like a rite of passage, you know, New York, Chicago, Philly, L.A., even Montreal, they all had their big organized crime inquiries, police corruption scandals, politicians using it for all kinds of press, but not Toronto."

"Ainsley would look good there," Garry said. "She comes out of the house onto the deck." They were standing below it now, looking up. "Shoot it from here, she's wrapped in a blanket, it's blowing open, we get a nice look up her legs, follow it right up, use the crane."

"Kevin follows her out. You want to do the fight out here?"

"I was thinking the make-out, the one with her and Kevin and Brittney."

"You want to try and shoot a threesome sex scene outside? You don't think that might be tough? Continuity might be an issue?"

"Right, who's going to notice anything but three naked movie stars making out."

"So now you agree Brittney Dineen is a movie star, good, but if no one's going to notice, why do it outside?"

"No risk," Garry said, "no payoff. It'll get people talking, be the scene they remember."

Abigail opened the door under the deck overhang, looked like it was some kind of rec room, pool tables and a fireplace, and said they could come in through there, see the rest of the house, and Garry was saying right away how this had potential, too, maybe do something with the pool table.

Kristina was still thinking about crime. This movie she was producing, Garry was directing, was supposed to be a light crime caper about some trophy wives pulling off a robbery, proving to their rich old husbands they were more than just pretty faces and fake boobs, though as Garry said, what's more than that? The more they worked it, though, every rewrite coming in from Allison, chick used to write sitcoms, was darker and more serious. Garry was always talking about the sex scenes, that may have been what he liked right from the start, the trophy wives banging each other, too, Kristina saying this porno, or what, and Garry saying we've got tough chicks pulling off all this crime, got to give something to the boys, but Allison was always going on and on about the effects of the crime, how it would change the women.

Kristina thought all that character arc bullshit was way too screenplay 101, but what she really wanted to tell this Allison was, look, I'm seeing this guy, involved with this guy, fucking this guy, she didn't know how to describe what she had with Richard and never cared with any guy before, so why did she now? Anyway, he's *involved* in crime and it's not making him all serious and, what did Allison say, disconnected?

Of course, Kristina really didn't know for sure that Richard was involved in crime, or how involved. Now she was laughing at herself, thinking that's funny, she back in denial about the men in her life?

Garry came outside saying, you've got to see this, "I know where we're putting the scene," and Kristina followed him through the house to the kitchen and said, "Here?"

"Come on." The room had a fireplace and a huge aquarium, six feet long at least, full of tropical fish, a big double oven like a restaurant and black marble counters everywhere. Garry said, "Picture Ainsley's pale butt on this. Brittney's. If I can convince her to show off that red bush."

"It'll be cold."

Garry said, it'll be sexy, "And look," pointing at the double glass doors leading out to yet another deck, this one facing east and south, no other houses in the eye line, just tall trees and downtown buildings off in the distance. "Perfect."

"At least," Kristina said, "you're a director who likes something."

"Oh, come on," Garry said, "we're making silly movies with sexy stars, it's fun. I don't have time for any of that bullshit baby-angst, we're-so-bored, everything's-dull crap. Really, this whole generation's just so fucking scared to try anything, they might fail, can't admit that, though, too easy, has to be some big, complicated *issue*. Shit. Wake me when the shooting and fucking starts." He laughed and walked into the dining room and Kristina heard him say, "Oh now, wait a minute, you could have an orgy on this table, serve up some fine Hollywood flesh, I love obvious symbolism."

The location manager, Abigail, had been standing by the door to the pantry with the maid and now she said to Kristina, "They want ten grand a day and we have to put four people up in a hotel — separate rooms."

"Sounds like this movie. Four Seasons?"

"Or one of the boutique hotels."

Kristina, still thinking like a line producer, figuring it'll take four days to shoot the scene, at least, the base camp'll have to be two miles away because there's no way these neighbours'll put up with trucks lining the street and fifty people walking all over the lawns, they'll have to have a dozen shuttle drivers to get people back and forth from makeup, it'll be a nightmare, and expensive.

Oh well, Kristina figured, at least with Garry shooting it, it'll look expensive and it'll be sexy, not one of those cold, alienated sex scenes like so many Canadian movies. Have to make sure Garry starts the rumour the stars really got off.

They looked over the rest of the house, finding a couple of bedrooms for other scenes and even the garage would work for the scene with the young wife, Ainsley Riordan, pulling the gun on her husband, taking it out of the trunk of her sports car so casual, Kevin kneeling on the concrete, the gun in his mouth, Garry saying it'll be fine, we'll cut to his piss going into the drain. Kristina thought it'd be good and she was happy Garry agreed to have it in the garage instead of outside in the driveway, they could use it for weather cover if they needed.

Now, back in the van, going to the next location, the restaurant that was supposed to be in Chinatown in New York, Kristina was back thinking about Richard and crime and she said to Garry, "How much money you think gets spent on drugs in this city every week?" and he said, wait, "Aren't you the Princess of Pot?"

"What?"

"Isn't your dad some kind of big-time international drug smuggler? Don't tell me there's a Hollywood rumour might not be true?"

Kristina said, for Christ's sake, Garry, "My dad's a hippie," but thinking, yeah, he was the King of Dope, smuggling tons of it back in the day, back when it was a real weed grown by old guys in Afghanistan and Pakistan, a little Mexican, some Thai stick. That seemed so different, though, so innocent. She knew her father never touched a gun, never got into wars over it, he was pretty much the banker, filling out phony customs forms. Wrote a book about it and retired to Gibsons Landing in B.C. to make organic bread.

"Well, there's no more hippies," Garry said, practically reading her mind. "Nowadays drugs are sold by professionals."

"Okay, and how much do you think gets spent on them in Toronto?"

"You mean all drugs? Pot and coke and X and stuff?" and she said, yeah.

Garry said, "More than gets spent on movie tickets, that's for sure."

"You really think so?"

"Come on, what do you think the average pothead spends a week? Hundred bucks? You talking the whole GTA, Hamilton to Oshawa?"

"Yeah."

"Okay, that's like four million people, maybe closer to five, you go all the way up to Barrie, Guelph, all that? All the potheads, anywhere from fifteen years old to fifty, fifty-five, say it's one in twenty."

"Five per cent. You think that many?"

"How many people you know smoke dope?"

"How many do I know don't?"

"Say it's only one per cent, one dope smoker in a hundred, that's still like, fifty thousand."

Kristina said, "Shit."

"Times a hundred bucks a week, what's that, like, five hundred grand?"

"Try five million."

"Hey," Garry said, "that's why you're the money and I'm the art. Then, you've got to add the partiers, the coke-heads — I can't believe people are still doing coke —"

"Are they?"

"Oh my God, get out more. And crack and X and meth, you want to count all the speed at the casinos?"

"I'm trying to figure out how much money gets spent on illegal activities a week."

"*Activities?* You want to include hookers, escorts, massage parlours?"

"Shylocks, are they still around?"

"Every club I've ever been in, and they are legion, had a 'partner,'" Garry actually making the air quotes, "came in with the money."

"So, it's big."

Garry said, "Honey, no city in the world could operate without it. Nothing would get done. I thought the only reason you were in the movie biz was to launder money."

Kristina said, "What the fuck?" But Garry was laughing, saying, kidding, honey, I'm kidding. "But now," he said, "I'm not so sure."

"I think I may be the only person trying to do this legit."

"This for a movie, you thinking about some kind of *Serpico* thing?"

"First we'd need some cop to get himself shot in the head and survive, take on the whole corrupt force."

Abigail was driving the van and she said, "Last year a bunch of the narcotics cops got arrested."

Garry said, oh yeah, that's right. "It was news for about a day and half. Nobody got shot, though, no drama."

"Okay," Kristina said, "but you think there's like two or three million dollars a week spent on illegal activities in Toronto?"

"Tax free, baby, tax free."

Shit, that was true, too. Pretty much doubles the take-home. She thought that could be something for a movie, but really what she wanted to know was how big a piece of that was Richard getting. She never saw him worry about money, never saw him even think about it, he just always had some and a lot of it was cash. Thinking about it now, Kristina realized he was the only guy she ever met paid for meals in restaurants with cash, dropping two, three hundred bucks on a table and never bothering with a receipt, paid for his last trip to Costa Rica cash, gave the travel agent twenty-five hundred bucks in cash. She knew he was involved in crime, organized crime, the minute she met him, the first time she slept with him, saw his tattoos, his Saints of Hell skull and the others, but she really didn't know what he did, how high up he was.

The truth was, she'd never thought she'd still be seeing him, figured he was a fling at best, a rebound after that asshole she was married to made her look like a fool, couldn't keep his dick in his pants. Now she was thinking the smart thing to do would be break it off, make some excuse and stop seeing him before she got in too far and couldn't get out.

The smart thing. Never really Kristina's specialty. Really, how bad could he be? Like Garry said, this was Toronto, nobody worried about crime here, it was New York run by the Swiss.

But then the restaurant in Toronto's Chinatown looked just like a restaurant in New York's Chinatown, they wouldn't even have to dress the place.

CHAPTER SIX

HOMICIDE DETECTIVE RAHIM 'Ray' Dhaliwal said, "I don't want to fucking talk about it," and then he said, "I just can't fucking believe it."

Beside him at the bar his partner, Lou Mastriano, said, "Do you not want to talk about it, or don't you believe it?"

Dhaliwal lifted up his beer, said, "It just pisses me off so much, you know."

Levine walked up beside him and said, "What, working with Lou?"

Mastriano said they'd been in court all day, the sentencing. "That kid."

Levine said, oh yeah.

"Makes me sick. Fuck."

Mastriano said, "He doesn't want to talk about it."

Dhaliwal said, "Eighteen fucking months." He drank some beer, shook his head. "Aggravated fucking assault, he killed him, fucking murder."

Levine said, "This the old man?"

"Sixty-eight, not old."

Levine said, yeah, that's true. His own father died at sixty-five but his father-in-law was going strong at seventy-nine.

"Guy was walking on the sidewalk for fuck's sake."

Mastriano said, yeah, he knew.

Dhaliwal said, "You know, maybe the old guy was a pain in the ass, every day he walked past these kids, every day he said something to them."

No one said anything. They all knew Dhaliwal had to talk about it, get it out.

"Get a job, lazy kids. He probably gave them some of that 'in my day' bullshit everybody hates."

"Probably."

"But you know, those lazy fuckers *should* have jobs."

"Yeah."

"And maybe he called the kid a Paki, so fucking what? You think nobody ever called me that? You think I never heard that a million times? Since I was five years old, go home fucking Paki."

Mastriano said, "You know it."

"So what, the kid's fucking Tamil, who even knows what that shit is?" Dhaliwal picked up his glass but then he put it back down. "Eighteen fucking months. Kid is seventeen years old, he's a man. Pleads to aggravated fucking assault. He knocked that old man down on the sidewalk in front of his own fucking house he'd lived in for forty years and stomped on his head till he fucking bled to death."

Mastriano said, "Yeah."

"And I don't even know, maybe it's the right thing, maybe the kid has his whole life ahead of him, maybe he's going to straighten out, be something, never do anything like this again."

"Maybe."

Dhaliwal said, yeah, maybe. "But it just feels wrong. It makes me fucking sick."

After a few seconds Mastriano said to Levine, "So, how the fuck are you?" and Levine said good.

He said he was meeting McKeon and Price, but they weren't here yet.

Dhaliwal said he wanted to get really drunk and beat the crap out of someone and Levine asked Mastriano if he could make that happen.

"Sure, we'll do it."

They acted serious about it, Levine knowing Mastriano would stay sober enough to keep his partner out of trouble and get him home.

And this was one they'd won.

The bar was crowded a half hour later when McKeon and Price sat down in a booth and ordered their beers.

Levine said, "Your buddy, Loewen, the kid, he went up to Owen Sound with his girlfriend."

"If you're talking about the Mountie," McKeon said, "they're on the task force together." The Combined Forces Special Investigation Unit, made up of Mounties, City of Toronto cops, and Ontario Provincial Police. Jason Loewen had been partnered with Price while McKeon was on maternity leave and then he'd been sent to narcotics — till pretty much that whole department got busted by the very same combined force that was now looking into the murder of eight members of the Lone Gunmen motorcycle gang.

"Some task force, everybody sleeping with each other."

Price said, hey, yeah, "Maybe we should ask them about these clubs."

McKeon said, ha ha, you're funny and Levine said, "Oh right, your drive-by, the swingers club."

McKeon said, "Lifestyle club." She was the lead investigator on it, the Major Case Manager. She said, "We met the owners of the club. Nice people."

Levine nodded like he was serious and said, "I'm sure they are. I'm sure they'll be very helpful, you'll get a lot of people coming forward with statements."

McKeon finished her beer and waved at the waitress for another round even though Price still had half a pint and Levine hadn't touched his. "Oh yeah, we're flooded with calls."

Price said it was weird. "These people had no enemies, there was no reason for anybody to kill them."

"Who knows," Levine said.

The waitress put three more pints on the table and was gone before anyone could say anything. The place was filling up now that it was after seven, a lot of downtown office workers finishing for the day, not wanting to go home and be alone. Like the cops.

"You know," Price said, "I would have thought something personal, but I don't see how you can have a jealous spouse when you're doing it together."

McKeon said, yeah, she didn't think it was personal. "Plus," she said, "the shooter was good, it wasn't like some amateur, firing a hundred rounds into the car. Looks like every shot hit someone."

Levine said that was weird, but he'd already lost interest.

"So," Price said. "You got something?"

Levine said, "You going to order any food or anything?" and McKeon said no hard enough that Levine said, "Okay

118

then. Right to the point. Your car dealer, Sheldon Kichens, was involved in some nightclubs downtown."

McKeon said, "He had that kind of money?"

"Surprisingly," Levine said, "no, he didn't. But he knew some people who did. And some people who needed it. He was putting them together."

"These the people," Price said, "he was supplying with stolen cars?"

"You know, not a single one of those allegations has been proven in a court of law," Levine said.

"No, eh?"

"But the thing was, Sheldon was having some personal problems."

"No kidding," Price said, "he was a drug addict."

Levine finally took a sip of his Caffrey's, nodding, and saying, "Yes, well, that was how he was dealing with his problems. Maybe not the best way to deal, but very popular. Well, that and hookers. Lots of hookers."

"So, let me guess," Price said. "He owed a lot of money."

"I'm not giving you a prize for that, it was too easy. Whoa, Maureen, slow down."

She put down her empty glass and said, "You want another one?"

"I'm fine, thank you." He looked at Price who shrugged. Levine said, "Okay then. What I heard is that maybe Sheldon approached somebody in law enforcement about helping him out of his jam."

Price said, "In exchange for some information," and McKeon said, "Who?"

"I don't know for sure, but somebody involved in narco, on the task force."

"That whole thing's fucked up," Price said.

"There are many rivalries in this multicultural city of

119

ours," Levine said. "It's not easy keeping a lid on a potential turf war."

Price said, yeah, "Especially with just as many rivalries on that task force," and Levine shrugged, what are you going to do?

Price said, "And it's just gotten worse since they brought in that Mountie to run it, what's his name, Monette?"

"Yes, well, whatever."

Price looked at McKeon who'd already waved the waitress over for another beer — and this time a shot of Johnny Walker, too — and saw she wasn't paying any attention so he said, "Hey, Maureen, this is your deal, you know, you're the one interested in this."

"Yeah? Really?" She shrugged like she didn't care but she wouldn't look at him.

Levine said okay, well, if that was everything, Mrs. Levine would be waiting up and he left half a pint on the table.

When he was gone and McKeon downed the shot and sat there drinking the beer in long gulps, Price said, "You know, Maureen, this isn't really like you, and I'm a little concerned," and she said yeah, well.

He said, come on, what's going on, and she said, nothing, the usual.

Price leaned back in the chair, they were sitting side by side, both with their backs to the wall, no one across from them now that Levine was gone. He looked at his partner and saw someone settling in for a drunk, someone who wasn't going to stop till they didn't know who they were. Price sipped his beer and figured the thing to do was let her have a couple more and then take her home. Her husband, guy named Morton they called MoGib, had been staying home with the baby since her maternity ended. Price figured they probably weren't sleeping too much and were probably fighting a lot. Shit, he'd been down that road himself with Cassie, but that was ten years ago, he couldn't remember what worked. He probably stayed away a lot then too, he was in the Fraud Squad, could be close to office hours taking statements, filing reports. Nothing would have helped.

Looking at McKeon, though, Price realized it was a whole different dynamic if the husband was staying home and the wife was working. Especially this job. Everybody she meets some kind of lying crook, scheming bastard, and her husband hanging out in the playground with the moms.

Fuck it, Price thought he could use another drink himself.

● ● ●

Louise O'Brien said she didn't think it was right, that's all, and Levine said, "What's that, women's intuition," and O'Brien said, something like that.

They were standing beside the car, a purple Beetle with big yellow flowers on it, down near Cherry Beach. The ambulances and fire trucks were still there and the first patrol car on the scene, driven by Anjilvel who said Brewski was off sick. "More like hungover," Levine said, and no one said anything about that. The Beetle was off the road, Unwin Avenue, across from the old power plant, and pretty well hidden in the weeds and trees.

On the other side of the brush was Lake Ontario, a bike path running all the way downtown, but the old industrial area, all the way up to Lake Shore, was a wasteland.

Two guys had found the car and seen the woman inside. They said they banged on the door and she never moved. The driver's seat was reclined all the way, looked like she was sleeping. The two guys were waiting over by the patrol car.

"It's just not right," O'Brien said. "There's no purse."

"So, we can get the ID from the plate."

O'Brien looked at Anjilvel and said, "But there should be a purse, right?"

Anjilvel said, probably. It was close to three in the morning, the place deserted, except for the gay guys out cruising. The two who found the woman, one had been on a bike, the other in his car, told Anjilvel they'd only been there a few minutes. The car was already there. The one on the bike said he saw something taped to the tailpipe so they looked closer. Anjilvel told them they'd have to tell the story a few more times.

Now Levine was sitting in the passenger seat of the unmarked, pulled right up into the brush beside the Beetle, saying it was leased by a Rebecca Almeida, "Got an address, 10 Yonge," and O'Brien said that would be those condos right on the corner of Queens Quay. Levine said, yeah, "Right across from the Star building."

"With the big egg beater out front. Some kind of art."

"That's the one."

"What floor?"

Levine said, twenty-six.

"Why didn't she just jump?"

"Didn't want to splatter such a nice body."

O'Brien looked over her shoulder at him, shook her head, and went back to looking through the car. She said if it was a suicide, though, a young attractive woman committing suicide, there should be a purse. "And probably pictures. And music playing, but the radio was off. And a note. Something. All she had were her keys."

"And priors. Couple of possessions and a fraud against the phone company, looks likes bad cheques, and a prostitution."

"Not much to drive you over the edge."

Levine said, no. "But you never know."

O'Brien said they should talk to the witnesses so they walked over to the patrol car. One guy was sitting sideways in the passenger seat with his feet on the ground outside the car and the other guy was leaning on his bike, kind of sitting on the crossbar.

"Hey there, I'm Detective Levine, this is Detective O'Brien." He held out his hand and the guys glanced at each other before the guy in the passenger seat of the cop car reached out and shook, saying, "Brian Bondar." He was in his early thirties, clean-cut, looked like he went to the gym every day after working in an office cubicle.

The other guy, the guy on the bike, said his name was Michael Canton and he shook hands with O'Brien and then Levine. He was younger, late twenties, and he looked like he also worked at some white-collar job but he put a lot of miles on that bike.

O'Brien said they really appreciated them sticking around, it was such a tragedy, and Levine said they also really appreciated that they called it in.

Canton said, "What do you mean?"

"Well," Levine said, "you know, with a lot of crimes, people just keep moving, don't want to get involved."

Canton said, oh right, "Suicide's a crime. I forgot that."

O'Brien said, "You didn't see anybody else around the car, did you?"

"Anybody else?"

123

The guy in the car said, "No, it was just sitting there."

"It was locked," Canton said. "We tried to open it, you know, when she didn't move. When it looked like she wasn't sleeping."

"Well, when we saw the hose on the exhaust," Bondar said.

Levine looked back at the Beetle in the brush and said, "You could see that from over here?"

Canton said, "We were over there," and pointed to a spot off the road.

"Still," Levine said, "to see the tailpipe." Looking over, only the purple roof of the Beetle was poking up out of the brush.

"From a lower angle," Canton said, and Levine looked from him to the car and then he got it, right, like if someone was, say, on their knees.

Bondar said, "We kind of ran over. We banged on the door and tried to open it, but you could tell."

O'Brien was nodding, writing down that they saw the hose taped to the tailpipe and ran over. She said, "What time was this?"

"A half hour ago, maybe, forty-five minutes."

Levine said, okay thanks, and started to walk away.

The guy in the police car, Bondar, said to O'Brien, "It does seem like a strange place for a suicide."

Levine stopped and looked back. He was out of the circle now, it was just O'Brien and the two gay guys.

O'Brien saying, "How do you mean?"

"Well, it's like the car's hidden in the brush there. You'd have to be right in the brush to find it," Bondar said.

Then Canton said, "But it's down here, so close to the water, there's plenty of places over there, you could sit in the car and look out at the water."

"Yeah, but what difference does it make," Levine said, "if you're just going to kill yourself?"

All three of them looked at him and Bondar said, "Then why not just do it in a garage?"

Levine said people do strange things. "They don't always think them through."

Bondar said she got all dressed up, did her makeup and her hair.

"And," Canton said, "she didn't jump off a roof or jump in front of a subway. Why would she want to look so good if no one's going to find her for days?"

Which Levine knew would have happened if these two guys hadn't called it in. The car could have sat in the brush for days. Weeks.

O'Brien said okay, thanks very much, shook hands again, and started to walk away.

Bondar said, "Can we go now?"

O'Brien said yeah, sure. "And we really appreciate you guys calling it in and sticking around."

Levine was already back at the Beetle when O'Brien walked up beside him and said, "See what I mean."

"Yeah, you got your experts on it now."

"Makes sense, though. I bet anything we get the tox back on her, there's roofie."

Levine was looking in the car. The dead girl, Rebecca Almeida, was maybe twenty-five, long curly hair, fresh makeup, it was true, subtle but effective. Nice cheek-bones, nice glossy lips. She was wearing a short skirt, kind of frilly, and a white blouse and a bra showing through.

O'Brien said, "The boots don't go with the outfit," and Levine said, you want to bring your experts over, and O'Brien said, "Teddy."

Levine said, "Okay, okay. It just would have been a lot easier if this was suicide."

"Since when is this easy."

● ● ●

Sunitha had Universal Flow on her iPod, filling her head so she couldn't hear the steady hum of her purple Venus G. The last time she used it the batteries, bullshit triple As, died before she finished, so at least that wouldn't happen again. On her back with her knees pulled up, looking out the window at the sun coming up, she was hitting her spot but not getting any closer.

Thinking about this guy, Get, was what got her so close and also why she couldn't finish. Bastard. Hadn't met a guy like this in years. Or ever, really. Now she knew she used to think guys were cool, they were put together, but she was a kid then, a baby. Since she quit drinking and stopped doing coke, stopped working the rub and tug parlours — since she started, as Lydia would say, thinking like a man — since then she hadn't met any real men.

She rolled over onto her stomach, onto a pillow, one hand on the vibe, one on her clit, thinking, fuck him. Then laughing, thinking, yeah, fuck him slow, her ass moving up and down.

He'd just sat there on the bed when she said she wouldn't fuck him, and they talked. Fucking joking around. What they wanted to do with their lives.

She'd almost told him.

Now she was moving the Venus G faster, humping the pillow. She'd almost told him how she just knew J.T. and the boys must have at least a thousand ounces of gold — at today's price of six hundred and twenty-eight fucking

Canadian dollars an ounce.

This guy, Get, seemed like he could handle something like that. He didn't get all weirded out when she said she didn't want to fuck. He didn't slap her around or beg her like a kid, he just said okay and they talked. Made a connection.

No, shit, she didn't want to think that. She kept humping the pillow, slowed down the vibe, pulled out her other hand and bit her knuckle. She didn't want her fucking life to spiral down that hole again, end up dependent on some asshole, pimped out and strung out. Not when she was so close.

Fuck it.

She rolled onto her back, pulled out the vibe and thought, fuck it. So close, but she just couldn't put it over the top by herself.

Just like this goddamned gold. Every time she handed the fucking rings and chains over to J.T. she saw the price going up on the markets, knowing it was six twenty-eight today, it'll be seven hundred soon, a fucking grand before long.

The vibe was still humming in her hand, Perpetual Loop still in her head, now it was "Be Happy." Ha, that was funny. She rubbed the vibe on her thigh, right at her crotch, moved it slow. Yeah. This Get up from the Motor City, he could be the real deal. He talked to her like a grown-up and she thought she saw something in his eyes, like he wanted something more, too.

Oh stop it. She laughed at herself, that kind of bullshit's what got every whore on her knees. She let the vibe trail over her puffy lips, though, back and forth, back and forth, up and down, up and down.

She could stay on her game, keep her guard up. She

could use him, he was in tight with J.T., he could find out where they kept the stash, where they melted it down. She reached down with her other hand, put the vibe in a little, then a little more. No, think about the gold, the score. This Get, that's playing with fire, just think about what *you* want.

A little faster. You can do it, you can do it all by yourself. This asshole Richard from Montreal sitting on all that gold, you can find out where it is, just take it. Set up the life you want, the life you deserve.

And when she did get it done all by herself she had her eyes closed and she was looking at Get's face. Last thing she saw before she fell asleep, thinking she'd never see him again, just forget it, could only be bad, screw everything up.

When her phone beeped a few hours later and it was Get asking if she knew any decent restaurants in this town she said, "Sure, I know a couple," and suggested they meet at the Shanghai Cowgirl on Queen West at seven.

● ● ●

Richard's movie-producer girlfriend Kristina was saying people always say how movie stars love to come to Toronto, they like the atmosphere, they like the professional crews, they like not being hounded by fans. "But the truth is," she said, "it's all about the money."

Richard said, "You think?"

"The actors, the big stars, they go wherever the big money is, they go to Spain, they go to Manila, they go to fucking Africa. When the exchange rate was better, when the Canadian dollar was worth sixty cents American, Toronto was a great place to go."

Richard was driving his new car, his Volvo hard-top convertible, Ontario plates. He liked it, it had enough power and it didn't look too flashy with the roof up. When he first got it, he wanted to sit there and put the roof up and down, watch those three pieces come apart and fit behind the seat so you'd never know they were there, but you had to wait fifteen minutes to do it again. Well, it did look pretty complicated.

He said, "Sixty cents on the dollar, makes a big difference with movie star money." He wasn't really listening. He was driving Kristina downtown so she could go to the spa with a woman from some American distribution company. Richard had asked if it was business and Kristina'd said it's always business. He pictured fat old men sitting in the sauna, chewing on cigars, making deals. Now it was thirty-five-year-old chicks, looked like movie stars, faces covered with five-hundred-dollar mud, making deals. He wondered, did they really put cucumber slices over their eyes?

Kristina was saying, "The movie stars get paid in U.S. dollars, no matter where they work. You see twenty million, it's twenty million U.S. But the crew, they get paid local, wherever they are. So a Toronto crew at sixty cents on the dollar looks a whole lot better than an L.A. crew at the full buck."

Richard said, yeah, and thought about his place in Costa Rica, the Gladiator Club, and thinking he might open another one, maybe in Panama, see how that worked out. The locals all paid local and the women they brought in, the escorts, all paid in U.S. dollars. Or their agents paid, those sleazy Russian bastards. Now they were starting to try and sell what they called hot Latinos so they could use local women, pay them next to nothing, but the market was tough, guys still wanting blondes.

Kristina said, "So when we had the exchange, and the tax credits on top of that, it was great. People still blame SARS and 9/11 and Arnold fucking Schwarzenegger but it's all about the money. That exchange rate changes, we're back in business."

Richard said, "But it's not the Canadian dollar going up as much as it's the American going down." He was having exchange-rate problems of his own. Well, not problems, so much, but the bigger international deals were moving away from U.S. dollars and into Euros. And artwork, he could hardly believe it, the brokers in Europe putting together the deals, accepting stolen paintings. He wondered, did they sit and look at them by themselves, show them to their friends, oh yeah, that *Scream* got stolen, here it is, paid for all the heroin in Norway?

And now the gold. Doing the big international deals with gold bars.

Kristina said, "Come on, come on," half under her breath, looking at the cab in front of them, the driver some guy in a turban turned all the way around to talk to his passengers and Richard said, "Relax, honey."

"Well, come on, this was New York or L.A., all you'd hear would be horns."

"Yeah," Richard said, "but it's not," thinking shit, this one starts to be a pain, time to move on.

Then he was thinking he hoped that didn't happen, he liked her. He liked this idea of the movie business, seemed like a place where a lot of cash moved across borders with not much trail. Already she'd told him about deals where guys bought foreign rights to her movies for half a million bucks, money getting wired and a computer file handed over. She said it was up to them to dub it or subtitle it, whatever, but all Richard could think about was what a great business cover that would make.

Richard was still thinking of a good time to tell her what he really did, but he had an idea she was starting to figure it out. She didn't seem too impressed with the phony bad boys, but he wasn't sure how she'd feel about the real thing.

The passengers got out of the cab, two chicks in their twenties, well-dressed in business suits but with short skirts, walked into the office building. Richard watched them go, thinking, these days in this town you couldn't tell if they were a couple of working girls off to give a guy a duo show in his office or a couple of lawyers. The cab moved slow and Richard followed.

Kristina said, "Well, we knew it wouldn't be fun forever."

Richard said, "We did?"

"Sure, you know, when we were kids, when I first started, it was such a rush to be on set, all those people with walkie-talkies, coming and going all the time, everybody in on it, trying to get the shot, get the coverage for the day. We used to celebrate every day, like as if we were all on the same team and we all won something."

Richard thought about that, the way it was fun when they were kids. He wasn't about to tell Kristina, but he felt the same way, before everything changed, before it was all business all the time, it was fun. Such a rush, get a few guys together, pull a job, go into one of those big discos in Montreal, the Limelight or Foufounes Electriques or the Metropolis when it went from being a porno movie theatre to a disco, go in there, let everybody know they were the suppliers now, either the dealers bought their shit, or they moved along, got moved along. Up and down St. Denis and St. Laurent and Crescent, all the clubs. And always there were a few of them, Richard and Pierre and Claude and Denis. Mon Oncle always setting things up, telling them where, making sure they had a steady supply from the Italians, coke and heroin in those days, and so fucking expensive compared to now, the shit just flowing into the country from all over the world. Sometimes he wondered how the street dealers made anything at all, no wonder they were killing each other for an extra block of territory.

Back then it was a party. It was even fun when somebody would try and tell them no, try and fuck with them. Pierre saying, it's all about supply and demand, and we demand that you take our supply. They brought baseball bats and chains and sewed lead into the fingers of their leather gloves. Spend the night handing it out, getting their dealers in line then end up back at Les Amazones, first strip club Mon Oncle opened on the island of Montreal. Four in the morning, eating souvlakis and poutine in the restaurant upstairs with the strippers, chicks up from the Maritimes and in from little French towns all over Quebec, back before Eastern Europe became the white Third World.

Kristina was saying, "So, of course, you want to move up, you go from PA to third AD to office coordinator to PM to line producer or associate and you want to be a producer."

Richard didn't know what all the letters meant, but he understood the moving up, the way you went from hangaround to prospect to patch to road captain with your own crew, maybe even further, sergeant-at-arms, treasurer, vice-president, see how good you were, how ruthless. Kristina was going on about what you missed — what she missed — the hanging out, the being one of the gang, getting loaded at the wrap party, not giving a shit what anyone said, and Richard was starting to see it wasn't her or him, it was just the way things are. You're good at something, you move up, things change.

He turned off Bay onto Elm and stopped in front of the old brick building that'd been turned into the spa and Kristina said, "Wax, massage, manicure, pedicure, facial, the things I do for my art."

"The price you have to pay."

She smiled at him and it made him feel good, made him feel like she knew what it was all about and she could do it anyway.

"So, dinner?"

"With the movie star?"

"Ainsley Riordan."

"Make it a girls' night, I've got things to do, call me later."

She was opening the door, saying, midnight, and he said okay, he'd be at home.

She stuck her head back in the car and he said, "Long day, you really work for it," and she said, "You know it," and leaned all the way over the front seat and kissed him.

Driving down Yonge towards the Gardiner Expressway Richard was thinking it was just like the Kiss-n-Ride, dropping off for a meeting, going to work. Like businessmen.

Like Mon Oncle always said they'd be.

Traffic was stop-and-go on the on-ramp. Richard was still getting used to Toronto, finding his way around. He'd actually got lost a few times, ended up in subdivisions, row after row of brand-new houses all looked the same, everyone he knew, a bored guy with money, just another customer.

He was thinking, if it was one of Kristina's movies there wasn't really a place to get a good look at the skyline of Toronto like there was for Montreal, it'd have to be a helicopter shot. Well, Montreal being an island it was easy. They used to come up from the old farmhouse Mon Oncle had, way out in La Prairie, the first chapter, drive into town and Mon Oncle would pull over before they got on the bridge, the Champlain, sit there on his old Harley and point to all the buildings, Place Ville Marie, Place Victoria — and lots of new ones going up then, too — and the lights on the cross on Mount Royal up above everything else and say something stupid like, it's all going to be ours, or, we're going to own this town, and rev it over the bridge.

Richard would have laughed at a scene like that in a movie, assholes on wheels, man, but it was like Kristina said, it was fun. They were rebels. They were building something, even if they didn't know it then.

Mon Oncle knew it, though. In the movie in his head Richard saw Mon Oncle played by a star, Jack Nicholson probably, but younger, like he actually was in those biker movies in the sixties, or somebody with a little more heft to him, Russell Crowe maybe, or even George Clooney, had to be somebody when he said something quiet, matter-of-fact, you fucking believed him, like you did Mon Oncle.

Maybe the movie would start earlier, if it was the story of Richard Tremblay, the survivor. It'd start when he was a kid, fourteen, fifteen, living on the south shore of Montreal, out in Châteauguay, maybe look like that Coppola movie The Outsiders, tough kids, but Richard would be the one standing off to the side, other kids didn't even notice him. Not till the scene in Weredale, that fucking kids' jail that looked just like the real thing, that'd be in the movie of his life. The day the Guillemette brothers kicked the shit out of him, knocked out his teeth and broke his jaw and his elbow, but he gave as good as he got, would've taken them if it'd been one-on-one, and then Richard never said a word to anybody, not a single counsellor and for sure not a cop. The scene would probably be a montage, dissolve over time till he was getting out and Pierre came to talk to him, said he respected him and knew he was from Châteauguay and did he know any native kids and Richard said, sure, he knew a few at Howard S. Billings High and that's how him and Pierre got into cigarette smuggling.

Now Richard was on the Gardiner heading west out to Hamilton, the traffic finally moving, and he was thinking this movie in his head was too jumpy, had too many dissolves and not enough dialogue, but he liked the scene where he and Pierre walked into the strip club out in that little town, that Pointe-au-Pic, St. Cesaire, Pierre's older sister dancing naked on the stage and she came off and took them to the big booth in the back.

Maybe it would be one of those long takes, a tracking shot all the way from the parking lot, getting out of Pierre's Parisienne, walking past all the Harleys lined up, going in, picking up Francine on stage, following her nice naked ass to the back, panning across the six or seven guys sitting there, all wearing their colours. They were the Coyotes then, all on their own, one of fifty little gangs all over Quebec, and Mon Oncle was maybe twenty-five, old to Richard at the time but nowhere near as old as the president, Marcel Turcotte, must have been thirty, thirty-five. Richard and Pierre just sat down next to the booth and watched the bikers, not even looking at the chicks on stage.

Right away they were hangarounds. If it was his movie, Richard would skip over a lot of that and the prospect stuff when they were gofers, doing the shit work, cleaning up the blood and piss and puke after the parties, taking the overdosed chicks to Emergency at the Charles Lemoyne, and taking all the risks on the job. There'd have to be some of that, hell, some of it was fun, kicking the shit out of some asshole thought he was tough — Pierre always loved that, always gave a few extra shots. And then the vote when the full-patch guys decided if they'd be members, Richard and Pierre waiting outside. And the fucking party when they got their colours, shit, Richard thinking, that scene would be for the DVD only, xxx baby, what a night, couple of nights non-stop.

Going fast on the Gardiner, then the QEW, Richard was thinking maybe it would be like that movie *Traffic*, cool Don Cheadle and that Mexican guy playing cops, different parts all have a different look, washed out blue, and what's it called, *sepia*, looks like faded brown, the movie of his life would get darker then, sharper contrasts, Turcotte shot fifty fucking times by a couple assholes brought up from Texas, Mon Oncle and Stephane Vachon going to jail for a year and a half, looked like the whole thing'd fall apart before it even got started. But then Mon Oncle got out and took over, in his quiet way, like he was your uncle, helping you out, giving advice, bringing in more guys who knew what they were doing.

That's when there'd be that scene coming up to the bridge. When everybody, the cops, the Italians, those fucking Irish Point Boys running the port, all the dealers, everybody figured they were a bunch of losers, assholes on wheels. Nobody seeing what was coming. Richard remembered watching the prospects cleaning up after those monster weekend parties, seeing there was still so much money left over, shit, after all the girls got paid, all the booze, that guy from Ste. Adele roasted a whole pig on a spit, after everybody got their cut at the end of the week there was still so much left, fucking bags of money. Richard thinking, we really couldn't spend it as fast as we made it, and we were trying.

The Italians paid them to be muscle, they hit trucks coming up from the states, and they were running a couple of strip clubs then, and agencies booking the chicks, and the escort business was picking up, but nothing made money like dope. Coke, or weed, hash, they couldn't get their hands on enough. Started making their own meth and X, but a million people wanting to get a little high every day, they could always use more. That's when Mon Oncle, sitting there on his bike looking at the skyline of Montreal, saying this is going to be ours, what he meant was, just ours. That's when he started looking to go around the Italians, go down to Venezuela and Colombia on his own, saying, why not? Who they going to send after *us?*

That's when Mon Oncle really turned them pro, said, come on, you can't have a bunch of cokeheads selling dope, it's like putting a dog in charge of a butcher shop. Turned them into businessmen, took them international, went down to California, the whole club prospects again, this time for the real thing, the Saints of Hell. Using their rules, their charter, said things like, no hypes, must have running motorcycle, males only, no explosives thrown into the fire at parties, fights between members will be one-on-one — the penalties all laid down, usually just "an ass-whipping." But Mon Oncle was savvy enough to know things were different in Canada, in Quebec. Their own charter said stuff like "no members of African descent" instead of "no niggers," "no rapes," and "a member is allowed thirty days without a running motorcycle," the riding season being so much shorter up north. And some bigger differences. The no-ex-cop rule got dropped when they recruited a couple, they started letting in guys of African descent, hell they started letting in Haitians if they could make their quotas, and they would've let in Indians if any of the Warriors at Kahnawake wanted in. A lot of dealers were chicks, fags down in the gay village, some shylocks, too, all backed up with their own crews, a lot of guys started driving SUVs year-round.

That first time Mon Oncle took Richard to California would be a scene, too, explaining the different situation in Canada, saying black guys aren't so many but there are more Greeks in the business and lots of Chinks coming on and those old-timers in Oakland saying, *black guys?* The next time they got together at the world meet in Amsterdam, those old guys were gone, it was a whole new generation, whole new operation, worldwide.

Mon Oncle saying the first thing they had to do was get their own house in order, get rid of anybody looked like they could bring us down, so they cleaned out some of their own chapters. Richard's first bloodbath, all those guys, nine of them from Hull up near Ottawa, snorting their profits, only collecting half the debts owed to them, making them all look weak, easy for the cops to just walk in. Invited them for a weekend party in La Prairie, had that reggae band Smiley's People, bunch of white kids and a black guy on the drums, playing all night, "Cherry Oh Baby," and "Buffalo Soldiers," a reggae "American Woman," and a reggae/funk of that one, "Will It Go Round In Circles," the one about having a story with no moral and the bad guy winning every once in a while, can it fly high, like a bird up in the sky? Just before the sun came up, everybody passed out, took those Hull boys into the old barn and slit their throats, right there where they killed the pig, so stoned they never even saw it coming. Put them in sleeping bags, filled them up with bricks, and dumped them into the St. Lawrence at Cote Ste. Catherine.

Now Richard was passing through Mississauga and Oakville, remembering it, seeing the whole thing like a movie, the next few years, everybody getting cleaned up, haircuts, long beards becoming trimmed goatees, the party houses getting renovated, turned into mansions, the strippers getting classy, yeah, people got in line, the Saints got straightened out, that's for fucking sure, but then those asshole Rock Heavy morons wouldn't get on board. Mon Oncle's old friend, Gus Soare, Gustave, thinking he could run the show.

Now Richard thinking this movie really has too many montages, jumping ahead now almost ten years, fighting a fucking war with the Rock. Lost a lot of good guys, full patches, Pierre blown up in his Cherokee, a few good Road Captains; Andre Leduc, fucking Duck, sergeant-at-arms in Terrebonne, shot in the head five times and Jesus, a couple dozen prospects and even more hangarounds. Wolfman turned informant, lost a chapter out of that in St. Hubert. Whole time Mon Oncle saying don't worry, it makes us stronger, weeds out the crap. Weeded out some good guys, too, but not Richard and Mon Oncle, and he was right, it made them stronger. The new guys they took in, the new prospects all realized it was business and there was fucking huge profits to make. By the time they got rid of the Rock Heavy they were so big and so strong they could take over the whole country.

So they did.

Going over the Skyway bridge into Hamilton Richard was thinking, maybe a lot of that stuff with Sylvie would be too schmaltzy, but every movie needs a hot chick and that was Sylvie Gagnon. First time he saw her, standing naked on the stage at Les Amazones, hands on her hips, yelling at them, saying, hey, look, naked chick over here. They were watching the hockey game on the TV that usually showed porno, a playoff game against Boston, lot of money on the Habs. She had a tight body, nice tits standing right up and in those days hair between her legs. Richard said, hey, and she said, oh, you notice, huh?

Now he was thinking a lot of the movie scenes with Sylvie would seem like too much talk because they really talked to each other. It was freaky how she knew him right away, or got to know him, not thinking he was just another goon on a bike. They stuck together, talked about everything. He moved up, started making real money, saw how that did as much damage to guys and the chicks — especially the chicks — than no money did. Not Sylvie, though, she just went with it, got richer, bought a house, had a baby, called the lawyer when Richard got busted and bailed him out, like it was just part of his job. Like it was.

No, Richard knew, Sylvie would be the star of his movie. She was the one he could talk to, the only one. He knew on his own he would've never done shit, probably gotten himself killed or spent twenty years in the slam, but with Sylvie he became the number two in a national organization. If they were listed on the stock market, fuck, he couldn't even imagine it.

Richard was pulling into Hamilton, his kind of town, steel mills and truckers and breweries, an industrial port, and like Mon Oncle said, they owned it, it was theirs.

There was still a lot of work to be done, but they had it going on, good-looking prospects, lots of capital, they were ready.

If Sylvie was still alive Richard knew he'd still be the number two, he'd still be in Montreal living in that three-hundred-year-old stone house on Rivière St. Jean Sylvie'd turned into such a fantastic place, the whole fucking estate so nice. When she died, shit, he didn't know what to do, didn't have anyone to talk to. Fifty years old and like a kid. So he took over the whole thing.

Now Mon Oncle's sitting in a prison cell in Quebec. Oh well, they got him a flat screen, a laptop, and a couple of hookers twice a month, he was doing okay.

Still, Richard didn't think it was the big Hollywood ending yet, he had more work to do.

141

CHAPTER SEVEN

Louise O'Brien was more interested in what they found on Rebecca Almeida's laptop than Levine was, him saying he'd seen all the internet porn he needed to, if he wanted to see that stuff, he'd get the real thing.

O'Brien said there was no way any of these guys could have known about the cam. She had everything that was on the laptop, a purple iBook with yellow flowers on it, same as the Beetle, copied to her desktop and she was going through everything. When they'd gone through the condo they found the laptop in a hundred plastic pieces on the kitchen floor and O'Brien said that was something, only thing broken in the place, but Levine said it looked like it just fell off the counter by the stool, an accident, and it could have been. The money stuff was a lot less enlightening than they'd hoped. O'Brien said it looked like it wasn't a completely cashless society yet after all, but there were pictures and videos of pretty much every guy who came through the door. There were at least two cams; one in the living room getting the exchange of money — all the guys left envelopes on the little table beside the leather couch, some of them greeting-card sized, Levine said, putz, sometimes the scene ended there — and another one in the bedroom usually caught the whole date. Like the one O'Brien was looking at now.

Price walking by said, "Hey, I know that guy," stopping and looking over O'Brien's shoulder.

She kept looking at the monitor, said, "Yeah? He a homey?"

"Oh, come on." On the screen Rebecca was on her knees, facing the cam, sometimes looking right into it, which made it seem like she was looking right at whoever was watching the vid, smiling and winking like she'd look at it later with someone else, eating popcorn. Behind her, pounding away, his eyes closed, the young black guy had no idea. He was skinny with a lot of muscle definition.

Levine didn't even slow down, walking past the desk, saying, "Little Man."

O'Brien said, "He's a banger?"

Levine was almost to the coffee room, saying, "Raptor, second stringer. He plays if Johnson's hurt. Or says he's hurt."

Price was nodding now saying, yeah, that's right, "Leonard Little, Little Man. Doesn't see much court time."

O'Brien said, shit. "Looks like he's the last one on here, nine to ten the night she died. Shit."

Price said, "Oh, this'll be fun. They only got a hundred and fifty lawyers in that organization."

O'Brien said, "Shit."

Levine was coming back with a cup of coffee and he said, "Hey Louise, you owe me a buck, no roofies."

"Shit. Nothing?"

"Plenty of red wine, and our friend, THC."

"Still doesn't mean she didn't do it herself," Price said. "Got herself relaxed so she wouldn't chicken out."

O'Brien said, "Right, sure, I can sell that, all these famous clients, press gets hold of it." She was staring at the monitor, Little Man flopped on his back and Rebecca looking into the camera making funny faces, crawling off the bed and walking into the bathroom. O'Brien said, "This look like a girl who's going to kill herself in a couple hours?"

Price said, "Anything could happen. She get any phone calls?"

"She had two cells, one was pay as you go, no records."

"Oh there's records," Levine said from behind his own monitor. "And if it was TV we could type in right here and get a list of all the calls she got."

"You might be able to get DNRs," Price said. "Take a couple of weeks. Course, if the phones were illegals, who knows. Maybe she even had more cells she dumped."

O'Brien said, "Thanks, Andre, I'm glad you're enjoying this."

"Just trying to help."

O'Brien had been clicking back through the other video files and pictures. Sometimes the cam was set to take a picture every ten seconds or every twenty seconds, made the scenes look like old-fashioned slapstick comedy porn. She said, "Well, there's where she got the tape," and stopped on a shot of Rebecca, spread-eagled on the bed, her wrists and ankles taped to the posts with grey duct tape. "Same stuff she used to tape the vacuum cleaner hose to the exhaust."

Price said, "Was it in the car?"

"Yeah."

"Lou, this is looking open and shut."

"Yeah."

Then Price said, "Hey shit, is that Big Pete Zichello?"

O'Brien clicked the mouse and moved through a few still shots of Big Pete, dressed now, cutting the tape off Rebecca's hands and feet. He had a cigarette in one hand and she took it from him, smoked, leaning back on the pillow.

"Looks like."

"We're still looking at him for the Eddie Nollo hit."

O'Brien said, "You think he was the shooter himself?"

"Looks like it, good help is hard to find. We had some taps, ran some surveillance but we didn't get anything."

"How long ago was that?"

Price thought about it, looked a few desks down to. McKeon who was staring at her own monitor and he said, "Hey, Mo, how long ago was Eddie Nollo?"

McKeon jumped a little, startled, then looked at Price and said, "Eddie Nollo? Got to be six months at least."

"Big Pete was with that hooker killed herself down by Cherry Beach."

O'Brien said, "Him, half the Maple Leafs, and a bunch of the Raptors." She looked at McKeon, who was back staring at her monitor.

Price said, "Shit, she had rich enough clients, what'd she charge?"

O'Brien said, "Three hundred an hour. Got a few here with a girlfriend, that went for five hundred."

"I'm sure," Price said, "these gentlemen are big tippers."

"Oh yeah, she was making money."

Price sat down and leaned back in his chair, settling in, and said, "She seemed to have things under control, she seemed to be doing what she wanted. Seems an unlikely suicide."

O'Brien said, "You got that right."

"So, Andre," Levine said, "now you've got women's intuition too? You still have a dick? Look, the hotshot lawyers down at the ACC will keep this out of the press, write it up as suicide, you'll never hear about it again."

Price said, "Who's next of kin?"

"Mother," O'Brien said. "Father went back to Portugal years ago."

Levine said, "Officially."

O'Brien said, sure, he could be back, "We don't know. We talked to the mother."

Price said she must be pretty broken up and O'Brien said, sure, of course, and Price said, "So, maybe for her you could work it a couple of days, talk to Big Pete, he knew about the tape."

O'Brien thought that was a good idea, she wanted to, she looked at Levine and said, "We have anything else to do?" and he said, "What? In homicide? No, we're just sitting around," and she said, "So, okay, let's go," and he said he was being sarcastic and she said, "Yeah? I didn't get that."

Price leaned over and put a disc on McKeon's desk next to her monitor, which she turned off the second he did. He looked at her and waited but she didn't say anything so he said, "Got some traffic camera stuff on there from Lake Shore, night of the drive-by blow job shooting. Haven't gone through it yet, don't know if there's anything there."

McKeon stood up and said, "Okay, well, I'll be back in a couple of hours," and was gone.

O'Brien looked at Levine who looked at his monitor like it had the secret to Middle East peace. She looked at Price and he shrugged so she walked over to him, sat her ass on the edge of his desk.

Price said, "I don't know, she's moody. Time of the month?"

"That's all you got?"

"Postpartum?"

O'Brien shook her head and started walking away, saying, "It's a good thing we don't get too many real whodunits, that's all the detecting we can do."

● ● ●

Danny Mac's wife, Gayle, took one of the new Camaros off their rental lot and headed east on the 401 out to Whitby, thinking she could talk some sense into Spaz's wife, Sherry.

Gayle liked the car, sitting low in the bucket seat, it felt like the one she drove when she was twenty-one, first going out with Danny Mac, back in the eighties. She loved to drive that car, open up the T-top and just go. Back when they were young and wild and free.

Now she was pulling into the express lanes, the V8 humming, four hundred horses, six-speed manual, thinking it was cool how all the old muscle cars were coming back, the Charger and Challenger and the Mustang. She'd like to see a new Maverick with some real power or a Duster with a v8.

She pulled right up onto the bumper of a brand-new Lexus, the car doing maybe a hundred and ten clicks in the fast lane, Gayle saying, "Come on asshole, let's go," and jumping back to the middle lane to get past, some rich-looking chick in the Lexus making a face. Gayle gave her the finger and cut back in front, saying, "What a waste of horsepower, bitch."

Led Zep on the radio, ten in the morning, the classic

rock station. The ten till two DJ was just back from maternity leave, Gayle thinking imagine that, the rock chick having a baby and coming back to work. The world sure changed since "Black Dog" was new.

Fifteen minutes she'd be in Whitby and what would she say to Sherry? She had a few things in mind, ways to ease into it, try and find out exactly what Sherry said and who all she said it to, find out what she really wanted, but as soon as they sat down on the big deck off the kitchen, looking out at the giant backyard, the stakes in the ground where the pool was going and the jungle gym already up, Gayle said, "What the fuck are you thinking?"

Sherry didn't even seem that surprised. She said, "I'm just so sick of it."

They were drinking white wine, some kind of Sauvignon Blanc from New Zealand, Villa Maria, Sherry said was really good. Gayle would've rather had a cold beer, neither one of them saying anything about drinking before noon. She'd only been to Spaz and Sherry's place a couple times since they'd moved in. It was a new subdivision north of the 401, farmland that had been expropriated for an airport that never happened, the sign still up at the turnoff, bragging about the four-thousand-square-foot houses on half-acre lots. When they came out for the housewarming barbecue, Danny asked Gayle if she wanted a house like this and she said, why, who we hiding from?

Sherry looked right at home, though. All her painful looks and shaking her head, and being so tired, it all seemed like an act to Gayle, and when Sherry said, "It's just not what I expected," Gayle said, oh no?

"What did you expect, Sherry?"

"I don't know, but not this."

Gayle was thinking, no? She said, "It seems okay."

149

Sherry waved her hand, her big wineglass looking like it was going to fall out, and she said, "It seems."

Gayle said, "Are you high?"

"What?"

"Did you smoke something, or take something?"

"No."

"Okay, so what the fuck do you think is going to happen?"

"What?"

"What? What the fuck do you think? You start telling people you're going to kick Spaz out, you're going to get a divorce, you're going to get your share."

Sherry looked right at Gayle, plenty sober now, and said, "That was in confidence."

Gayle thought, okay, so it was true, not rumours at all. She said, "Oh come on, how long have you been with Spaz? You think you can talk to some lawyer, he won't find out?"

"That's *my* lawyer."

Gayle drank some of the wine. It was still cold enough she didn't have to really taste it. "Okay, you thought you could go to a lawyer, tell him you want a divorce and you want half the money. Then you tell him how much money and where it comes from."

"I only want what's mine."

"And you really think that's how it's going to go? You really think Spaz will say, oh okay Sherry, you want to keep the brand-new, half-a-million-dollar house, the brand-new Volvo SUV in front of the three-car garage and half the money — half the *real* money — and that'll be fine. You think he's going to write fucking alimony cheques?"

"He has to take care of his kids."

Gayle said, "Sherry, honey, I don't know, nobody told

you, but we married the bad guys."

Sherry said, I know, I know. "But not like this."

"No." Gayle was thinking, not like this at all. No one expected it to go like this. To be this big, this good. She said, "You remember when they first bought that place up on Crow Lake? That old marina?"

"Yeah."

Gayle finished off the wine in her glass and poured some more. Sherry's glass was still half full, but Gayle filled it up, too, saying, "We had some wild parties, you remember?"

"Vaguely."

"Place was so private, we got some all-over tans. We were some hot chicks." She could tell Sherry didn't want to take any trips into the past, but Gayle kept going, saying, "You remember that tat Wendy got, on the inside of her thigh, all the way up to her puss, got her lips pierced?"

Sherry shivered like she was cold, took a big drink from her glass and said that must have really hurt.

Gayle thinking, what's up with you? "You remember, she snorted, then she rubbed coke all up and down herself. She didn't feel a thing." Shit, Gayle remembered how jealous Sherry was at the time, Griz carrying Wendy around on his shoulder, everybody cheering the tat — looked like ivy with butterflies and little birds on it — and the ring through her clit, Wendy saying they better watch out for the hungry pussy.

It was a great party. A lot of great parties, but now Gayle was seeing Sherry different, though, maybe seeing her the way she really was, jealous and possessive. Gayle said, "Is this all because Spaz is fucking some stripper? You know that doesn't mean shit."

"That's not it."

151

"You know that's just part of the game, show the prospects what a man he is."

Sherry shrugged like she didn't care and Gayle saw how serious she was. How serious this could be.

"Are you just pissed off because we're not twenty anymore? We can't walk around topless without our tits hitting our knees?"

"Speak for yourself."

And there was a little smile, which Gayle thought was good, Sherry not having completely given up. But also not so good because she hadn't moved on to full-time grown-up, either.

Gayle said, "Yeah, well, not like I have to worry about much sag in a teaspoon, right?"

"Hey, more than a handful," Sherry said, "is a waste."

"Yeah?"

Sherry finished off the almost full glass of wine in one long drink and then filled up the glass, not even looking at Gayle's, saying, "Yeah. A waste."

What Gayle was seeing was somebody who didn't know what they wanted. Or somebody who actually got what they wanted — how rare is that? — and then couldn't admit they didn't like it. Now that she was seeing Sherry like this, sitting here in her huge, brand-new house, her little tennis outfit probably cost a thousand bucks, the whole thing so Martha Stewart, Gayle could see Sherry was confused.

Probably just like every other woman in this subdivision.

Gayle said, "Okay, well, you have to work it out."

"Work it out?" Like it was funny.

"Yeah."

Sherry drank another half glass of the wine and said,

"You know who he's fucking? You think it's some stripper? Well, of course, it's some stripper, lots of strippers, some fucking Russian sixteen-year-old hooker, too, but I don't give a shit about that. No, it's not the fucking that pisses me off. It's the going to dinner with the reporter. That's what pisses me off."

Gayle said, "Reporter?"

"Fucking bitch. Writes for the paper, one of those columns. She's forty-five fucking years old, wrinkled up, got no tits. Shit."

"Yeah."

Sherry said, "Yeah."

Gayle drank the rest of her wine and said, "Okay, you're right, that's not going to happen, nobody's going to talk to any reporters, but this, this talking to lawyers, talking about the money, that's not going to happen either."

"I don't want him to come back here."

"Well he's going to Sherry, so start liking it. Because you and me, and Spaz and Danny and Nugs, we're not like the people around here. We didn't choose this life, and there are different rules in the one we did. You like your big house and your cars and your clothes and always having a few grand in your purse, you like it. Well, you get to keep it, Sherry, you get to have it all, but stop talking to people. Fuck, you think the way these guys made the money, they're suddenly going to start playing by the rules?"

"They play by the rules in their legit businesses."

"Come on, Sherry, you're smarter than that. Even if they do once in a while, they sure don't at home, do they? You keep talking to lawyers, how do you think it'll end?"

Sherry looked Gayle right in the eye, saw she was beat. A little drunk, and probably a little high before Gayle got there, now she was really starting to slide. She said, "I'm the mother of his children."

"Yeah, that's why we're sitting here having this talk, Sherry. Otherwise, it would've been done by now."

"So now they send you? If I don't stop, will it be you comes out to do it?"

"Oh stop it. I came out because I'm your friend. If anybody else knew what was going on there wouldn't be any talking."

"You're the only one knows?"

Gayle thought about J.T., cute young J.T. and her own situation, and she said, "Yeah, just me. I was talking to Mitchell Fucking Morrison's girl, the Chinese one."

"Stephen, though, he's acting so weird."

Gayle thought, Stephen? She said, "Sherry, this is Spaz we're talking about. How can you tell it's any weirder?"

They laughed about that and Gayle could feel it moving back to the right place. Sherry talking a little about old times, the mountain run they did to Alberta when the Wanted Men became a chapter, that was something, took over that old-west-looking hotel in Wayne, had to cross all those little bridges to get to it, and then talking about her new house and the yoga room that got all the morning sun.

But Gayle was thinking about this reporter Spaz was seeing. Something would have to be done about that. Thinking shit, if Danny pulled a stunt like that she'd take care of him, make it look like an accident.

Or get J.T. to do it, then get rid of him, she was going to have to do that anyway.

She smiled at Sherry, thinking how the poor girl made some changes to the new ways, but maybe left too much of the old behind.

Knowing what happened to the guys who did that.

154

• • •

Isobel Fredericks turned out to be a woman about fifty, short and carrying a few extra pounds but well put together with a nice smile and short red hair. She was saying, sure there can be jealousy. "There can be jealous couples, detective."

McKeon was drinking a latte, holding the mug in both hands and looking at this Isobel, thinking she dressed a little young with her tight jeans and red silk blouse with maybe one too many buttons undone and her leather boots with the spike heels, but it wasn't too flashy and it worked. She could be the hip high-school teacher all the girls liked. Hell, maybe she was. Along with being a woman who liked to go dancing with her husband, meet other couples and have sex with them.

Isobel said, "People are people, even in the lifestyle. Oh, we're open and honest about some things that other people aren't, but not everything."

"But how can there be jealousies?"

McKeon had gone back to the Club 4420 website and found the discussion forum. She'd followed a few threads, expecting it to be all sex and titillation, but they were talking about good places to go on vacation, passing around the same lame internet jokes and dieting tips. She'd been visiting the site enough to start to see some personalities and she had to join to send email to one of them. Didn't like using her real name, but it was for the job, right? The club owners might have been able to help, but McKeon wanted to talk to someone else.

Isobel smiled and McKeon was thinking it was genuine. Here they were, a couple of women at the Starbucks on Bayview, they could be taking a break from shopping, looking at shoes and kitchen gadgets.

"Well, detective, what can happen is one couple can meet another couple and play together." She looked at McKeon, waiting for her to ask, and when she didn't, Isobel said, "And then maybe one of those couples can meet another couple and play with them."

"Isn't that what it's all about?"

"Like I said, people are people. Sometimes a couple can act like a jealous girlfriend."

Isobel sipped her espresso and McKeon nodded, thinking she knew perfectly well the Lowries weren't killed by a jealous girlfriend, or a middle-aged couple acting like one, but she wanted to keep talking to this Isobel.

McKeon had picked her because she seemed to have been around quite a while and knew a lot of people. And because some of her posts in the forum were funny and when threads got too tense or started to get too personal she always used a joke or some lighter comment to get everybody back on track. McKeon liked her.

And now, in person, she liked her even more. Like the big sister she never had, maybe.

"Okay," McKeon said, just to keep it going, "do you know of any jealous girlfriends the Lowries may have had?"

Isobel said, "No."

The Starbucks was almost empty, two-thirty in the afternoon. McKeon hadn't told Price she was meeting this woman from the club. She didn't expect to get anything very useful to their investigation. So why was she here?

Isobel wasn't rushed or in a hurry or anything. She kept looking right at McKeon, waiting for her to say something, and when she didn't, Isobel said, "This wasn't something personal, something someone from the club did."

"No?"

Isobel smiled again and said she watched *CSI*, she read mystery novels. "And this is Canada, I doubt anyone at that club has ever held a handgun, let alone fired one. Whoever killed Sandra and Mike knew what they were doing, isn't that what the news said?"

McKeon said that could be true, they didn't know for sure. Then she said, "But it must have been someone who knew what Sandra and Mike were doing, where they were. Why would someone want to kill the Lowries?"

"Some people don't like the lifestyle, detective, but they usually stop at writing silly letters to the editor."

"No one from the club has ever been threatened?"

Isobel kept looking right at McKeon, smiling a little and shrugging, saying not that she'd ever heard, and McKeon felt like the woman was flirting.

"How well did you know them?" McKeon said. "The Lowries?"

"Not very well." Then Isobel leaned in closer. They were sitting side by side in the two big armchairs by the window and she put her hand on McKeon's arm and said, "I mean outside the bedroom."

And McKeon thought, oh come on, this is so lame, but she didn't pull away. She looked at Isobel, at the smile, and she couldn't tell how much of it was a put-on. Well, most of it, for sure, it was pretty much a punchline, but there was a little bit . . .

Then Isobel laughed a little and said, no seriously. "We never got together. Wouldn't have minded, it just never happened."

McKeon was starting to think that even these open relationships were hard to manage. She said, "Did anyone know the Lowries very well?"

"Outside the club? I doubt it. They came to a few

dances, and they were on the cruise, of course, but I don't know anyone who got together with them."

"But they kept going?"

"It's not uncommon, detective. It's not just one big orgy, you know."

McKeon said, oh yeah, she knew that, and Isobel said, "Which is too bad," but then she smiled again, another punchline.

"We didn't find any reference to the cruise in any of their calendars," McKeon said. "Or day planners or anything. Is that the way it usually is, they never tell anyone?"

"Well, they're going to be discreet, certainly, it's not the kind of thing you tell the babysitter, people don't need too many details."

"No, of course not."

McKeon said she'd been looking at the website, at the discussion forum, and people had been talking about the Lowries, but no one knew anything about them, and Isobel said they were probably just normal, average people, like you and me, and McKeon felt that flirtiness again.

She said, "You never know about people, something like this happens, we start digging, all kinds of stuff shows up."

"I think you've already found the biggest secret in Mike and Sandra's life."

"If it didn't have anything to do with why they were killed, there must be some other secret."

"Jealousy, infidelity, lies — aren't these usually the reasons people kill each other?"

"And money," McKeon said. "And drunken rages, and some of the stupidest macho bullshit you can imagine."

"I can imagine."

McKeon was thinking about gangbangers and assholes

shooting each other on dance floors because some other asshole looked at his bee-yoch, or because some chick came on to more than one of the assholes, trying to play them.

"Well," McKeon said, "thanks for meeting with me, but I think you're right, this didn't have anything to do with the club."

Isobel was still leaning on the arm of the chair closest to McKeon and now she crossed her legs and leaned back, more settling in than getting ready to go. She said, "How long have you been married, detective, five, six years?" and McKeon said, "Five," before she thought about it, and Isobel said, "I thought so."

Now McKeon leaned back in her chair and looked at this Isobel, thinking, I don't want to have this conversation, but I do, knowing it was the real reason she'd emailed and now just waiting, letting it happen.

And Isobel knew it too, she was comfortable, easygoing. She said, "Everyone's a little curious, Detective McKeon."

"Maureen."

"And it's even weirder for women, how could you possibly bring it up with your husband? What kind of a woman would you have to be?"

Bored? No, maybe more just in a rut, or starting to think that every day was too much the same, never very exciting, putting "make out" there on the calendar with the dentist appointments, joking, calling it "the chore," but wondering about that.

"You'd be surprised how many couples are at the club because the wives were interested," Isobel said. She was talking quietly, but not like she was telling a secret. "Oh, usually the husband makes some jokes, or some kind of not-so-serious reference, but a lot of wives think about it. A little variety, a little excitement, something naughty and wild." She was smiling and leaning close to McKeon. "Put on a sexy dress, flirt a little with some other grown-ups, no sleazy guys looking to cheat on their wives, no so-hip-it-hurts kids in the room. It's a great environment."

McKeon sipped her latte and said it sounded interesting.

"We all start out with fairy-tale images," Isobel said, looking away, looking at the young baristas making the lattes and mochaccinos. "And then we have to live our real lives. Even the best relationships change over time, detective. There's no reason it should be less fun, less exciting. In fact, we're older, we're smarter, we have more experience." Now she was looking at McKeon again, saying, "It should be better."

McKeon said, yeah, it should, and thought about another Saturday night with a DVD and a pizza, MoGib watching *Kink* on Showcase and falling asleep on the couch.

Isobel said, okay, detective, okay Maureen, you think about it, take it slow, there's no rush. "It's your life," and McKeon said yeah, and Isobel said, "And as far as I know, it's your only life."

They put on their coats and walked together outside and stood on the sidewalk on Bayview, lined with stores and restaurants, most of them trendy and new, but there was still a hardware store and a place selling hobbies — toy trains and models.

Isobel leaned in and gave McKeon a hug and said, "Good luck, Maureen," and McKeon was about to say something about how she really was just curious, she wasn't really that interested in the club, and Isobel said, "I'm sure you'll find out what happened to Sandra and Mike. You seem very good at this."

McKeon said, well, they'd keep working on it till they

did find out and Isobel said she knew she'd keep at it and then she said good-bye and McKeon watched her cross the four lanes of slow-moving traffic and go into a bookstore, something called Sleuth of Baker Street. Nothing but mysteries.

McKeon thinking she had too many mysteries in her life.

Then Price called on her cell and said they had a breakthrough.

●   ●   ●

She didn't bother being late, none of that keeping him waiting bullshit, and when Sunitha walked along Queen West right at seven, there was Get standing by the door of Shanghai Cowgirl.

They went in and Sunitha thought, yeah okay, when Get walked right to the back and outside because people were sitting up front at tables across from the counter, which they'd never do if there was a place on the patio. She held back, waiting for him to come back in, looking embarrassed, but there he was, sitting down at a nice table for two.

Sunitha went and sat down, every other seat on the patio taken, of course, and then the waitress, Cecily, came over smiling and saying hi and Sunitha was really surprised she was saying it to Get. Sunitha said, "Hey Ces."

Now it was Cecily looking surprised and saying, hi, Sun, how you doing?

"Fine." She ordered a vodka tonic and Get asked for a beer, saying something local, what would you recommend and Cecily said to try the Mill Street Organic and Get said all right, casual, like he'd been here a hundred times before. Sunitha was thinking, shit, she'd said this place because it was young and hip and urban and so Queen West. So art gallery and indie band, served something called Trailer Trash Sushi, and Geisha Grill Steak, and she was sure Get would be out of his element, knocked off balance.

But here he was saying, "I don't think you can get a Courvoisier and Coke here," and she said, "Fuck you," but smiled at him.

Then Cecily brought them their drinks and Sunitha relaxed. She laughed at nothing and shook her head and saw Get was laughing, too. So he wasn't too cool to laugh, that was good.

He ordered the Shanghai noodles and Sunitha thought about the Ghetto Chicken, right there on the menu, with fried mushrooms and gravy, but thought, no, that might be pushing it, and ordered a salad and some spring rolls, said she might get something else after, she'd see.

Get said, "Yeah, we see."

Part of her was pissed he seemed to be having a good time, like it might have been at her expense, but she couldn't tell. This was different, usually she could tell everything about a guy in the first five minutes.

So she asked him how he met J.T., and expected him to say something like, the Army, and be all mysterious, but he said, "Playing golf."

She said, "What?"

"Yeah, on a golf course. Afghanistan's only one."

"There's a golf course in Afghanistan?"

"I was there on leave."

She said you must have signed up, volunteered for duty, there's no draft these days and he said, wait and see. Then he said, "Yeah, I signed up," leaving out how he was the only one in his crew could get in, even with the Army lowering standards, looking for ninth-grade graduates and only misdemeanours, not letting the felons in yet. Wait and see on that, too.

"So was it," she said, "like on TV?"

"All that shit, that playing soccer with cut-off heads? Picking people off in the desert, see how far they can get before you fire on them? Yeah, that's all true. We did house-to-house, bust in the middle of the night, pull out the men, strip 'em naked and throw them in the Humvee. Some guys like to rape the women."

"But not you?"

"Terrorize the kids, you see it in their eyes, they grow up all they want to do is kill Americans."

Sunitha said it makes the projects in Detroit seem good and Get said, "We don't know how good we have it," and she couldn't tell if he was kidding, being ironic like the hipsters in the Shanghai Cowgirl, but she didn't think so.

Then she said wait a minute, you were in Baghdad and you went on leave to Afghanistan? "Why not Dubai, or Thailand, you were halfway there."

"Lot of guys went to your homeland," Get said, "some city, Goa. Lot of Israeli soldiers there, you can make some deals."

Sunitha said, "Yeah, and screw a Bollywood wannabe, she'll tell you secrets of the Kama Sutra."

"Some casinos, too. Like South Africa," Get said. "Lot of guys went there, even black guys, it's all cool now, got Beyoncé concerts. That's not why I was there."

"No," Sunitha said, "you were there to play golf."

Cecily brought the food then and Get offered Sunitha some of his noodles, big wide flat ones with lots of chicken and shrimp and she said thanks, putting a little

163

on the plate with her spring rolls, thinking how many times had guys said to her, you want some, order your own?

"I was there to meet people, make some deals. Lot of deals get made on golf courses."

"Yeah, in big business."

Get said, "This the biggest business in the world." He ate some noodles and drank a little of the Mill Street, nodding, yeah. "Kabul Golf Club, was in the Paghman Mountains, just outside Kabul. Looks just like it does on TV, all desert. I notice on TV in Canada you get a lot more Afghan in the news than you do Iraq."

"That's where our soldiers are."

"Yeah, but we kind of forgot about it back home. So this golf course, was around a long time, years and years, plenty of my kind of deals got made there. Then the Russians came and closed it down, thought anyone who played golf was an American spy."

"Weren't they?" Sunitha used the chopsticks, picking up her spring roll and dipping it in the sauce, looking up at Get with those big brown eyes, long lashes. She was starting to think the way to flirt with this guy was straight on, but then she wondered why she wanted to flirt. She might just be able to tell him her idea, see if he'd go for it.

"They liked American money, that's for sure. Guy who runs the place, Mohammad Abdul something, they all Mohammad something, what was his name?" Get used the fork with his noodles. "Afzal, that's it. He went to Pakistan. The whole idea of a border is different over there, you know? No Ambassador Bridge, that's for sure. Anyway, old Afzal, he tells us when the Taliban kicked the shit out of the Russians — those poor bastards, guys grew up in fucking Moscow, barely seen hash in their lives

164

suddenly stoned every day on the world's finest — anyway, those Taliban, they hate Americans even worse."

Sunitha said, "Everybody hates you guys," still flirting.

Get said, yeah? Smiling. "Who gives a shit? We got there, ol' Afzal came back opened up his golf course. Got J.T. and his boys to get rid of the land mines, paid them American cash, then he tells us, you know, so we feel safe, tells us he got a shepherd to walk the course with fifty sheep for a week and none of them blew up. We say, oh, not a one? Okay then, we play." Get shook his head and Sunitha realized he liked it. These were happy memories for him.

He said, "So that's where I met J.T., playing golf in Afghanistan."

"On your three-day leave."

"Yeah." Then he looked right at her and said, "You gonna tell me how you met J.T.?"

She said, "You know all about me," and Get said, "Honey, I don't know a thing about you."

She watched him drink some beer and look right at her, patient, waiting, like he really didn't know anything about her and he wanted to. Most guys, knowing she worked in a massage parlour, knowing she was hooked up with a couple of dykes robbing spas, that's all they'd need, think they knew everything there was. But not this guy. This really was different but she wasn't ready, not yet, so she said, "You know all about my skills," and waved her fingers at him, long and thin and brown with bright yellow nails, "and now I have this other thing," looking around the hip Shanghai Cowgirl at the trendy kids going to college on Daddy's money and the artists living downtown in crappy apartments not even knowing they'd be moving out to the burbs soon, thinking how

165

they'd all think it was so cool what she did, like she was some kind of rebel. But not Get. Sunitha looked at him sitting there waiting for an answer, knowing he knew. He knew there was nothing cool about it.

She said, "Come on, I'm the immigrant dream come true."

"Yeah?"

She thought maybe, though, she could tell him something. She said, "That was my father's plan, anyway. Come to Canada, make a lot of money, go back to India, get a big house with servants."

"Didn't work out, huh?"

"Does it ever?"

"You tell me."

"He hated it here. He was only using the place, but still, he was so pissed off he couldn't be one of them."

"One of what?"

"Canadian."

"It's like back home," Get said. "Like the man said, every blue-eyed thing is an American the minute they get off the boat, we been here four hundred years, we still waiting."

"Who said that?"

Get said, "Malcolm."

She laughed, more nervous now than flirty, but she turned it around, made those big eyes and Get said, "Malcolm X? Didn't you read the book?"

"Saw the movie, I like Denzel," all the way flirty now, and Get said, "I bet you do."

"Anyway, we've only been here fifty years."

"Three fifty to go, it won't help, take my word." She looked at him and wondered when he read any Malcolm X, wondered when he started thinking like this, and if it was working for him. She still didn't really know what he was doing in Canada, hanging out with J.T. and the Saints. It had to be a deal, a drug deal or something, moving dope down through Detroit, but this Get, he didn't seem in any hurry to get back home.

Really, he didn't seem to be in any hurry at all, he seemed like he wanted to know and she figured maybe she'd tell him a little, so she told him about her father giving up on the legit immigrant dream and going to work for Akbarali Samanani. "The Indian Godfather."

Get said, oh yeah, is he related to Russell Akbarali and Sunitha said, shit, "You been in town three days, you know everybody?"

"Small world."

"I knew Russell when he was a little kid, offering girls five bucks to see our boobs."

"He's doing better now."

Sunitha looked at Get and thought, well sure, he's a guy, but thought she didn't need to say it, Get knew. She liked that. She said, "Yeah, the MoneyChangers, they'll clean your money quick. They've got escorts, massage parlours. I thought about working in one of theirs."

"Just to piss off Daddy."

"If he was still alive. I'll tell you, one time, when he was doing good, he took me and my sister to Disney World. You ever been?"

Get said, no, he hadn't.

"I was eleven, my sister was thirteen, a little too old maybe, but we'd never been on a vacation. My father, he was doing pretty good then, I think smuggling cigarettes from the States, or it could have been electronics, I don't know exactly. He might have been smuggling people into the States, that's what got him killed. Anyway, he booked two rooms, one for me and my sister, one for him. You know why?"

"No, why?"

"My sister said because we were getting too old to share a room with him, just the two double beds."

"Right."

"It was right in the resort, the hotel is inside Disney World, you know? So we go to bed and he goes to bed, but I can't sleep and I'm scared, that fucking mouse is after me, you know?"

"I always worried about Dumbo, shit, a flying elephant, he could do some damage."

"So, I go out into the hall, I'm going to my father's room, but the door opens and there he is, saying good night to the hooker."

Get said, no shit, smiling like it was funny. Well, Sunitha thought, if it wasn't you, if you weren't some eleven-year-old brown girl in a strange country on your first and only vacation, maybe it was funny.

"She wearing a costume," Get said, "like a princess or the Little Mermaid?"

Now Sunitha could see it really was kind of funny. She said, "No, she was not wearing a costume. She looked like every other chick in Florida, wearing shorts and a halter."

"Maybe it was just a date."

"I was eleven, I wasn't stupid. But that's what my sister said when I told her. She actually said, 'Mom and Dad are separated,' like they might get back together, like he didn't dump us in a shitty townhouse in Brampton, my mom cleaning up puke, changing diapers in a nursing home. So the next night I kept my sister up, we listened at the wall. You have any idea what it's like to hear your father try and talk a hooker down in price? Negotiate for anal?"

Get laughed, said, shit, you had it all the way bad, girl, and Sunitha said, "You know it," but she liked the way he made fun of it and still understood that it messed her up. She got the feeling he'd never call her a psycho bitch and flip out on her.

Ces was at the table then, asking them if they wanted any dessert, and Get said, no, not right away. Maybe they should go for a walk, see the neighbourhood, and Sunitha thought that was a good idea. She knew if they kept talking she'd tell him her plan and it was too soon.

CHAPTER EIGHT

BACK AT SUNITHA'S THEY WERE IN the bedroom doing it right away, missionary, like, Get said, "regular folk," just a couple out on a date, and Sunitha liked it, it was good, but she knew she'd never finish that way. They had a good rhythm and she had her knees pulled right up to her tits and Get, Lord have mercy, had the widest shoulders and the strongest arms, she barely felt him on her body, and muscles on his back but it's just the way she was, so she did what she hardly ever did, she pulled him close, kissed him on the mouth and slipped out from underneath, saying, "Just lay back, baby, okay," and got on top, slipped him back in like he was never gone. Closed her eyes and rocked back and forth a little, then leaned forward, put her hands on his chest and squeezed and squeezed.

He said, "You like it on top, cool," and held onto her nice round ass. She was grinding then, pressing down on him and moving, eyes closed, the two of them in sync right away, and she was thinking, yeah, she liked it on top, that's what this was all about, coming out on top for once in her life. Thinking how nobody ever gave a shit about her, nobody worried about her, thinking she could walk in, take what she wanted.

If this Get could work with her, they could do it, she knew it. She knew it would work. She opened her eyes, saw him looking up at her.

"Oh, baby, yeah," he was laughing, "come on, come on," and she did, riding him right to the end, falling onto his chest, breathing hard, covered in sweat.

Now she was sitting up, Get still not finished, still inside her, and she smiled at him, saying, what does my baby want, and Get said, "This is good, I like looking at you," and she gave him a 'who me?' look and started moving again.

She kept looking right at him, right in the eyes, and she pressed her hands onto her own breasts, squeezed, and moved her hands around, her arms hugging herself.

She said, "What are you doing up here in freezing cold Canada all by yourself, baby," and he said, "I'm getting fucked," and she said, "You know it," and moved in the rhythm.

Then she said, "You ever want to just get out, just take off," and he said, "Every day," and she said, "Why don't you," and he said, "You know."

She ran her hands all over herself, stopped between her legs and leaned way back touching herself, saying, "What if you could, what if you had a million dollars, millions and millions," and he said, "In a truck, just drive away," and she said, "In gold."

She shook all over, shivered and tensed up, squeezed him like a vise, held on and held on till the breath just emptied out of her and she fell forward onto his chest, grabbing his shoulders and kissing him.

After a couple of minutes he said, "Baby, I'm not done," and she slid off him and piled up the pillows in the middle of the bed and lay face down on them, her ass in the air, and she said, "You the man," and he laughed a little and said those vodka tonics were too much, and she said yeah, and felt him moving around, getting behind her, lifting her up and she was thinking she never wanted to be on her knees again, but Lord have mercy that's not what this was at all, and damned if she didn't finish again, one more time, just before he did.

A few minutes after she watched Get stand up and stretch, his back to her, and she almost grabbed his ass. He walked into the little bathroom taking off the condom and she heard the water run. Then he was coming back, lighting the smoke in his mouth and tossing the pack and the lighter on the bed beside her.

173

Sunitha got out a cigarette and lit it while Get stretched out on the bed beside her.

She lay back so they were side by side, looking up at the cracked ceiling, listening to the streetcar go by down on Queen, smoking their cigarettes. She knew he was waiting for her to say something, not like, you were so fantastic, she knew he didn't need to hear that. She never knew a guy before who did what he wanted and just enjoyed himself but wasn't an asshole about it. The jerks in the rub and tugs, half the time they were more worried about her, always asking if she was enjoying it, she wanted to say, yeah, giving hand jobs to fat losers really gets me off, just wishing they'd shut up. She took a deep drag on the cigarette and let the smoke out in a long slow stream, watched it rise up and thought, shit, even when she tried dating those white U of T boys they were all about being liberated, about making sure her needs were met, what the fuck was that about? One of the reasons she liked J.T. and his boys, they were honest about who they were, those guys, didn't give a shit about meeting her needs, but then they never did get met, did they.

She looked sideways at Get, wondered how come with this guy he wasn't all clingy and needy, he wasn't worried at all did she get all the way home, and wow, did she. She kept looking at him and heard him say, "You want to tell me, so why don't you."

She laughed.

He said, come on, you want to.

She said you know all about it, why don't you tell me.

He took a drag, flicked the cigarette in the general direction of the coffee cup on the bedside table and said, "No, this is your thing, you tell me."

"But you know what I'm talking about."

"You don't tell me soon, we'll fuck again, then it might be too late."

She said, "That might not be too bad," all flirty and smiling up at him and he said, shit and she said, okay, okay. "You know what I'm talking about, you saw me give the gold to J.T., you know he's buying it up all over town, paying top dollar. You know what he's using it for?"

Get said, "What?" and she could tell he wanted to know. She could tell he was thinking maybe it wasn't what he thought, just fencing the chains and rings.

She said, "He's melting it down, making gold bars."

She saw Get smile a little, saw his head move a little. She said, "Yeah, that's right. Can't be traced, can be used anywhere in the world, you can take it a lot easier, you know they have dogs sniffing for cash at customs now?"

"Could just use girlfriends."

"With gold you don't have to worry about exchange rates."

"But gold, it can go down."

Sunitha sat up on the bed, cross-legged, right beside Get, looking right at him. "And it can go up. It could be a thousand bucks an ounce in a few months. It could be two grand an ounce next year."

"Or it could be shit."

"No, honey, it'll always be gold."

Get took a drag, let out the smoke, and dropped the butt in the coffee cup. He took his time turning back to look at her and she waited, knowing he was interested. She nodded, yeah, looking at him, he never even looked at her tits, just looked right at her and said, "And you want it."

"Yeah, don't you?"

"You talking about stealing from these guys?"

"Yeah, why, you got a problem with that?"

He laughed. "Not if you think you can get away with it."

"That's the beauty of gold, you get it, you can take it anywhere."

"Once you have it."

She said, right, yeah, that's the thing. "Once you have it."

"And you don't know where it is."

"They don't exactly advertise."

"No," Get said, "I don't expect they do."

Then Sunitha said, "But I bet you could find out," and Get laughed. She slapped his chest, harder than she expected, but he didn't budge, and she said, "This isn't funny."

"No? You don't think so? Coming up with a plan to steal a few million bucks worth of gold from guys whose official motto is, what is it again? Oh yeah, 'Three people can keep a secret if two of them are dead.' They have a special club in the club, you have to kill somebody to get into. You don't think that's a funny idea?"

She looked right at him and said, "Not if you get away with it."

Yeah, then she was nodding at him, noticing he wasn't laughing anymore. Now she knew he was picturing gold bars, put a couple in his pocket, carry around a million bucks, just like that.

It was getting him ready to go again, too. She kept looking him right in the eye and she reached down, wrapped her long fingers around his hard dick.

Nobody laughing now.

•   •   •

176   Big Pete was thinking he should've taken the whore's laptop, but just pushing it, stupid thing, purple with the big yellow flowers, off the table, it fell apart easy enough, looked like an accident. He liked the suicide look of it, put an end to it right there, nobody asking any questions.

Not even her good friend, Stacy, sitting here on the couch crying her eyes out, sobbing and holding Kleenex like it was a fucking movie, saying, but she was so happy.

Big Pete saying, well, you can never tell, right? Wanting to get past this bullshit and start asking his questions. Would've been a lot easier if Becca had just told him, flat out said it, who did she tell about Big Pete, who knew he was gonna be there? Had to be a fucking biker, that's who she paid her protection to, assholes taking over the whole fucking town, but which one, there were so many of the fuckers these days. Or really, it could have been Eddie Nollo's guys, though Pete doubted that, they weren't showing any backbone at all, just folding over like everybody else. It could've been Angelo, though, for sure, getting rid of the only guy wants to stand up to these assholes on wheels and in that case Big Pete wanted to know who he sent, find out who's on what side. Fuck.

He'd have to ease into it with this Stacy, he knew that, but shit, how much more blubbering could he take? She was the only other person knew he saw Becca. He knew that because Becca invited her over one time and they both did him. They liked each other, too, he could tell, they weren't faking that. If this one knew, she'd give it up, he wouldn't have to do anything but ask questions. Thing was, he hadn't wanted to kill Becca, either, he hadn't planned to, she was just already so stoned when he got there and she wouldn't tell him anything, pissed him off.

Now Stacy was saying, "She just moved into that condo, she loved it, it was so close to the bike path, she used to ride out to the beach," and more wailing. Shit.

Big Pete got up and walked around Stacy's place. All these condos looked the same to him, there were so many going up downtown now, these ugly towers. Thinking, shit, Becca kept saying to him no one, nobody, she didn't tell anybody, saying, what do you think I am, stupid? And Big Pete saying, no, greedy, and Becca crying, saying, I swear, I *swear*, for fuck's sake and her goddamned eyes wouldn't focus. The minute he walked in, the look on her face, she was so shocked to see him, he knew. He said, yeah, I'm supposed to be dead, right, who'd you tell? Who'd you call, say, yeah, he's leaving now?

Now Stacy was getting up and walking to the bathroom and Pete was thinking, *finally*. He heard her blowing her nose and the water running, then the door closed.

He was thinking it must have been Angelo, who else would Becca have been more afraid of than him? She kept

saying, I didn't, I didn't, over and over, and he got more
and more pissed off and he grabbed her and shook her.
He was holding her by the shoulders and she spit in his
face and said, fuck you, and he grabbed the sides of her
head and shook, lifted her up off the ground by her head
swinging her around and threw her on the bed and she
bounced off. She looked passed out there on the floor, like
she fell off. He thought he could just leave her there, just
walk out, but he knew he'd have to come back. Whoever
she told, whoever was trying to kill him would try again,
he'd have to find out.

And for all he knew she had a fucking concussion,
laying there on the floor, and she might never get up and
that would look like a crime and the cops would be all
over it, the papers, too, it'd be on fucking TV. Thought
about dumping the body but he just knew as a missing
person she'd be all over TV — good-looking chick like
that, the papers'd keep the story going for fucking weeks.

Stacy came out of the bathroom and now she looked
fine, like she'd never been crying or freaking out at all,
and she said, "You want a drink?" and Pete said, sure,
whatever you're having.

It seemed smart at the time, dump Becca in her own car
down by Cherry Beach, off the road in the weeds there,
tape up the exhaust pipe into the car and let it run. Could
be days before anyone looked inside and called the cops
and then they'd just call it suicide, probably wouldn't
even find the concussion or any bruises on her head.
Seemed fucking brilliant for Big Pete.

He heard Stacy getting ice out of the freezer and
making drinks. Shit, he should've said beer, just pop one
open and get this done.

The longer this went on the more he thought about it

and the more worried he got. He started thinking about all those fucking TV shows Lorraine watched, those goddamned science cop shows on all the time, they could take blood and piss and find out everything, they'd be able to tell he was there and killed her. No, he wasn't sure, maybe the cops in Toronto didn't have all that fancy shit. Fuck, why did he have to be banging a chick all the way downtown, why the fuck didn't he stay in Vaughan where he owned all the cops. Goddammit, thinking with his dick.

Stacy came into the living room then with two glasses, celery sticks in them, saying, "Caesars, start the day," and handed him one. She sat down on the other end of the leather couch and picked up her cigarettes.

Pete watched her put a smoke in her mouth, realized she'd put on makeup while she was in the can, pale pink lipstick and eye shadow, maybe something on her cheeks, and brushed her hair. She looked good.

He said, "It's a shame," and Stacy, turning her head to him and lighting her cigarette, taking it out of her mouth and blowing smoke out in a steady stream, said, "What is?"

Pete thought, right, what is. It's over now, done, who's going to look hard into the suicide of a whore?

He said, "You like it downtown? It's expensive, no?"

Stacy smoked and said, "Yeah, it's expensive, you have to work all the time, you never get ahead."

Pete said, "You ever think about management"

"You saying I'm old?"

"I'm saying you're smart, you could run a place, a few girls in a house up in the burbs, make some money for yourself. Or a massage parlour, a spa."

"One of yours?"

"Maybe."

Stacy took a drag on her cigarette and blew smoke at

179

the ceiling. She crossed her legs, showing them off, and looked like she was thinking about it. Then she said, "Becca didn't tell anybody about you."

"No?"

"That's what you want to know, right?"

"Why would I want to know that?"

"She told *me* everything, yeah, but she never told anybody else. She didn't even tell me who you were."

"You just figured it out."

"I knew you weren't a client."

"No?"

"After that time when the three of us did it, we talked. She actually liked you, she thought you could have some fun together."

"We did have fun."

"She thought there could be more."

Pete thought, holy shit. He knew she was only a part-time whore, she had that Raptor Dance Pack thing going on and she did some online porn, classy stuff, but still, and she called herself an actress, even did a commercial, he thought, but he knew, like all the others, pretty soon it would be a lot less of that stuff and a lot more whoring. She was hot, and he liked her, but he'd never thought there could be more.

He said, "Now we're talking about you."

"I know what's coming," Stacy said. "My sister did this for years."

"Yeah?"

"She got herself a dentist, some Iranian asshole, worked out pretty well."

"Could work out for you, too."

"If I can put up with that." She turned and looked right at Big Pete and said, "Honest to God, Becca never told a soul she was seeing you. I don't know if that's why she . . . did what she did, but I know she never told." She took another drag and butted out her smoke in a big glass ashtray on the glass table beside the couch. "Why do you care, anyway? No one gives a shit, she's dead."

Pete said, yeah, I know. "That's too bad. She have any family?"

"Just her mother. Father got deported back to Portugal, didn't talk to him since she was a kid."

Pete was looking at Stacy and he was sure she believed Becca'd never have set him up. This Stacy, she was a pro, it would never occur to her, do something like that. But Becca? Shit, Pete knew she still thought she could get out. Yeah, and the more he thought about it, the more he figured it was Angelo, guy liked his big deal with these bikers, was so afraid of going to war, he'd want to get rid of the only guy didn't like it.

Then Stacy said, "We could still have some fun," and Big Pete said, you think? And she said, sure, and put her hand on his thigh. He noticed her fingernails were each one a different colour.

181

● ● ●

When the Italian finally got dressed and left, no shower she noticed, wondering if he goes home to his wife like that, Stacy got on her cell, the disposable, right away.

J.T. answered and Stacy said, "He thinks it was Becca called. He's not sure who."

J.T. said, good. "Is he coming back?"

"Didn't make a date, but he left happy."

"Good."

"So, I'll see you?"

"Yeah."

"Good." She hung up and went into the bathroom, thinking she could do a whole lot better than some Iranian dentist.

● ● ●

Driving north on Jane they passed Finch and Get said, "Look at this, you got your own little Canadian projects, way the fuck up here," and J.T. said we got them all over town.

He pulled into the parking lot of a place called the Driftwood Community Centre right next to a high-rise apartment building and said, "She's in there, come on."

Getting out of the car Get said, "Driftwood, figures," and J.T. said, what do you mean, figures? and Get said, "Not exactly built to last. Not like the one we saw yesterday, out by that rich kid's place, called that the Granite Club. Make it out of stone, lasts forever, not some driftwood piece of shit, floats out to sea."

"You're a real philosopher," J.T. said. "Thinking deep thoughts."

"You see enough of it, you can't help but notice."

They crossed to the apartments, Get watching a couple of kids, boys maybe ten, riding bikes through the lot, the lot that might hold fifty cars for a building twenty-five, thirty stories, and said, "The projects, man, they all look the same."

J.T. said, "Like going home," playful about it, smiling, but wanting to know.

"Yeah, like where I grew up, the Jeffries," Get said, "but they're gone now, city knocked them down a few years ago."

J.T. said, "We've got some downtown, Moss Park and St. Jamestown, but they're small. Used to be Regent Park but it got bulldozed."

"Cities smarten up, get this shit out of the high-rent districts."

"Out of sight," J.T. said, "out of mind."

Get said, yeah, but you need it, you can find it.

"Couple of high-rises and then townhouses all around, two stories, sidewalks in front, but no streets. There's no road goes right through this place."

"So you here," Get said, "you must have business here."

"And the minute you get here, everybody knows. Like one of those villages over in Afghan."

"Or a prison yard."

J.T. said, yeah, or that, and walked into the building, Get following, thinking yeah, they're all the same, a project's a project, but here, the rest of this Canada, they don't seem to have any idea they even have places like this. Even this Toronto, it's in the middle of nowhere, not messing up the shiny high-rises downtown at all. Then he saw the graffiti on the wall beside the door and said, "Crips?"

J.T., holding the door, said, "Not affiliated, they just use the name. Got Bloods, too, Street Thugs, all the names."

Get said, "Shit," going into the lobby.

J.T. led the way up one flight of stairs and down the hall. There were people all over the place, all of them black, some women looking at J.T. suspicious, doors to their apartments open, little kids going in and out. A couple of girls, maybe sixteen, smiling and giggly, said, hey J.T., all flirty, and then said, who's your friend, looking at Get, and he nodded, not saying anything, thinking yeah, it was all the same.

They turned into another hallway and Get saw a big black guy sitting in a La-Z-Boy chair watching TV way at the end, right there in the hall, couple of pit bulls beside him. Get said, "That's security?" and J.T. said, "Hey Malcolm."

The dogs growled and the big guy in the chair, must be Malcolm, said, "Shut up, you," and then, "can you believe this motherfucking judge, that bitch say anything, he believes her," and J.T. looked at the TV and said, "You would too, looking at that those tits," and Malcolm said, "Them lumpy-ass silicone tittie-bags," and J.T. said, "You'd ride that ass all day," and Malcolm said, "Fucking right," and held up his hand for J.T. to slap as he went through the door into the apartment.

Get walked a few steps behind, looking in Malcolm's lap, seeing the .45 there, bits of popcorn on it, and wondering if these Canadians were for fucking real.

Inside, though, right away he saw it was for real. The living room had a double desk in it, the kind two guys sit facing each other, and that's just what a couple of young black guys were doing, looking like college students, laptop computers open, typing away. The bedrooms, there were two of them, had tables lined up, no chairs, and were piled with vacuum-sealed bags of dope, a pound of weed each, must have been hundreds of them. The place looked like a store.

J.T. said, "They've got every apartment, one on top of each other, all the way to the top. Next floor up is the drying room and packaging and after that it's all growing."

"So, not the first floor, and not these two, leaves twenty-three storeys of grow rooms?"

"Twenty-two, there's no thirteen in the building, people are superstitious." J.T. nodded at the two kids who nodded back, barely taking their eyes off the screens, and went into the kitchen. Get followed, shaking his head. "Last year there was a chick, had the whole top floor of a building down in Parkdale, down by the lake. It was a good idea, but she had to have vents all the way across the roof. Some asshole jumped off and the cops went up, looking around, saw them."

"But this operation, they all vent out straight up."

J.T. opened the fridge and got out a bottle of blue Gatorade, tossed it to Get and got another one for himself. "And all the fertilizer and shit gets hauled up to the top floor and there are holes lined up all the way down, pipes in them."

"Nice."

"You want to see?"

"What I'm here for." Check out the supply, but really Get'd seen enough. He already knew he'd be telling his mom and his Uncle Main that these bikers, these Canadians, they had it down. They could deliver steady supplies and probably buy ten times as many weapons as Tommy could get his hands on.

He followed J.T. back out of the apartment and into the hall. There was a stairway right by the door and Malcolm was already standing up, running a plastic card through a reader, just like in a hotel, to unlock the door. The little light went green and Malcolm pushed the door open and Get followed J.T. up to the next floor, the hall, everything looking exactly the same except there was no Malcolm in a La-Z-Boy.

The apartment had the same layout, and a couple of black girls in it, but these ones were taking the dope out of plastic drying bins — looked like big white garbage cans on their sides — and laying it on trays on the floor.

One of the girls, Get figured she was in her twenties at least, looked at J.T. and said, "Marika's not here."

J.T. said, "Yeah, I know, she will be." He turned to Get and said, "They bag it here, four hundred fifty-four gram bags, that's a pound. Cops say they can get three grand for it, maybe they can. We get closer to two."

Get was thinking he could get three for it in Michigan, four or five the farther south he went, down where they're still fighting the war on drugs. Not like up here where it's practically legal, or where nobody seems to give a shit what's going on. He said, "How many plants you got in each unit?" and J.T. said, "Come on."

They went up another flight of stairs to another apartment with exactly the same two-bedroom layout but this one was full of plants, nice big leafy ones under thousand-watt bulbs. The stoves had been pulled away from the walls and the lights were running off the two-twenty circuits. There were holes about a foot around cut into the ceiling and silver flex tube, like from a dryer, was running up.

Get said, "This isn't hydroponic."

"Soil, easier to manage."

"Once you get it in here. You got what, fifty plants to a room?"

"Average a hundred thirty-five an apartment."

"Twenty-two apartments, that's over twenty-five hundred."

"And that's just this building."

They walked back down the stairs to what J.T. called the office, Get trying to think how this would work back home, but not seeing it. Since they knocked down the Jeffries there weren't many high-rise projects. He thought about those trailers out by the armoury on Eleven Mile,

186

but they'd need so much security, have to pay off so many people, something solid in place like this takes three months to bring out a crop, be sitting ducks the whole time. No, you'd have to really be running things. Like these bikers, have the whole city, or so they say. That's really the thing here, Get thought, how much control these guys really have.

In the office Marika Hare was waiting for them and not looking anything like Get expected. She was black, yeah, but she was tall and skinny and wearing some kind of business suit, grey jacket and pants, a pink blouse buttoned all the way up, which he thought was too bad because it looked like she had a nice rack, even for somebody as old as she was, he figured in her forties anyway.

J.T. introduced them and she held out her hand like a white guy, shaking like a businessman.

Get said, "You got a nice operation," and Marika said, "We do."

J.T. said he was just showing Get around, giving him a feel for things, seeing if he wanted to put in an order.

Get said, "How often could you get me fifty pounds?"

"We call that about twenty kilos," Marika said, "charge you two grand apiece. You come up with the forty grand, we be ready once a week with it."

"You deliver?"

"That's extra."

Get said, course it is, but still, and Marika said, "J.T. here can arrange that. The money goes through him."

"Can't have the merchandise and the cash," J.T. said, "in the same location."

Get said, "Course not," thinking he'd have to talk to his mom and Uncle Main, but man, this operation was slick, better than those crazy Klan farmers and the

Indians, and at half the price, this is what they wanted, for sure. He shook hands with Marika again, but she was already on her BlackBerry telling somebody she'd have to check and call them back but the person wouldn't stop talking so she just waved at Get and he left, following J.T. into the hall.

Outside, walking back to J.T.'s Avenger, Get liking the look of it even if it was four-door, J.T. said, What do you think? And Get said, Was decent of her to let us see the operation and J.T. said, "Hey, we're the bank, it's our fucking money set it up," and Get thought, yeah, but she's out there in front of it, probably guaranteeing every cent. He said, "It's good, it looks good."

In the car J.T. said, "You like deli?" and Get said, "No Coney Islands in this town," and J.T. said, what?

Get said, "Hot dogs with chili on them, and onions."

J.T. said, you want a hot dog in this town you get it off a cart on the street, spicy sausage or all beef, all kinds of shit to put on them, cheese, hot peppers, corn relish. "Shit, you can get vegetarian, if you want, eat on the run, everybody here in such a hurry." No, he knew a place they could sit, so they drove east on Sheppard instead of south back into the city. Right away they drove past the campus of something called York University and Get thought it was just like back home, his neighbourhood growing up so close to Wayne State, like rubbing their faces in it. Then this neighbourhood they were driving through wasn't black anymore at all, the street signs and storefronts were all in some kind of Russian or they said to buy Israel bonds and support the United Jewish Appeal, and pretty quick the houses were a lot bigger and there weren't any apartment buildings or townhouses.

Then, on one of the benches by the bus stop, Get saw

Marika's face looking back at him, the words underneath saying she could sell him his dream home, not just a house, and he thought, yeah, this city is fucked up, big-time dope-growing real estate agents looking like the mom in that Fresh Prince sitcom.

Well, at least now, Get was thinking, he could tell Sunitha he was getting close. He was seeing the big dope farms and he'd be seeing the meth lab soon. He could see her big brown eyes looking at him, though, saying, but no gold? No kiln melting it down into bars? And he'd say, no, not yet, but he was starting to believe she was right, that it was at least going on, and what would they do when they did find it?

●　●　●

The breakthrough Price was talking about came from the temporary partner he'd had while McKeon was off on maternity, Jason Loewen, who then went to work narco and was one of the only ones left standing when that whole department got arrested by the Mounties last year.

Now he was on some super-secret task force investigation, but Price managed to talk him into a little off-the-record meet, so they were in the Tim Hortons on Lake Shore and Leslie, things still way too tense to get together on College Street, and he was telling them about Sheldon Kichens and his connections, how the guy started out with customers on both sides — cops and crooks — and got to know them all. "Sometimes," Loewen was saying, "a guy would want to buy a fancy car and the banks wouldn't give him the money."

McKeon said, "Because they were drug dealers," and Loewen said, "Or they were on cops' salaries," and she said, oh, right. She had a headache, still pounding from her coffee talk with Isobel, the swinging housewife.

"So anyway," Loewen said, "this Sheldon could always hook you up with somebody willing to loan a little cash. And the thing is, a few people are happier he's not talking anymore."

McKeon said, yeah, "Who?" She noticed this Loewen was a lot more confident now, more comfortable in his cop skin. When she first met him, day she brought Nathaniel in to show off in the squad room, Loewen was like a jealous teenager, all nervous and defensive, but now he was cool. When Burroughs and the narco squad went down and Loewen didn't get touched, there was a lot of gossip, McKeon remembered, she was back then, a little suspicious herself, but now it looked like that whole department had been dirty a long time and they weren't letting the new guy in on anything.

If he'd wanted in.

Loewen was saying, oh you know, city's upside down. "These bikers are coast to coast now and most of the drugs are going through them. It's giving them a nice base to expand from, they're putting a lot of money on the street. This Sheldon, he was moving up, too, going from brokering cars to moving all kinds of money. It looks like he was involved in getting some big downtown clubs financed."

Price said, "With this new money?" and Loewen said, yeah, the Saints.

McKeon drank more coffee, the last thing she needed right now, and tried to concentrate, but she really couldn't focus. She heard Price say, "This Sheldon, he start getting money from more than one source?" and Loewen said, "That's what it looked like," and Price said, "Well that's fucked up, that'll get you killed."

The Tim Hortons was busy in the late afternoon, people coming and going, lined up at the counter, and the Wendy's in the other half of the building was starting to hop. It was too noisy for McKeon, but also made her think about going home, having dinner with her husband, MoGib, the baby crying, trying to get him to bed, crashing herself. Shit, what a life. Maybe she should go back to the office, write up some notes, have a beer with Price or maybe O'Brien.

Loewen was saying guys like Sheldon tend to think in the short term. "Or, like everybody else it seems, he saw the changing of the guard in town, new players, big movers, and he wanted to change teams."

Price said, "Moron," and Loewen said, "Well, you know. So, he was stressed, then he got himself in more debt, the drugs really picked up."

"As they do," Price said, "when you're stressed."

"And he was starting to get out of control."

Price said, "You seem to know a lot about this guy," and Loewen said, "Yeah, well, we were sure looking at him."

"Close?"

Loewen said, "He'd been on the radar for a while, you know, small-time, but the thing is, maybe, he had a meeting with someone."

"Someone on your task force?"

"It could be a coincidence," Loewen said. "But we had a new informant registered, gave him a number and everything, started paying him."

"And when the car salesman died, so did the informant."

"He became inactive," Lowen said. "I wouldn't have noticed, you didn't call me. I mean, it could be a totally different guy, a lot of people sign on, then don't pan out."

"A lot?"

"It happens."

But McKeon was thinking, oh yeah? She'd been thinking maybe there wasn't anything to this, maybe the guy just OD'd, but she was having a tough time selling that to herself, and now, shit.

Price said, "Anybody else know?" and Loewen said, "Shit, I'm just the gofer. We got so many forces on this fucking task force. So many jurisdictions, we spend all our time bumping into each other and filling out fucking forms. No one looks at them all."

Price looked at McKeon and she said, yeah, knowing it was up to them now, they could do something with it, or not.

Price said, "You think any good could come from it?" and McKeon was thinking, sure, we could bust some more crooked cops, hell, it probably goes all the way to the top, get all kinds of evidence against this new-order organized crime in town, shut that down and walk off into the sunset.

It could happen.

Price was nodding then, looking at Loewen, and McKeon tried to remember the last time she just went home after a day at work, had a nice dinner with her husband and watched TV, some reality show about people trying to get a date, or even a Leafs game, she didn't care. Used to be MoGib worked longer hours than she did, always full of stories about Bruce Willis buying the whole crew lap dances or major screw-ups on set, some starlet's hissy fit, then just the two of them getting home late, making out in the living room.

All that was before the baby, before Nathaniel. Now

MoGib was full of stories from the sandbox, him and the moms in the park. At least the women were finally talking to him, weirdo unshaven guy pushing around a stroller, little blonde-haired boy pointing out every piece of construction equipment on the street.

She didn't say anything and she could feel Price and Loewen start to wrap things up, heard Loewen say, "I just wish we'd arrest somebody, you know?" and Price say, what do you mean, and Loewen said, "You know, it's like we're on the sidelines watching all this happen. We're taking notes while these assholes take over the city."

Price said, "Somebody's got to sell the drugs and loan money to people the banks won't."

Loewen said, "Ha ha, you're funny, you sound like Levine. I just mean, we're always going after the top guy, you know, we always keep these huge investigations going just a little longer, months, years, Crown lawyers always asking for more evidence, but we never seem to get anybody."

"Hey," Price said, "we got Mon Oncle, the top guy."

McKeon watched Loewen agree with that, nod, and say, yeah, we got him, "And half our force, but it didn't stop anything, these guys didn't miss a beat."

"It's not like you get paid by the arrest."

Loewen said, "I wish we did, we'd be busting guys every day."

"Small-time, petty-ass shit."

"So? It'd be something. How long you think it took for somebody to replace Mon Oncle, five minutes? You think getting him put a dent in anything? I don't know, shit, it might be tougher for these guys to replace fifty small-time, petty-ass worker bees. We spend years, millions of dollars building a case against a guy, once in a while we

193

get him and so what? We might be doing this all wrong."

Price said, yeah, well, "That's not really our place, is it?"

"No. I guess not."

McKeon wanted them to keep talking, even though she knew it was over. She just wanted to say something to keep them there, something so she wouldn't have to go home, but Loewen was standing up saying he hoped he helped and if there was anything else to let him know.

Price said, "Sure, I love coming out here. Maybe next time we can meet at Starbucks."

Loewen was walking out now, saying, "You find one with parking," and McKeon thought, yeah, he had the swagger now.

Then she and Price were back in the Crown Vic, Price driving down Lake Shore towards downtown. She knew they'd be in the office in fifteen minutes, it'd be pretty much six then, and Price would be heading home.

She said, "So, that's pretty much that," and Price said, pretty much.

McKeon said, "It's fucked up, though."

"What else is new."

Yeah, what else. She said, "You know Keirans and Roxon, went to meet the guy?"

"Not Keirans. I know Barb Roxon, though, knew her when she was with sex crimes, we worked a serial rapist when he moved on to murder."

"Yeah?"

Price kept looking straight ahead, driving on Lake Shore under the Gardiner, no lake in sight from where they were, saying, "One thing I learned, Mo, you never know anybody as much as you think you do."

"Anything's possible."

"From anyone."

McKeon thought, you got that right, but what can you do about it? As if she didn't have enough on her mind, go looking into this. It could have been a murder, sure, guy was going to turn informant, make a lot of people worried, but it could have been an OD. Then she was thinking she'd only agreed to look into it at all because the cop who brought it to her, Anjilvel, was a woman. Hadn't even thought about that but she realized it was true, show some solidarity. If Price had brought it up, said they should look into it, she wouldn't have agreed. But she wanted to show this young female cop what a great organization she was in with, no more glass ceilings or special treatment.

She hadn't really thought what that meant, where it might go.

Price turned up Bay, saying, "You know, we don't have to do anything right now."

"We don't have to do anything at all."

"No, but you will. You might as well write this up, do a little CYA."

"I'm not thinking about covering my ass, Andre."

Price said, "No? You should. Anyway, this is a tiny part of something much bigger. Like Loewen said, they got all kinds of people working this from every angle. Now that he talked to us, Loewen'll write something up, too, he's got to think CYA."

"That what you teach all your partners?"

"What the great Ali Nichols taught me," Price said. "Only reason I'm still here, doing any good at all."

McKeon thought, right, got to do some good.

He pulled the car into the parking lot behind police headquarters on College Street and said, "You park here?"

"Yeah, you going home?"

"Christopher and Akim are playing basketball tonight, starts at seven."

"Oh yeah, what is it, that East York league? How old do they have to be?"

Price was getting out of the car. "Supposed to be ten, but when Christopher started they saw how tall Akim was and put him on the team, too. You got years, Mo, don't worry about it."

She said, "Yeah, years," thinking how the hell do you last that long.

Fifteen minutes later the car was signed in and they were signed out. Price took off and McKeon walked out to the parking lot where her Neon was parked, knowing she should just get in and drive home, be there in half an hour, forty minutes. She stood there looking at the car for a minute then went inside to make a phone call, telling herself it was for work, pretty sure about it.

●　　●　　●

Sunitha was sitting at the table in the breakfast nook in White Girl Brenda's condo, laptop open, looking at a website by a guy calling himself the Great Mogambo. She was thinking this guy's been predicting the economic collapse of the U.S. for years now, every time the debt goes up and more people go bankrupt — which was every day now — he keeps saying he's hiding in his closet, shivering, the door bolted shut. Made some sense, she thought, can't just keep moving the money around forever, every empire falls, and then Lydia came into the kitchenette saying, "If it's a tramp stamp on the top of your butt, what's it called on top of your puss?"

Brenda came in behind her then, saying, "I'm hungry, let's go out," and Lydia said, "You never have any food here," and Brenda said, "Well, yeah."

Sunitha said, "I don't know what it's called."

"Anything," Brenda said, "below the waistline, front or back, is a tramp stamp. Next time we hit a spa, let me get a Brazilian first and then I'll get one way down there."

Lydia said, "Why don't I just shave you," and Brenda said, "Ooh, I'd be too scared to let you down there with a razor," and Lydia said, "I have to tie you up first."

They were all giggly and tickling each other, Lydia grabbing for Brenda's puss and Brenda trying to stop her and then sticking it out and they banged into the table and Sunitha said, "Will you two stop it," and they made faces at each other and at Sunitha.

Then Brenda said, "Ooh, better leave her alone, she's working so hard," and Sunitha couldn't stand it when she used that little-girl voice and she said, "Yeah, why don't you go get something to eat?"

Lydia said, "You coming?" and Sunitha said, no, I'm not hungry. "Maybe bring me back something," and as the other two were going out the door she said, "And not some fucking Mickey Dee breakfast burrito bullshit, either, bring some real food," but the door was closed and she knew it'd be junk.

The night before they'd hit a massage parlour way out on Finch and Meadowvale around three in the morning and come back to the condo. Those chicks, those Chinese or Korean or Vietnamese, whatever they were, pissed-off chicks screaming at them in those high-pitched voices, shit, Sunitha just about lost it on them and started shooting. Lydia was calm, though, Sunitha liked that. She could see what Brenda saw in her, standing there with the .45 in her hand, telling the main mama, it don't make no never mind to me, I shoot you or I don't, I'm taking the money with me. The old lady believed her. Hell, Sunitha believed her.

They left with a little over five grand in cash and a pile of jewellery that Sunitha was looking at now, sitting on the glass table next to the laptop. Big chunky gold chains, bracelets, rings, must have been twenty grand worth. The deal was, the massage chicks found out where the customers with the big ticket items lived, mostly Asian guys, and then somebody robbed them. Brenda found out, she wasn't saying how, and Sunitha didn't give a shit, but Lydia was pissed about it, wanting to know who her *source* was, saying, was it some chick, some fucking Chinese chick you're doing, but Brenda wouldn't say. She just knew where the stash was, that's all, the two of them fighting for a while, then Lydia saying let's go to Slack's and Brenda saying, no, it's porno night at Goodhandy's, let's party with the trannies, and they didn't get back till the sun was practically coming up.

The Great Mogambo was saying again, like he always did, buy gold. Buy as much as you can. Cash is trash. Not worth the paper it's printed on, worth less every day. Gold is where it's at. Sunitha believed some of it. Some of it was crazy, these guys, the gold bugs, were one step away from survivalist freaks living in the deep woods getting ready for some final showdown, but no doubt, the price of gold was going up, people buying it all over the world.

Sunitha picked up her cell phone and flipped it open thinking she'd call J.T. and set up a meeting to sell him what they got, but she was thinking, shit, *give* it to him is more like it. What would he say, five grand? In her dreams. He'd more likely say two or three and take the bills out of his wallet, count out twenty or thirty hundred-dollar bills, wouldn't even put a dent in what he had.

Living for the moment, Lydia and White Girl Brenda, still pissing off her daddy, would be fine with their share, Sunitha thinking she'd give them a grand to split, and they'd be on their way, but shit, it wasn't right.

She flipped her phone shut and then right away it rang and she jumped. Then she shook her head and said, "Shit," out loud and opened the phone, saying, hi, and then, "Hey, I was just thinking about you," hearing Get's deep voice tell her, yeah, he'd been seeing the sights in this Toronto the Good and she said, "Oh, like what?" feeling herself start to flirt even though she didn't want to.

Get said, "I got more to see, maybe we can hook up later, talk about it," and she said, yeah, that'd be good, thinking right away how she was coming on too strong, hearing someone else talking to him, sounded like they were in a car, had to be J.T., and she said, "You with J.T., I need to see him, too," and right away wished she hadn't, feeling like she wanted to see Get alone.

Then Get said, "Naw, he's busy," and she could heard him joking, could tell he was making a face at J.T. who was probably driving and looking pissed off, Sunitha thinking, little boys, out playing.

She said, "Okay, call me when you're ready," and Get said he'd do that and they hung up.

Sunitha sat at the little breakfast nook then, looking out the window at all that traffic going nowhere, and she picked up the gold chains, feeling the weight in her hand, and thought, yeah, this Get, when he starts to see how much they could take, he'll be right there with her. And then she'd have to figure out how much she wanted to be with him.

She put down the gold, closed her laptop, and put it in her bag. Then she put the gold in there and figured she could worry about Get later. First thing first, find out where J.T. and the boys are keeping it and get it.

●　●　●

They were leaving the boat, the barge, Get said, one time, "I was a kid, my cousin, Griz and me, we busted in this old lady's house, everybody said she had all this jewellery, diamonds and shit she brought from Romania or Transylvania or some shit, what she had, man, was cats, hundreds of them. Smelled just like that," and J.T. said, well, you know, "Meth labs, they smell like cat piss," and Get was thinking, yeah, but melting that gold, that was something.

That's what he came to see. Goddamn, that Sunitha was right.

Get said, "Meth, man, it's really a white man's drug."

"Because we think it sounds like a real medication, something a doctor might prescribe."

"Had it in the Army."

"We still think they're part of the establishment, you know, the Man, and he's on our side, only worried about you, keeping your black ass down in the ghetto."

Get said, "The Man, the only truly colour-blind motherfucker there is."

"We don't know that yet."

"You catching on," Get said, stopping beside J.T.'s Avenger and looking back at the barge. From the outside it didn't look like anything, an old hunk of steel, nothing but a big floating hull. J.T. told him how you hook it up to a tug, the smaller boat with the engine, and six guys could

200

pilot it all over the Great Lakes. That's what he said, pilot it. They could go from Minnesota to Cleveland, Buffalo, Detroit, Chicago, Rochester — and all over the Canadian side, looking just like all the other boats on the lakes.

Except along with using two of its cargo holds for hauling salt and grain, the other two holds were full of weed, tons of it, and the pilothouse had a huge meth lab and kilns melting gold down into bars.

J.T. was opening the door of his Avenger, saying, "You should look into the meth, though, big profit margin, good sales approach, you know, makes you skinny and you have great sex."

Get sat in the passenger seat and said, now you're a salesman, and J.T. said, come on, meth heads get addicted faster and harder than any other drug. "And there's over a million addicts in the U.S. now, it's moving up the charts."

"Don't you get, what's it called, crystal dick? Can't get it up anymore?"

"I know potheads," J.T. said, "can't get it up anymore." He put the car in gear, the big engine hardly making any noise at all, and Get was thinking how he liked the car more than he thought he would, even if the interior was a little cheesy, looked like the original Shaft. J.T. said the new Camaro was good, too, had a ragtop and the new Challenger had some real balls.

"It's really a white thing," Get said, "meth."

J.T. drove them out of the port and onto Kenilworth Street in Hamilton, heading towards the Skyway bridge and back to Toronto in less than an hour. He said, "You could move it south, hillbillies love it, and it's always been big with fags, but it's really getting big. These new cooks," J.T. said, "really know what they're doing. We

201

got a guy, makes one he calls Strawberry Kwik, it's pink, the little club girls love it. Got some with Coca-Cola in it and some tastes like chocolate."

"Shit, everybody doing it."

J.T. said, damn straight. "All these kids, the cooler they think they are, the easier it is to fuck them up."

"You know it," Get said. "This does look good."

"Distribution is good, too. The boat really helps. These guys, these bikers, they used to have labs all over the place, apartments, basements, shit they had some in the backs of trucks. I heard," J.T. said, "about a lab they had on an island up in Georgian Bay, place used to be a hunting lodge."

"Shit."

"Had them on Indian reservations — that's a good market, too, Indians, and prisons."

Get said, "It is tempting."

"The problem used to be the ingredients, you buy big supplies of the stuff, like iodine, Benzene, chloroform, ammonia, ether, and you know, those pills you take when you've got a cold?" J.T. looked at him and Get thought, shit, he is a salesman, said, yeah? J.T. said, "All that shit, man, Red Devil Lye, drain cleaner, paint thinner, it's some nasty shit. But you buy that stuff in bulk, cops start following it. In Ontario last year they busted over fifty labs."

"Pain in the ass."

"That's another reason why the boat is so good," J.T. said. "We buy the stuff as we move it around, get some in Wisconsin, some in Michigan, some in Ontario, New York, Illinois. None of it stands out."

Get said, "Nice." He was really starting to see how big-time organized these guys were. Like J.T. said, coast to coast. People really underestimated them, still thought they were fat, dumb guys in leather jackets. Hell, Get hadn't seen a motorcycle yet. And he was starting to see how good it could be to have people underestimate you.

Get said, "Add it to the coke and smack?"

"It's even better," J.T. said, "because we control the whole manufacturing and supply, don't have to worry about dealing with assholes halfway around the world."

And Get thought, no, maybe just assholes next door.

J.T. said the way he understood it — "and it was all before my time, you understand" — was that in the early days in the sixties when the bikers in California started to deal they sold weed that was grown in California, but those old bikers, they were such racist bastards, and didn't trust anybody, they wouldn't deal with Mexicans or South Americans.

"Or Negroes," Get said.

J.T. said, "Oh fuck, no, those bikers, they were worse than the Klan. But they needed money and there were so many kids looking to get high any way they could. I think the truth is the Mafia had the heroin totally controlled, that whole *French Connection* shit, and the bikers didn't want to deal with them either."

"Probably called them wops. Times change, don't they?"

They were on the Skyway then, the bridge high enough to let huge boats go underneath, way bigger than the little freighter J.T. and Get were just on — it'd pass through here, no one would notice, J.T. saying, "Yeah, but the change didn't start in California, it started here in Canada. Those guys, American bikers, they had military contacts, you know, Air Force, and meth was always big in the forces, give it to the pilots keep them awake for days, give it to the grunts run them up the hill."

Get said, "And some things never change."

203

J.T. said, yeah. "So they had this drug just sitting around, they could make it themselves and they wouldn't have to deal with spics and wops."

"Or smuggling."

J.T. said, right, or smuggling, and Get thought, this guy wasn't even seeing shipping from Canada to the U.S. as smuggling, it was just crossing the street.

J.T. said, "And it was easy to sell, meth, the effects right away are great. Confidence, big sex drive, man, supposed to be great, all you can think about. One chick, she told me she didn't mind being a hooker at all, loved to get laid all the time, the worst part was waiting on the sidewalk. Said she fucked herself for hours and hours, it was all she did, wore out all the batteries in her vibrator and the damn thing got so hot from all the rubbing she had to wear an oven mitt."

Get said, "Damn."

"But you know, when her teeth fell out, she was puking all the time, skin just hanging off her bones, it was some sad shit. Meth heads don't jump off the roof, you know, they don't OD, they just go zombie, practically dissolve."

"And they never get clean?"

"No," J.T. said, "they never do. Once a customer, always a customer."

Get was looking out the window, J.T. changing lanes, passing everybody, and seeing this QEW highway lined with warehouses and new office buildings and big-box shopping centres, the whole place looking like new money. The closer they got to Toronto the more condo buildings they passed, twenty, thirty storeys, all brand-new, covered in glass and looking out at Lake Ontario, New York State right there.

Get thinking, yeah, once a customer always a customer was true about pretty much anything. Whatever you start out as you pretty much stay. His mom, his Uncle Main, everybody he knew back in Detroit, staying where they started, doing what they do, it is what it is. His mom dreaming about the big house out in Washtenaw County, working at it all the time, but was she really getting any closer?

J.T. said, "We get back, you want to go out, get something to eat, get laid?"

"Naw, man," Get said, "I've got a date."

"You been in town a week, you have a date? This like a date-date, like somebody you're seeing?"

Get said, yeah, maybe. "We see." We see. Just don't tell J.T. she's got this plan, take the gold and run, take it anywhere in the world, be free.

Then he was thinking it could work by himself, too, change what he is, a whole new start anywhere he wanted. We see.

205

• • •

McKeon let two guys buy her a couple of drinks, vodka tonics, and tell her all about the fascinating world of bond trading. They had all that fake cynicism of Bay Street players, all that pretending they were bored and that it was all bullshit, but they couldn't help it, they were so full of themselves they came off like excited teenagers.

Really, McKeon liked it at first. The bar was full of twenty-something skinny chicks, spent every dime they had on their Jimmy Choos, so she didn't think anybody'd even talk to her. Then this Andy, who was probably into his forties and his young friend — she forgot his name as soon as he said it, didn't look thirty yet — started hitting on her. She thought it must have been some office game, some kind of find the sad, single chick closest to forty and see how excited she gets, but she drank the vodka tonics and laughed at their lame jokes and loosened up.

Then Andy was saying something about, you make a million, you lose a million, it doesn't matter, and McKeon said, "What's a million?"

"In the grand scheme of things," Andy said, "not a fucking thing."

The young guy, McKeon really couldn't get a read on his age because he was wearing a nice enough suit and not saying much, he could have been a rich student, an intern, or he could've been thirty-five, just led a pampered life, was starting to look really eager. She was waiting for one of them to ask what she did, wondering what she'd tell them.

The bar was right downtown, place called the Irish Embassy, another one of those places trying to look like a pub but it was in a building that used to be a bank so the ceilings were twenty feet high and there were big screens showing the baseball game all over the place. McKeon had taken a seat at the bar, thinking she'd wait a half hour, if Roxon didn't show by then it meant she didn't get the message or she had nothing to say. Now McKeon was thinking that might have been an hour ago, or maybe two. She'd already had a drink before the Bay Street boys started buying them and she wasn't sure how many she'd had since.

Andy was still talking about money, she figured it was about all he ever talked about. Looking at him, though, she could see he had a lot of it and he liked to spend it on himself. He was a good-looking enough guy, McKeon figured, if you went for guys who got manicures and, looking closer at him, she was thinking, facials.

Then she realized he was looking right back at her and she just knew this was his sincere face, his "I'm going to say something important" look and she figured it'd be something about watching the sun come up over the city from the fiftieth floor of some condo on Lake Shore, or if she was ten years younger, maybe watching the sun come up from the deck of a sailboat in the Caribbean.

But then the kid came back with three shooters in his hand, saying, "Liquid Cocaine," and McKeon looked at the gold flecks in the glass and knocked it back just like the guys did.

Andy still had his sincere look and he said to McKeon, "Have you ever been with two guys at once?"

She didn't laugh, she just looked from Andy to the kid and back and said, "No, I never have." Andy was nodding right away, thinking she was interested, and she said, "But if I ever do, it'll be with a couple of guys who want to be with me, not just with each other and I'm only there so they don't freak out thinking they might be fags."

Still looking at her all sincere, Andy said, "Why don't you fuck off, you old, fat cow," and he smiled and turned and walked away.

"There's nothing wrong with it," McKeon said to his back. Then she looked at the kid and said, "Honey, you can do a lot better."

She was thinking she might as well go home when Barb Roxon walked up and said, "You eat yet?" and McKeon said no so they moved to a table and got menus.

Barb said, "How's Andre?" and McKeon had to think a minute to realize she meant Price.

"Good, he's good," remembering Price said they worked the serial rapist-murderer together.

Barb said, "I was downtown when he got out of uniform, him and Levine coming downtown to be detectives." She said how she was working with Nichols then, "Before he got political and promoted to the corner office."

McKeon said, "And now narco."

"Yeah, what a career path."

"What's next, internal affairs?"

Barb said, don't even joke about that, and the waitress came over and they ordered salads and crab cakes with sweet potato fries. Then Barb said, "You want another drink, I'm surprised no one's buying them for you in here."

McKeon decided not to tell her about Andy and the kid, but she did order another drink, back to the vodka tonics, and Barb ordered a ginger ale, saying, "I quit drinking when I started sex crimes. Well, not right away, first I had to hit bottom, you know, taking statements drunk, asking the same question five times. I was supposed to be the sensitive one, Harold Druckerman had to sit me down. Imagine being so far gone that guy thought it was a problem."

McKeon said, yeah, that must have been bad, looking at Roxon and trying to figure out how old she was, thinking early fifties anyway, but in good shape, nice grey suit, purple blouse and a good dye job. Kind of woman makes people say fifty is the new thirty.

"I'd like a drink now, though," Barb said, watching the waitress put down her ginger ale and McKeon's vodka. "I thought narco, you know, we might be dealing with some professional criminals, wouldn't be all emotional and all that." She took a sip of the soft drink, put the glass down. "Then on Monday, we bust a grow op with a half-assed meth lab in the basement, fucked up all the way. There's one guy there, he's fifty but he looks seventy, and two kids, maybe twenty, twenty-five. I don't think they'd been cooking it for very long, but they knew about using it."

McKeon said, yeah.

"And there was baby stuff in the house, half a pack of diapers, couple of bottles with sour milk stuck to the bottom. There was a crib in the corner of the kitchen, some baby clothes."

"Yeah."

"Yeah, but no baby. I ask the girl, where's your baby, honey? Says she doesn't know what I'm talking about. I say, come on, just tell me she's with your mother, something, but no."

"Nowhere?"

"There were some places in the back yard looked like it could have been, so we dug it up, but nothing. We had the dogs out for a while, but the house was so close to the ravine, ten-minute walk, could be anywhere."

The salads and the crab cakes came at the same time. McKeon picked at the food but Barb dug right in, saying, come on, eat, you need it. Then she said, "Oh shit, I'm sorry, here I am talking about missing babies and you just back off mat leave."

"It's okay," McKeon said, "it's been a while. You have any kids?"

"No."

"I don't even know, are you married?"

"I was, I married Mike Chapman, he had a couple of kids already. We talked about it, kept putting it off and then it was too late."

The name sounded familiar, but McKeon couldn't

place it, and then Barb said, "You remember Mike? He died a couple years ago?" and McKeon said, Oh, right, yeah, remembering the desk sergeant at 55 Division everybody liked. Some kind of cancer or heart thing, she thought, something happened quick, she remember the memorial service, the wake.

Then Barb said, so, "What's up? What you working on?" Then she smiled and said, "You're on the suburb blow job, right?"

McKeon said, yeah.

"In a car I can understand, but on the Gardiner? Not even on it, they were on the ramp, what was going on?"

McKeon started to giggle a little and when she tried to stop it got worse and she was thinking, shit, maybe ginger ale's not a bad idea. She took a breath, said, "Get this, they were on a booze cruise in the harbour, with their swingers club."

Barb smiled. "Swingers club? They still around?"

"More popular then ever."

"I guess," Barb said, "you can rule out jealous lover."

Serious now, McKeon said, "Trouble is, we ruled out everything."

"Yeah, nothing, eh?"

"Not a thing. Nichols is on us every day, but we've got nothing."

"Tough one."

"Yeah."

There was one of those awkward pauses in the conversation, no one saying anything, the sounds of the bar all around them until finally Barb said, "So, what is it?"

She was drinking her ginger ale, looking right at McKeon, McKeon saying, nothing, you know, well. "Yeah," Barb said, "Just tell me, okay."

"It's that car dealer, the guy who died in the hotel."

Barb kept eating, didn't react, or at least McKeon didn't think she did, but the place was starting to sway a little, McKeon thinking, how many drinks have I had, coming up with five, but then remembering the shooters.

Barb said, "Sheldon Kichens, yeah, what about him?"

McKeon couldn't tell if Barb was surprised that's what it was about or not. She watched her eat the crab cakes, cut off pieces with her fork and dip them in the creamy sauce, looking right at McKeon, waiting.

"You know people were looking at him?"

"Yeah, *we* were looking at him."

"He was into drugs?"

"He sure was the night we found him."

"DOA?"

"The paramedics worked him a long time."

Now Barb was sitting back in her chair, holding her empty ginger ale glass in her hand, and it wasn't going right. McKeon thought she could be casual, just us girls, joke around about guys on the force, maybe they'd even dated a couple of the same ones, Ed Sanderson probably, then slide into it, but now, all the drinks making her dizzy, or maybe Barb threw her off, talking about missing babies, whose drug-addict parents couldn't deal with or help them. McKeon thinking she was only here to avoid going home to her own kid, her own house that'd be a mess, smell like baby puke and just depress her. Maybe it was postnatal, standard stuff, but she just didn't want to deal with it. She wanted to stay at work, just stay busy and not think about it.

Now she couldn't think of anything and Barb was still looking at her, waiting, so she said, "There's some talk. Was Jurevich ever alone with him?"

Barb said, "You have any idea what the fuck you're saying?"

"I saw the report. He had a lot of drugs in his system."

"He was a drug addict, Maureen."

"Too much drugs to be walking around the hotel smashing lights and yelling at people."

"You should stop right now."

"It's in the report."

"The file's closed. Why the fuck are you reading it?"

McKeon said, yeah, you're right, there's nothing, and Barb said, You know I'm right, and looked around, holding up her empty glass to the waitress. Then she looked at McKeon and said, "Who put you on this?"

McKeon said it didn't matter, it wasn't official, it was nothing. Then she said, "Look," and looked at Roxon.

The waitress showed up then with another ginger ale and another vodka tonic. Barb never stopped looking right at McKeon.

McKeon said, "I wanted to let you know. I just wanted to . . ." and she stopped, trying to remember what she'd wanted to do. She couldn't think what she was trying to get out of this, she wanted to have a drink with Barb, have her say something about the dead guy, something about how it was an accident? She didn't expect Barb to come on so strong, but everything was so fucking fuzzy. She drank the vodka and looked around the bar, all the bankers out getting loaded, pretending they were such big shots.

Now Barb was saying she could recommend a couple of good meetings, one right downtown near College Street, saying, "You'd be surprised at how many familiar faces you see."

McKeon said, "I better go," and Barb said, sure, I'll get you a cab, and McKeon said, no.

"Maureen, how do you think you're getting home?"

She had no idea. She didn't even want to go home. She said, "I'm fine."

But Barb was taking charge, getting out her credit card, calling the waitress over, saying, "Sure you are, I know that," standing up and putting on her coat.

McKeon went with it. She couldn't focus and she had no strength at all, no energy. She didn't know how, but they were outside and she was getting into a cab and Barb was saying something about making sure she got into the house. McKeon closed her eyes and a second later she heard her husband, MoGib, saying something and a guy with an accent that sounded so phony saying something and then she was in her house.

Smelled like dirty diapers and McDonald's french fries, enough to make her puke, so she headed to the bathroom and almost made it and heard MoGib say, "For fuck's sake, Maureen," and decided to just take a nap in the hall there.

213

CHAPTER NINE

Roxanne said to Nugs, "All business, really, is relationships," and he said, yeah, you got that right.

They were standing on Queen Street East looking at a
couple of buildings on the north side, corner of
Broadview, Jackie's strip club and the New Edwin Hotel
next door. Roxanne was telling Nugs that since the Drake
Hotel way across town got renovated it was doing great
and even the old fleabag Gladstone Hotel was fixed up.
"They're both packed on weekends and even some nights
during the week. The Gladstone," she said, "has the Hump
Day Bump on Wednesdays, pretty much all gays, it's like
Queer Street West out there."

Still, Nugs wasn't convinced, he just said, "Yeah."

"This is an even better location," she said. "Closer to
the village for gay nights, and closer to downtown, Riverdale, even the Beaches. It could be really classy."

"Just managing it, though," Nugs said. "Think of how
many people you'd need."

Roxanne said, yeah, and Nugs could see she was thinking she was losing him. She'd called him up with this idea she had, buy the New Edwin and renovate Jackie's which they already owned, turn it into a nightclub, a classy place, sell ten-dollar martinis. She told him how popular places like that were in town, like the Drake, and how there were new private clubs in town, Spoke, and Verity, all trying to be London or New York. Nugs had asked her, how did you get my number, and she'd said they knew some of the same people. Told him she was in real estate development before, did he know the Toy Works office building on King West, that was hers, and then she got into high tech, internet service providers, and Nugs said, oh yeah, she was the chick saw that fucking Russian kill the other Russian. He'd heard of her. She said the internet stuff didn't really work out, she got back into real estate, so he agreed to meet, hear her plan.

216

It's all relationships.

But he wasn't going for this.

"We could buy it, renovate it and then sell it again," he said, "wouldn't have to manage it," and Roxanne said that would work, too, but then he said, "Jackie's does all right, though. Come on," and saw she didn't blink when he walked into the strip club.

Middle of the afternoon there were only a few customers, a mailman and a couple young guys in suits, a few other guys scattered around. One chick was on stage, a couple others were sitting at a table, one of them eating poutine.

Nugs sat down at a table on the other side of the bar, in the back, away from the action. The bartender came over fast anyway, asking them what they wanted, and Nugs said to him, "You sell martinis?"

The bartender said, sure, and Nugs said how much are they and the guy said, "For you? On the house," and Nugs said, no, for customers.

"Eight bucks."

Nugs said okay, what the hell, a couple of martinis and looked at Roxanne. She was wearing a suit, but the skirt was pretty short and the blouse was tight.

A dancer came over to the table, asked if she could get them anything and Nugs looked at Roxanne who said, oh, I don't know, I don't think so right now, and Nugs thought, shit, business must be fucking bad she's even thinking about it. Too bad, looked like when she was in control she was all right.

He figured she must be pretty much at the end of her relationships if she called him, tried to sell him on this plan.

But he liked the idea that he was the one making the decisions now. Jackie's was owned by a numbered company and Nugs's name wasn't on any of the paper-work, it was all other companies, wives, girlfriends, and lawyers. It was complicated, like all relationships were, but this Roxanne found him.

The bartender came over, put a couple of martinis on the table, said, "These are your classic martinis, gin, vermouth, and an olive. There's a million kinds now, apple, chocolate, whatever you want. Let me know," and he was gone.

Roxanne said, "I've never been here before, this is a nice place," and Nugs said, it's a dump, it's a tittie bar, no one's looking at the decor, and Roxanne said they must have been sometime, "Someone put some thought into it, all this western stuff."

Nugs said, "Before my time," but she was right, some-body fixed the place up once to look like it came out of a

Clint Eastwood movie, all old west. Since it'd had the naked chicks, though, nobody bothered to keep that up.

Roxanne drank her martini and said, "Wow, that's good." Then she said, "You know, this whole neighbourhood's changing, it's really on the verge," and Nugs said, yeah, there a neighbourhood in this town that isn't?

He watched her keep smiling at him, keep up her professional business-lady look, tell him about resale values and interest rates and real opportunities and he had to admit, shit, she worked it. Here he was knocking her on her ass, probably her last resort saying no thanks, and she was still in there. He liked her.

He said, "What about further east, how's that going?"

"Further down Queen? Good. Looks like there may be a shopping centre going in where that movie studio burned down on Eastern, you know it?"

"I know Eastern," Nugs said, street the clubhouse was on. "What about condos?"

"Sure, like the warehouse got renovated at Eastern and Leslie?"

"I like condos," Nugs said. "You build them and then you sell them, don't have to think about them again." Long-term ownership being a big problem. Who owns what, all that.

Roxanne said, sure, "This would be a great location for condos, you kidding? Queen and Broadview, so close to the DVP, to downtown, this would be fantastic."

"Maybe we'll start with something else," Nugs said. "A little further east."

Roxanne said, sure, smiling at him.

And Nugs thought, okay. Now we're talking, now we're running the show. Richard and the boys from Montreal — joined them all up coast to coast — were the ones with the international relationships, they had the contacts in Colombia, this Moctezuma, and they made the deal with the Italians, but that time was done. Other than the relationships, what did Richard have? All this money they were turning into gold to ship down to Costa Rica was raised right here in Toronto, the coke that would come back would get sold here. They were even leaving part of the city for Colucci, him and Richard working out that deal and Nugs doing him the favour of taking out Big Pete.

But now Nugs was thinking they could make their own relationships. People were coming to them. The old Rebels, maybe they joined the Saints, but they were the biggest chapter in the country now, doing the most business. They had the soldiers, they had the power. Nugs was the fucking national president, time to really step it up.

He said to Roxanne, "Maybe we should talk about this some more, maybe over dinner," and she said, sure, that'd be great.

Relationships change, leadership changes. How much could this Moctezuma really like Richard? Not more than he liked the money.

219

●   ●   ●

"Toronto's always comparing itself to somebody," Sunitha said. "They like it to be New York, you know, or even L.A., but they talk about the waterfront being like Chicago's and now they're starting to mention Detroit more."

Get noticed she always said *they*, like she was already gone. He said, "Detroit?"

"Like as a warning, you know? Hoping they don't go the way of it."

Get thought, well, no kidding. Close down all your

factories, throw everybody out of work, anybody who can goes running to the burbs, or California or Florida, place ends up looking like a war zone. Not that far from the Baghdad he saw.

They'd left Sunitha's apartment on Beaconsfield and a block south turned onto Queen West, way out west in Parkdale, Sunitha telling him it was another part of Toronto getting gentrified, all the middle-class white artists, grew up in nice houses in the suburbs now getting government grants and teaching jobs at colleges moving in, pushing the poor immigrants out.

"That's perfect for them," she said, pointing across Queen at the sales office for a new condo building called Bohemian Embassy. "It's so fucked up."

It was different, he'd give her that. She was different. Woke up in her bed this morning after meeting up last night, having a few drinks and not talking about going to see the boat or J.T. or any of that, Get's dick standing up poking her ass, she was pressed against him. He thought she'd say something, be pissed off, or just leave him there and go in the bathroom acting like she was in control, but she just rolled over and got a bottle from the nightstand, poured something in her hand and took hold of him.

He'd said, "You all business," and she said, You don't like it, and he said, "No, it's good, it's hot," dropping his head back on the pillow.

She said, "They call it warming fluid and personal lubricant."

Get was thinking he meant she was good, she was hot, but he just went with it. Sunitha put her head on his stomach, watching what she was doing, and Get touched her naked back, her smooth brown skin, running his hand from her shoulder down to her ass.

She was saying, "You think anybody uses it for shoulder massage, get the kinks out of your neck?"

Get wasn't saying anything.

"You put the word *lubricant* on the bottle, everybody knows what it's for."

First thing in the morning, it didn't take that long. Or maybe she was really just good at it. Get finished and Sunitha sat up and kissed him on the lips, saying, We'll do me later, okay, you hungry? I'm starving, and she jumped out of bed.

Get got dressed while she was in the bathroom, thinking this Sunitha was the strangest woman he'd ever met. Her apartment, what was once the attic of a big old house, was small and crammed with books, all kinds of books — little paperbacks, big paperbacks, hardcovers. Didn't have a TV or a stereo, just the iPod and a laptop, took them with her everywhere she went. No car, she took cabs everywhere, or she rode a bike, a bicycle, one of those old-fashioned one-speed Schwinn types.

She came back in the bedroom, walking around naked, she had to know how hot her body was but not acting like she knew, and started digging through a pile of panties on the floor in the corner saying, Don't worry, they're clean, I just never put laundry away, and pulling on a tiny white thong and then her tight, low-slung jeans.

She was digging through the pile again and turned sideways, looking at him. Now he wasn't so sure her tits were done, the way they were moving around could just be naturally big. And so nice. She saw him looking and said, "You getting ready?" and he said, Yeah, even though he had no idea what he was getting ready for. Felt good, taking on the day, see what happens. And he'd liked the idea of taking it on with this Sunitha.

221

Now, walking on Queen, Get stopped and said, "How much would that house go for?" pointing to half a brick semi a couple houses up from Queen with a For Sale sign taking up most of its tiny front lawn.

"Three hundred, maybe three-fifty if they put in a new kitchen and bathroom."

Get said, "Fuck. Gladstone Street."

Sunitha looked at him, said, "What?"

"Gladstone Street in Detroit, we got houses way bigger than that, way, way nicer, not half a house, a whole fucking three-storey red-brick house, four bedrooms, front yard, back yard, you can't give them away."

"You got other places, though, big old million-dollar homes."

Yeah, Get thought, true enough, and those two-, three-hundred-thousand-dollar houses right next door, calling it Jefferson Village, but he said, "We got plenty just falling down."

"Why don't you buy them?"

Get said, what? And Sunitha said, turn them into grow ops, fill them up with plants, you won't need to import so much, and Get was thinking, yeah, he could buy a couple of those houses on Gladstone, Eastlawn, Garland, all the way over to Jefferson, but maybe not grow ops, take too much security. He said, "Buy it for a dollar, sell it for two, that's business. Be nice to sell them for more."

Sunitha said, oh yeah? "You got ten thousand people a month moving into Detroit?"

"No, people moving out."

"People are coming here from all over the world, every country there is, somebody from there's in Toronto, you got that?"

Get said they had some Latinos, "Arabs on the west

side, some Chinese out in Warren, Troy, some Russians moving in that's about it."

"That's why you can't give those houses away."

Get said, true enough, but he was thinking they were still nicer houses than these, even fixed up, three-, four-hundred-thousand-dollar Toronto houses.

They passed the Gladstone Hotel, an old fleabag being renovated for the artists, and then a block later they passed the Drake Hotel, already reno'd but way upscale, Sunitha saying a real artist couldn't possibly afford a drink in there and Get saying, you a real artist? looking at her waiting for an answer, but she just looked at him like she thought he was being a smartass.

Get noticed, though, all over the place houses were being fixed up, stores, too. The buildings all looked old but the stuff inside them — art galleries and "design" stores and pastry shops — all looked new. Nothing like his neighbourhood back home, nothing new going in there, people wanted new shit, minute they could afford it they moved away, like his mom planned, out to Birmingham, past Twelve Mile at least, or St. Claire Shores or fucking Lansing.

Now, walking on Queen Street in Toronto, Get thought he could buy a house — a couple of houses — on Gladstone back in Detroit, pay cash for them with the money he was making on this trip, fix them up like these places, how much could a kitchen and a bathroom cost?

Sunitha took him into an old restaurant, what his grandfather called a greasy spoon back in the day, had a bust of Elvis in the window, little booths and some stools along the counter.

Sunitha said, "Hey Spiros," and sat down at a table by the window.

223

Get watched an older guy with slicked-back black hair, had to be a bad dye job, turn around from the grill and smile at Sunitha, everybody's friend. The old guy said, "You want coffee?" and Sunitha said, of course.

She looked at Get, he was thinking she was going to hold his hand on the table but she didn't, she said, "This place is one of the last hold-outs. We'll see for how long."

"Somebody make Spiros an offer?"

"All the time, pretty soon he'll take one, go back to Greece."

"Hasn't been there in fifty years, it's all changed, he's not used to it."

"He comes back, but his place is an art gallery."

"A Starbucks."

"Some restaurant where they stack the food in a pile, charge fifteen bucks for a salad."

"Everybody says what a great neighbourhood it used to be."

"Fucked up."

Spiros put down coffee in chipped white ceramic mugs in front of them and Sunitha ordered a western omelette and brown toast and Get said that sounded good, make it two.

He was thinking he would've guessed yogourt and granola or half a grapefruit or something, but looking at her he thought, no, that's what he would expect some chick living here with all these cool people, wanting to be one of them. Not this chick, though. He had no idea what she wanted.

Well, outside of stealing all the gold from the most ruthless motherfuckers he'd ever seen outside of Detroit.

And it was coming up to him trying to figure out what he wanted.

When the food came and they started to eat, Get watching her put strawberry jam on her toast and taking big bites of the omelette — which was a lot better than he expected — he was thinking this was the first time he'd been in anything that seemed like a scene in one of those romantic comedies Obie's girl Tweetie watched all the time. The morning-after scene, music playing, everybody happy, boy gets girl, before some shit comes along breaks them up, they spend the rest of the movie getting back together.

Then Sunitha was saying, it's weird, eh, sounding Canadian, and Get said, What, and she said, This. "Hanging out with someone, knows what you do, but doesn't care."

Get took another bite of the omelette, nice fluffy eggs and plenty of ham and green peppers, and thought it was like she was reading his mind. Or thinking like him, which might be even weirder. He said, "You think you know what I do?" and she rolled her eyes, looking cute in her black-framed glasses. He said, "You know some of it, yeah."

"And you know some of what I do," Sunitha said. "Some of what I did, and you never bring it up, like you don't care."

Get said, "We do what we do. What we have to do."

"We do what we think we have to do."

And she was looking right at him, serious, getting to it now, and he knew she wanted to talk about what he'd found out from J.T., if he knew where the stash was, if he was going to tell her, help her with her plan, but looking at her was making him think other things, too, like, do we *have* to do what we have to do. Since he was up in Canada, he was looking around. In Iraq and Afghan he was on a mission, get the contacts, set it up, get back

225

home. He was homesick, wanting to get back every day. Every time he got extended, always just a few more months, made him want to get home even more, it was all he thought about.

But this was different. It wasn't like the first time he went away. He wasn't worried anymore things would change back home. Now he knew wherever he went for however long, it would be the same when he got back. Not exactly the same, couple more guys'd be shot, new players trying to move in, but it would all feel the same.

He said to Sunitha, "You know what you want to do, don't you?"

"I can feel it's time for something new."

"New location?"

"I've gone as far as I can here."

Sounding like his mom, talking about her big house in the burbs, all that shit Get never took serious. What did he think? Day by day, no more. Now this plan, this big move, stepping up, buy all this dope from these bikers, sell them weapons, live big as long as possible and go out with no regrets. The same thing as always, only bigger, make yourself a bigger target. Nobody he ever heard of ever got out but two ways — jail or dead.

With that on his mind, this future that wasn't any future, he said to Sunitha, "What if I told you I saw it and it was just like you said."

"Yeah?"

"And I thought it might be possible."

"Then it is possible."

"Then what?"

"Then anything we want."

"So we're back to that?"

"We're so far from that," she said. "Anything we want

really means *anything*. The reason they're doing this is because it turns the money into something they can take anywhere in the world. We could go anywhere in the world."

"Have to be careful. As you say, this kind of money is good anywhere so a lot of people will be trying to take it from you."

"Get it and go. Take it easy for a while. You must know someone, could make you someone else."

"For a price, anything's possible."

She smiled, looked like a college girl just got an A. "You see, you know you want to."

Get was thinking, as much as I know anything I want.

She was finishing her omelette, wiping up the plate with the toast, getting every bit. She looked at him and said, "Well, it's something to think about."

And he knew she wouldn't be thinking of anything else.

He wouldn't be either.

●   ●   ●

Price watched McKeon walk through the weeds and broken bottles and said to her, "Are you hungover?" and she said, "A little, yeah, so?"

"So? Come on, Mo."

She said, "I'm fine."

The uniform leading the way, looked to be in his early twenties, Asian guy, said, "He was right up here."

They were just off the bike path along the Don River, under the Gardiner Expressway. All summer the newspapers had been full of pictures, artists' drawings, of what the area could look like gentrified: townhouses, lofts, art galleries, cafés, parks, nice wide bike path along the water. Price remembered his wife looking at the drawings and saying, you notice something about all these drawings? Not one of them has the expressway over top. No traffic jam, hardly any people at all, just a few young couples walking around holding hands, what's it going to be, some kind of gated community?

Now it was abandoned rail yards where homeless people lived.

And died.

The uniform stopped by the taped-off crime scene. Some old blue tarp was pulled over a couple of trees, more like big bushes, to make a kind of tent, and there were some beat-up shopping carts, garbage cans, torn-open bags of clothes and other junk. It was all thrown around like a hurricane passed through. Price said, "He live here?"

"The shelter guys think so," the uniform said, pointing back the way they'd come.

Price said okay. He looked around, figured the place'd been in bad shape before the paramedics got there and then they drove right up, tore the rest of it apart. The crime scene guys were waiting back by the bike path, but there wasn't going to be much for them to do, really.

The uniform said, "Guy was beaten pretty bad but he was still alive. The medics worked him for a while and then took him to St. Mike's but he didn't make it."

"Do we have a name?"

The uniform shrugged. "Pick."

"You mean, like there's so many, we can pick one?"

"No, that's what they called him, Pick. I don't know why, maybe they know."

Price looked back towards the bike path, there was a

white van with Na-Me-Res on it in black letters. He looked at McKeon and said, "You going to be all right?"

She said "I'm fine," but Price thought she was going to puke, so pale and hiding behind big sunglasses like the teenage girls were wearing. He said, "If you say so," and walked back to the van.

There were two young, dark-skinned guys sitting on the back bumper, looked clean-cut enough, short hair and well dressed, and there was a guy looked to be in his forties, also dark-skinned but different than the young guys, with a big belly and broad shoulders standing beside the van smoking a cigarette.

The uniform said, "This is Adam Charles. Detective Price."

Price held out his hand and they shook. Adam Charles said he was on outreach duty with the Native Men's Residence and Price said, so that's what it means.

Charles said, yeah. "People think it's a native word, Na-Me-Res. We do have Tumivut, the youth shelter. Means 'Our Footprints.'"

Price looked at the two guys sitting on the bumper and didn't think they were native, more like Tamil, or Sri Lankan, something like that. He said to Adam Charles, "So, was Pick native?"

"Don't have to be native for us to help," Charles said. "Just homeless."

"Did you know him well?"

"Not well. We bring hot food, coffee, try and get them into shelters. We have fifty-two beds in Tumivut and sixty-one at the main res."

"They usually full?"

Charles said, you'd be surprised. "It's got to be pretty cold to bring some of these guys in."

Price said, "You look familiar," and Charles said he'd been on TV a few times, "Reporters usually talk to me when a new report comes out about the homeless, I tell them the same things every time." Price said maybe that's it, but he didn't think so. Then Price said, "You found him?"

"Hadn't seen him around for a while, so when we were passing we stopped in."

"Was it unusual to not see him for a few days?"

Charles thought about it, looked like he could go either way and said, "I didn't really know him that well."

"But you were worried enough to stop by?"

"You know, detective, the poor diet these guys have, malnutrition, some drugs, alcohol, there's a high rate of paranoia, lot of mental illness, suicide."

Price said, right, sure.

"And sometimes," Adam Charles said, "there are people after them."

Price said, "What do you think happened?"

"Could be anything. Don't look too hard for something that makes too much sense, is what I'm saying. Too much sense for you and me, I mean. Whatever got him beat to death would seem crazy to us, you know?"

Price said, yeah, like some prison yard dispute, too many reps on the bench press, and the way Charles nodded, agreeing, Price knew he'd met him on the job.

Price said, "What do you know about Pick?"

"Not much. He came from down east somewhere, the Maritimes, Nova Scotia maybe, New Brunswick."

McKeon came over then and said, "Did Pick have a girlfriend? He was new, was moving in on anybody's girl?"

Price said, "You think this's a domestic?" and McKeon shrugged, said, they usually are.

Charles said he didn't think Pick had a girlfriend and

230

McKeon said, he have any friends at all?

"I don't really know," Charles said. "We're not really in their business that much, that way they can trust us a little."

Price handed him a business card, saying, "My cell's on there, if you think of anything else."

Charles said okay, he'd call him if he heard anything and then he got his volunteers back into the van and they drove off.

Price and McKeon both leaned against the bumper of the car then and watched the crime-scene guys work, slow and methodical, and, Price thought, thorough, which he liked to see.

Price said, "I think I busted that guy," and McKeon said, who, the native guy, and Price said, yeah. Then he said, "Maureen?"

She lit her cigarette and dropped the match, blowing out smoke saying, "What?"

"Nothing. Anyway, he's not going to remember anything."

"Because he's going to protect the homeless guy who's alive, the one who did it."

"So they can continue to trust him."

"Yeah, well, it's not like we're after anybody anyway."

Price looked at her, watched her inhale deep on the cigarette and blow the smoke up to the sky, and said, "What's that supposed to mean?"

"I had a drink with Barb Roxon last night."

"What the fuck did you do that for?"

"She's the handler, her or Keirans or both of them. They killed the car dealer."

"The guy OD'd," Price said. "Worst they did was didn't get him to the hospital fast enough."

"Sure," McKeon said. "You know it and I know it."

Price looked around the weeds and bushes and the Don Valley Parkway and the Gardiner Expressway passing over top of them, the Don River and Lake Shore Drive, steady traffic going in every direction, and he said, "Maureen, are you okay? I mean, besides the hangover? You drinking in the day? You drinking alone?"

"What about Roxon and Keirans."

"They'll wait," Price said. "What about you?"

McKeon looked at him, took another drag and said, "I don't fucking know, Andre."

"Okay," he said, "that's the first thing we have to worry about."

McKeon said okay, and Price thought that was a good sign, she wasn't going to have to hit rock bottom.

Price said, "Let's get a coffee."

● ● ●

Friday afternoon, Dufferin Mall was packed, teenagers, old folks, women pushing baby strollers. Richard parked by the Beer Store and the Winners, walked through the mall to the food court, bought a latte and a bran muffin with raisins, saw the guy he was meeting and sat down across from him, the guy saying, "So what do you think, we the only white guys here, the only ones born in this country?"

Richard said, "The babies, I guess, getting that citizenship."

The guy, Staff Sergeant Daniel Monette, an overweight Mountie wearing jeans and a Green Bay Packers jacket with the yellow leather sleeves, said, "It may not be America, but it's close enough."

"Everybody's second choice."

"Enough come here," Monette said, "looking for America, they'll just turn this into it."

Richard said, "Looking to get ahead," and put an *Entertainment Weekly* magazine on the table.

Monette looked at it and then back to Richard and then he picked it up, felt the envelope inside, the cash, and he folded it and put it in his pocket saying, "I don't really feel like I'm earning this, these days, we're fucking up all on our own."

Richard sipped his latte and broke his muffin into pieces, pushing the plate towards Monette, offering him some, saying, "I was thinking the same thing."

"But then," Monette said, "some assholes go and kill eight guys in one night, stuff them into the trunks of their cars, starts a war."

"More like finishes it," Richard said, "and it's not even in the papers anymore."

"Fuck the papers, we're getting pressure."

"How come they want you guys to do your jobs, it has to be in the paper, you have to get pressured?"

"We get the fancy red uniforms, pose with the tourists, we always get our man. We've got an image to protect." He sucked on the straw in his paper cup. "If it hadn't all been in one night, if it'd been spread out a little, fuck."

Richard said, yeah, "We've got an image to protect, too." He was still pissed at Nugs for doing it but he had to give the guy props, it sent a message. Even Richard was getting it.

Monette picked up a piece of the muffin but it didn't have any raisins in it so he put it back down and said, "The task force is all over it, but we've got fuck all. I don't know who you sent, but they were good."

233

"They got nothing?"

"Well, people are starting to suspect you're not the fuck-ups they thought you were."

"Was bound to happen," Richard said. "Eventually."

"Right now you got nothing to worry about. You prick."

"Keep working it," Richard said.

"Fuck that. It's not like we'll get our act together any time soon. You hear what happened in Lethbridge?"

Richard said, no, he hadn't heard anything, and ate some more of the muffin, not saying anything about the Saints chapter in Lethbridge finding out about the Mounties on them and walking away from half a million bucks in weed and a meth lab, but nothing else, no charges laid.

"We got nothing," Monette said, "some fucking leftovers. You know why? Cause we stayed on it too long. We had you fuckers nailed, we had wiretaps, we had surveillance photos, we had fucking video."

"Yeah," Richard said. "Not good enough?"

"Fucking lawyers. We run the investigation for months, we pile up all the evidence and we take it to the fucking lawyers. Do you know the way it used to work in this country?"

Richard said, "Tell me," wondering if he'd tell it the same way Mitchell Fucking Morrison, the Saints' top lawyer, told it, all about how the cops used to run an investigation, put together all the evidence and take a summary to the Crown attorneys and say, trust us, we've got enough. The lawyers'd put together search warrants and write up all the charges, the cops would make the arrests, guys would get bail, or more often lately, spend months in slam, and then Crown lawyers would take their fucking time handing over all the evidence, full disclosure, they called it, to the defence. Morrison said that's where they'd get them.

"It's this fucking full disclosure," Monette said, and Richard thought, yeah, it is gonna be the same story, funny, you don't usually get that from cops and lawyers. "Used to be," Monette said, "we could tell the assholes, don't worry, we have everything, it just takes fucking months to type up every goddamned wiretap, translate every fucking word because you pricks have too many fucking Vietnamese working for you." He pointed at Richard and Richard shrugged, what can I do?

"Used to leave out anything wasn't relevant, till your fucking lawyers were all over it, demanding, shit, that we turn over every fucking scrap." Monette was still pissed. "Now, these cocksuckers, they say they can't lay any charges until we provide them full disclosure, the entire fucking investigation, every goddamned expense receipt, every fucking picture we took."

"That doesn't sound right," Richard said. "You'd have to stop the investigation and write everything up. Could take months, people don't just stand still waiting for you."

"You think this is fucking funny, don't you?"

"Well," Richard said, "it's gotta be fair. Gotta follow the law."

"Fucking hilarious, you're fucking George Carlin aren't you?" Monette finished off his drink and crushed the paper cup in his hands, made Richard think of the little guy in *Jaws,* crushing his Styrofoam, trying to be tough. "All we're ever gonna get this way is two-bit dealers, fucking small-time shit, dumb-ass morons too slow to know what they're doing."

"Sounds about right for you," Richard said.

235

"Yeah, well, we're gonna fucking get you."

"No, you're not," Richard said, letting the cop have his little rant but bringing him back to reality. "These lawyers, once they go to court they don't want to lose a single one. It's bad for their careers, and it's not like they get points for trying. They'd rather let me operate the rest of my fucking life than go to court, spend five million bucks and lose. That's a career-limiting move."

"Fuck you."

"And you know perfectly well how much things have changed. How fast things happen, how things move. You can run all your fucking investigations, you can keep picking up the dregs, getting rid of all the dumb-ass morons you want. You thin my fucking herd, and I thank you. Keeps you in business, keeps me in business."

"Fuck you."

Except Richard knew it wasn't his herd anymore. He'd set up this whole move to Toronto, this whole new game and made himself so untouchable, so unconnected to any of it, he was expendable. The soldiers were all loyal to Nugs, and that guy was really stepping up. He said to Monette, "You had your say, that's enough."

Monette shook his head and looked around and Richard realized he was drunk, middle of the day. Shit, all the years he put into this asshole, getting him promoted, getting him transferred to Toronto and now he's going to blow it. Richard was thinking how he didn't need this shit, how he wasn't going to start over with another fucking Mountie, even if he could.

Which now, feeling like he was getting pressure from all sides, he didn't think was even possible.

Richard looked around the food court, all the faces of people from all over the world, kids wearing soccer shirts, teams he'd never heard of, old ladies wearing black, chicks on cell phones.

He said to Monette, "It's going to calm down, don't worry."

"Yeah? This was supposed to be over by now, you had everybody in line, remember, a nice corporate merger, all your fuckin' deals, nobody even notice."

"There's always adjustments."

Monette said, right, "But your fucking house of cards is going to come tumbling down. We'll all get fucked."

Richard said, don't worry about it, and Monette said he wasn't worried. "It's done, the Italians are going to blow up, fuck the whole thing."

Richard said, "Bullshit."

"You don't think? Oh no, that's right, you think you have a deal. That's not what I hear."

"What do you hear?"

"Even a blind squirrel finds a nut once in a while."

Richard said, what does that mean, and Monette said, once in a while, somebody on the task force does something right. "Sometimes we tap the right phone, sometimes we follow the right guy."

"Yeah, so?"

"I'm just saying, you assholes sent out a message, everybody got it." Monette looked at Richard and said, "And this is far from over."

Richard said, yeah, okay, that's what you want to believe fine, go ahead, looking like it was crazy, but he knew it was true. Big Pete was still walking around telling everybody what a shitty deal they made, how the Saints weren't even keeping up their end, and Richard knew he had enough guys agreed with him, thought Colucci was old and slow. The whole thing *was* going to blow up.

"Don't worry," he said. "It'll work out."

Monette said, "Not this time. We don't get you, this war will."

Richard said, "Get yourself some coffee, man, go to a rub and tug, have a nice blow job, you're tense," and he got up and walked away from the table.

Still, walking through the mall Richard knew he was right, Nugs wasn't fucking up at all, taking out the whole Lone Gunmen and not leaving a trace, he really did have the soldiers, that thinned-out herd looking pretty good.

And not taking out Big Pete, letting Colucci know they didn't have a deal after all. It would start a war.

Richard stopped at a place sold cinnamon buns and bought a small one, licking off the icing and taking a bite, thinking, he really didn't give a shit if these assholes wanted to go to war, kill each other, kill everybody, he just didn't want it to start for another few days.

He dropped the wrapper in a garbage can by the door, deciding he'd have to buy himself some time.

● ● ●

Sunitha was pointing at the screen of her laptop, saying, is this what it looked like, and Get said, no, it was bigger than that.

"Bigger, shit, how much have they got?"

"That boat's an operation," Get said. "I'm surprised they have everything in one place like that."

They were in a coffee place called the Mercury Espresso Bar on Queen East, Sunitha using the free Wi-Fi connection, looking at kilns, jewellery-making stuff, and precious metals investment sites. She said, "Kitco gets a million hits a day," and Get said, yeah, really, not that interested.

She said, "Yeah, well, you type 'melting gold' into Google and you get more than a million hits."

Get said, "Yeah?"

"All kinds of companies selling equipment to melt it down, showing jewellery designs and moulds, but when you get to the page to order stuff there's no more of that, just bars, ingots — all kinds of sizes. Like this," and she turned the laptop so he could see the screen, Get saying, no, bigger, and Sunitha saying, "Shit."

They were sitting on a couch against the back wall — a big map of the area painted on it, but Get noticed it wasn't there to help you find your way around, none of the street names were written in, this place being so trendy, expecting you to know where you were all the time. There was a Starbucks across the street, Get said why don't we go there, but Sunitha said, "I like being independent," and Get said, "I'll keep that in mind." She said, "You know what I mean," and he said, "I do," but he wasn't sure she did. People always think they know what they mean till they see the cash, or in this case gold, Get still surprised it was actual gold.

They'd been walking around downtown, went for lunch and to a couple of bookstores, Sunitha asking him if he wanted to pick up anything by that old guy in Detroit, writes the crime books, but Get said no. Didn't tell her he had them all. She took him into a bookstore called Indigo he said looked just like ones they had called Borders and she said, all the chains, they're all the same.

"Almost," he said, "this one doesn't have an African-American section."

"Even bookstores divided up like that?"

"Everything's divided up like that." He was thinking, at least the bookstores he'd been in, even that Borders

239

way up on Woodward, past Royal Oak, shit, in Birmingham, went all the way up there to see the old guy talk about a book he wrote about Nazi spies in Detroit in the forties. Was all right, had a sexy chick on the cover, and in the story she liked to show off her tits, even had a little mention of the first Detroit race riot, though it didn't say anything about the bump campaign — black people bumping into whites, nudging them out of the way, bumping them off the sidewalks. Get remembered his grandfather telling him about that, forgot if he was there or heard it from someone, but imagine that, white people shocked they getting bumped into on the sidewalk, scared of that. No wonder they so fucking petrified now.

Sunitha said, "So it isn't just jewellery getting melted down."

Get drank his latte, served in a tall clear glass, like a beer glass. The blonde chick that made it put a design on top, looked like leaf, and before he stirred it Get thought maybe it was a marijuana leaf, so now he was looking at the little blonde girl, tattoos on both her arms, her hair falling out of her ponytail, nice tits sticking up out of a low-cut tee under her apron and a big ass in tight jeans, thinking she's so funny, putting a little dope on top of his coffee. Everybody coming in, all the young artsy types, they all know the blonde and she knows everybody.

"I figured," Sunitha said, "they'd be making one-ounce bars, maybe ten-ounce, but what you saw, sounds like maybe a kilo bar."

"What's that?"

"If they're just melting other bars it's probably just to put another stamp on them. Maybe water it down, like they do the coke."

Get said, yeah, maybe, but he didn't think so.

Changing the stamp seemed more likely.

"Did you see anything that looked like this?"

"Yeah, some." Sunitha's laptop was showing a picture of little gold rectangles, size of a credit card, all stamped with the words "Credit Suisse."

"Ten-ounce bars, most popular in the world. Today worth six thousand four hundred and fifty U.S. dollars each."

Get drank his latte and watched the confident young white people come and go through the Mercury Espresso Bar. Sunitha was typing away again and Get was thinking how easy it would be to move millions in gold around. His mom and Uncle Main, when they went to New York to see MuMu, taking two hundred grand in twenties, ten thousand twenty-dollar bills, wrapped a hundred in a pile, a hundred piles, fill a gym bag. Everybody on the street knowing what it is. Imagine they tried to make a buy in Colombia, a million bucks, how would they even get the money there, they had nothing like the network these guys did. He said, "No, they bigger than that." Now thinking about this deal with J.T. and the Saints of Hell in Toronto, two hundred grand a month, maybe a lot more if they could move it all. Be nice to drive up with thirty of those little rectangles, fit in a CD bag, shit, he wasn't even sure if there was a law against it, take your gold for a ride.

"So, what?" Sunitha said. "Like six inches long?"

"I don't know what six inches looks like. Less than nine, I know that."

She was typing again, not even smiling at his little joke, shit, get this girl talking about gold she's got no sense of humour, then saying, "Like this?" And he looked at the laptop and said, "Yeah, that's it."

"Shit, kilo bars, very popular in Asia at the moment. Thirty-two point one five troy ounces. Times six forty-five today, could be more tomorrow, makes twenty thousand, seven hundred and thirty-six." She looked at Get, said, "And change," and he was impressed till he saw the little calculator in the corner of the screen.

"So it takes fifty of those bars to make a million bucks."

"Did you see fifty?"

He saw closer to two fifty, but he wasn't about to tell Sunitha that yet. He said, "Maybe."

"Maybe, you shit, you did. Oh fuck, they have more than a million bucks in gold bars," and she was off typing again.

Get said, what goes on in this neighbourhood and she kept looking at her laptop, saying, "Movies."

Get said, "What?"

"Movie studios down on Eastern, they call it the studio district. Lots of film company offices over on Carlaw."

And on Queen East, right outside the coffee place, Get had seen a lot of antique stores and new-looking restaurants in old buildings. They were all the way across town from Sunitha's place in Parkdale, place she was complaining about going upscale, but Get was thinking this part of town was going up too. He said, "How much the houses go for around here?"

Sunitha looked at Get and didn't say anything. She drank some more of her latte, put the glass down on the low table, and typed some on her laptop, saying, "Here, you never seen an MLS listing," turning the screen back towards him, scrolling down.

Get looked at the pictures of the houses going by on the left-hand side of the screen, not much to look at, clapboard semis, duplexes, triplexes, all squished close together, no front yards really, no porches. Not much to them. Except the prices. Get said, "You kidding?"

Sunitha said, "There isn't a house listed in downtown Toronto for less than three hundred grand."

"Try Detroit."

She typed and there they were. Get said, "Fuck."

Sunitha said, "This for real? Ninety-nine hundred bucks? Twelve-five? Where's Garland?"

"Look at that, Eastlawn, Fischer, Conner, they all less than twenty grand."

Sunitha said, "What do you want to do, pick up some gold bars and buy houses in Detroit?"

"You could," Get said. "Quite a few."

"You kidding? One one-kilo bar, get you two of these houses. Hell, go big, get this one, nineteen five. Where's Lakewood?"

"It's all right, 261, that's way the other side of Jefferson."

"So?"

"Right down by the water, Lake St. Clair."

"House by the water's always a good deal."

"Always?"

"Look around here," Sunitha said. "Couple blocks down you're at Lake Shore, used to be a big expressway over top, the Gardiner, but it got pulled down a couple years ago. This whole place is going upscale."

"Down below Jefferson, Alfred Brush Park, Harbor, it's not too different from around here."

"No?" Sunitha said, "Looks like it's about two hundred and eighty thousand dollars different."

Yeah, Get was thinking, fourteen of those gold bars different. Buy a lot more house in Detroit.

243

"Twenty grand, though, these places must be in bad shape."

Get said, "Shit, yeah, for the wrong buyer," thinking they were probably crack houses, squats, half a dozen people living there, desperate fuckers, but for the right buyer, able to get them out? The building was probably okay, it was bricks, had a roof, some windows.

"Okay," Sunitha said, finishing off her coffee and closing her laptop. "Now we have to figure out how we're going to get it off the boat."

And Get just looked at her, thinking, she is all the way crazy.

She said, "What do you think? Is there someone there all the time?"

"I don't know." It was almost funny watching her, like a movie, she was planning it out in her head. "You just going to smash and grab?"

"Why not?"

Get laughed. "You think these boys as easy to take as some chicks in a rub and tug?"

"Okay, are they getting ready to move it?"

Now he was starting to see it, too, like a movie in his head. He said, yeah, they getting it ready. "You wouldn't believe how."

"Tell me."

Looking at him serious.

"They're packing it in with scuba shit, tanks and wetsuits, those belts with the weights."

Sunitha was smiling. "Cool."

"They have some kind of resort in Costa Rica."

"With hookers, yeah, J.T. asked me if I wanted to help train the girls, be a boss lady."

"I guess they're expanding. Said something about a

golf course, too."

"Well shit," Sunitha said, "we better get busy."

Get said, "We better?"

"A hundred kilo bars, that's over two hundred pounds, I can't carry that myself."

Get was playing along, saying, have to get a couple of those suitcases with the wheels, and then realizing that might even work.

"We need to talk to Russell." She looked at Get and said, "But I don't want to tell him too much, I don't want to have to split this too many ways."

"No," Get said, "a couple million only goes so far."

Sunitha said, "You got that right," and stood up, still pretty much looking Get straight in the eye.

And he was thinking how far it would go in Detroit, twenty-thousand-dollar houses down by the water, could be good.

245

CHAPTER TEN

TURNS OUT THE LEXUS WAS ALL right. Plenty of power and the leather seats were big enough for Big Pete. He drove it south out of Woodbridge, taking Islington down to Finch and then across to Jane. It was like going over a border his wife never wanted to cross, he could hear her in the car as soon as they made the turn onto Finch, saying how it sure got dark all of a sudden. Big Pete not saying anything, but thinking, yes Lorraine, all the people here are black, who gives a shit? Lorraine saying something like, they better not even think about moving north of Highway 7 and Big Pete thinking, why would they want to, they all of a sudden get a craving for tacky marble tiles and furniture covered in plastic wrap? Cannoli? Shit.

This drive, though, it was Albert in the car with him looking to score points. Albert, twenty-five years old and ambitious, Big Pete said there might be some heavy lifting and the kid was the only one stood up.

Now he was saying, "I never come down here anymore, fuck it's dirty."

Big Pete hadn't even noticed, but now that the kid mentioned it he saw what he meant, the apartment buildings were falling apart, the storefronts looking old and tired.

"Yeah well, the economy's bad these days," Big Pete said.

"You're telling me. I like this car, though, Lexus is cool."

"Yeah," Big Pete said, "it's the Cadillac of cars."

Albert didn't laugh, but he smiled and nodded in rhythm to the music that was only playing in his head.

Big Pete said, "Okay, here it is," pulling into a strip mall on Finch. "She's waiting for us."

The storefronts that had been rented out were mostly West Indian groceries and clothing stores, new and used. One store sign said "Baby and New Mothers." The biggest unit at the end was a restaurant, the Caribbean Delite. Big Pete and Albert walked in.

Empty in the late afternoon, not a single customer, the lights were dim and reggae music was playing, Big Pete thinking it might have been Black Uhuru, old-time stuff taking him back to his teen years, coming down here to score weed, calling it ganja, being cool. Now he stood in the doorway for a minute thinking Albert was right, it'd been a while since the neighbourhood was new, felt new, like it was looking ahead. This place, this Caribbean Delite was brand new and looked good and Big Pete thought, about time, maybe it can start to turn things around.

Albert said, "So where the fuck is she?"

The big room was divided in two by a bar. One side was a restaurant with tables covered in yellow tablecloths and wicker chairs and the other side had a small dance floor and a wall of mirrors. In the middle of the restaurant half a huge neon palm tree went all the way up to the ceiling.

Then a black woman was coming out from the kitchen, looking like she could be anywhere from thirty to sixty, hard to tell with that smooth dark skin and some kind of cloth wrapped around her hair, looked like a big turban. She was smiling, saying hi to Big Pete, saying it'd been a long time and thanks for coming. "You want a drink?"

Big Pete said, sure, and told Albert to take a seat and wait.

The kid said, "It's okay by you, I'll stand," and didn't move.

Big Pete shrugged, looked back to the black woman and said, "So, what's up, you're not behind on any payments."

The woman, Nichole, she was a little taller than Big Pete in her platform shoes, said, "Beer?" and Pete said, "Rye and ginger, if you're going behind the bar."

A black guy wearing an apron came out of the kitchen carrying a plastic tub and started putting knives and forks — wrapped in white napkins — on the tables, one in front of every chair.

Nichole made Pete his drink and made one for herself and came around and sat on a bar stool, saying, "I'm sorry, Pete," and he looked around and said, "Fuck."

The black guy, the busboy in the apron, was standing beside Albert holding a gun to his head, looking like he'd done it a hundred times before.

J.T. came out of the kitchen and said, "You walk right in, this the only muscle you bring?"

Pete said, "Fuck you."

Nichole said, "I'm sorry, Pete, really," and Big Pete said, "Don't worry about it," and she picked up her drink and went into the kitchen.

J.T. sat down at the bar and Pete said, "At least this time you got the right guy," and J.T. said, "Do we?"

"On fucking Lake Shore," Pete said, "shot that poor asshole, his wife going down on him."

J.T. said, "But are you the right guy, Pete? We thought you were going to move on Colucci, but it doesn't look like you have the balls."

"You fucking punks, what do you know about loyalty, about running a real operation? Riding your fucking bicycles, your fucking leather jackets, you're just a bunch of fags, sucking each other's dicks."

J.T. looked at Get and said, "He talks tough, but when it comes time to step up, he can't get it up."

Big Pete said, "Fudge packer."

Get said, "Willing to stand by an old man, his time's past, and take the fall with him."

Big Pete didn't argue with him, what could he say? Asshole was right, Colucci was rolling over. But all this talk, Big Pete knew by now they weren't going to kill him.

"Happens all the time," J.T. said. "Guy stays on too long after the game's changed."

Pete kept looking at J.T., thinking what the fuck is this about.

J.T. saying, "Thing is, we're making changes, you're making changes. Keeps things fresh."

"Yeah," Pete said, "you're making changes?"

"We are."

They looked at each other and Big Pete said, okay, that's the way you want it.

J.T. stood up and said, "That's the way it is," and Big Pete said, "Okay," watched him walk to the door, the black guy going with him, backing away holding the gun, and they were gone.

The minute they were out the door Albert said, "Fuck, why didn't you move, I could have dropped him, bang!" Had his little automatic in his hand, Pete knew he couldn't hit a fucking cow from two feet away.

Big Pete sipped his rye and ginger, looked at the big neon palm tree and thought, yeah, he had enough muscle, he had enough guys with him, it was time. Some of them, they'd be pissed off, but if these assholes on wheels keep the business going, keep bringing in the coke and supplying the meth and weed, the money keeps flowing, guys would get over it in a hurry.

It's the only way change happens in this business.

Pete finished his drink, said to Albert, "Let's go," and they left.

• • •

251

McKeon was sitting at her desk in the homicide office looking at crime scene photos on her computer monitor. Clicking through a few dozen photos of the silver Dodge 300 angled back into the wall of the on-ramp and a bunch of pictures they got off a couple of traffic cameras that showed the car driving on Lake Shore a few minutes earlier.

Back at the office, trying to be a detective, thinking it would make her feel better.

And keeping her from going home.

What a fucking day.

Interviewing more people who were on the swinger booze cruise, Isobel setting it up, all those middle-aged women coming on to Price so hard, did they even realize it? In front of their husbands, half the guys seemed turned on. Another chick hit on McKeon, she was pretty sure, but she was trying not to pay attention.

And nothing about the Lowries, nobody mad at them, nobody jealous, nothing. One of the women they talked to, "Pdancer" on the message board, turned out to be for pole dancer because that's what she spent most of her time doing at the Friday night dances, said the Lowries were into "soft" swap. Then she explained it meant they really just flirted with other people, maybe a little kissing and petting but always in the same room. She asked McKeon if she'd tried pole dancing, said there were a lot of places to take classes, even gyms using it for workout routines and McKeon said, yeah? "High heels in the gym?" and Pdancer — Kathy — said, you want to see mine?

McKeon was glad when Price's phone rang and he said they had to go. Driving back downtown Price said, "You imagine a club, middle-aged couples go together and there's pole dancing?"

252

They were going to see Adam Charles, he'd called and said he had someone they should talk to. He was waiting for them at the hamburger place on Gerrard everybody called the Hooker Harvey's because it's where the teenage hookers hung out.

Price said maybe McKeon should take the lead and she'd said, this one's yours, isn't it, but Price pointed to the table and she saw Adam Charles sitting with a strung-out-looking teenage girl and said, "Yeah, okay." Talk to her woman to woman.

But then she blew it.

The girl, Tina, didn't want to tell her story, of course, but she wanted something hot to eat and Price got her a burger and a poutine and Adam Charles told her she didn't have to say anything, but it would help her if she did, and she looked at McKeon and said okay. Told her she was hanging out with another girl, didn't know her name, just called her Pokey, and they met Pick and McKeon said, "Who's Pick again?"

It got worse after that, McKeon not knowing any details, trying to get Tina to tell everything but really, the girl didn't want to say a word. McKeon got pissed off, said look, if you don't want to help, what are we wasting our time for.

Price had to step in, said to McKeon, why don't you get a cup of coffee and started over with Tina, going through everything they already knew, taking his time, letting her fill in little details one word at a time.

Price said did Pick take you back to his squat and Tina said yes. He said did he want something from you and she said yes. And you didn't want to give it to him? Tina said, Pokey said she would, and Price said, but she changed her mind, and Tina said, he couldn't.

McKeon watched the whole thing, Price taking forever but keeping the girl on track. The girl not so keen to be telling this to a man, and sure not to a guy as big as Price, broad shoulders in a nice suit, bald black head.

Price said, "Did he get mad when he couldn't?" and Tina said, "Yes." It went on and on, McKeon just wanting to get out of there, but Price waited and waited, saying, "Right, yeah," all soothing, and then, "You were scared, sure," and Tina said, "Yeah, I was really scared," and Price said, "Maybe that came out weird, like laughing or something?"

Tina said, "Yeah maybe." She said, "That's what Pick thought, for sure, and he started hitting us, hitting Pokey really hard, punching her and she hit him back. She just went crazy," Tina said, "hitting him and hitting him. Picked something up, a bottle I think, and hit him, and there was blood all over the place."

253

Price asked a few more questions and Tina told them Pokey left after that, she had no idea where, some people were talking about Calgary or Vancouver, maybe up north. Tina thought Pokey might have been from up north, Sudbury or Sault Ste. Marie.

Adam Charles asked if she was aboriginal and Tina said she wasn't sure.

Price asked Tina if she'd be okay to come back to the station with them, they'd get a youth counsellor to be there, but they wanted a real statement. Tina said she never hit him and Price said he knew that, he wanted to make sure it was official, written down right so it wouldn't get mixed up later.

Took the whole afternoon and then Price was done, heading home. He said, "You going home," and McKeon said, "In a while."

Price said, "Maybe you came back off mat leave too soon, you could take another six months."

"At no pay."

Price said, yeah, standing there by the elevators.

She knew the problem wasn't coming to work, it was going home. She thought Price knew it, too, the way he was looking at her. She said, "I'm going to do some work, I feel like I fucked up today."

Price said, you did. "But today's over. Start fresh tomorrow."

"I'm going to do some work. Type up some notes."

Price said, okay and left, saying, "You think about stopping for a drink on the way home, you call me," and she'd said sure, she'd do that.

She'd typed up her notes about the meeting with Tina and then typed up the stuff from the interviews with the swingers. Nobody knew nothing. She'd looked through everything on the Lowries, no reason for anybody to want to kill them.

Now she was drinking cold, stale coffee and looking at her brand-new pack of cigarettes, Rothmans, on the corner of her desk. She was thinking she should just go home, it was almost seven, MoGib would have fed Nathaniel already, probably eaten dinner himself. She could get there for bath and bedtime stories. If Nat would fall asleep. More likely she'd sit in the living room watching TV while MoGib sat in Nat's room with him in the rocking chair. Or they'd let the kid cry for half an hour, pick him up for a while, let him cry some more. McKeon had no idea what colic was, but she didn't think she could take much more of it.

Downstairs and out the back door for a smoke in the parking lot. She lit up and inhaled deeply, let the smoke out slow, enjoying it. This time she'd quit for over a year. Next time, next time would be the one. She was thinking maybe she'd walk over to Yonge, get a coffee at the Starbucks, maybe a bowl of Shanghai noodles next door.

A car pulled into the lot and Louise O'Brien got out, was walking towards her when McKeon saw it.

O'Brien said, "Hey, Mo," and McKeon said, "Fuck."

"What?"

"Look." McKeon pointed to where O'Brien had parked the Crown Vic right next to another Crown Vic, two unmarked cop cars in a row, not unusual at all in the parking lot behind police headquarters.

O'Brien said, "We get another car stolen out of the lot?"

McKeon took another drag on her cigarette, dropped the butt and stepped on it, saying, "Can't fucking believe it," going back into the building.

255

O'Brien followed.

At her desk McKeon clicked through the pictures, put two at a time on the monitor, side by side, a traffic-camera picture and the shot of the car against the wall.

"Fuck." She made the little dotted-line square around the licence plate of the traffic-camera car and kept enlarging it.

O'Brien said, what are you doing, and then, "Too bad, but so what?"

By the time the licence was big enough to see the letters and numbers on it they were too blurry to make out, standard Ontario plate, four letters and then three numbers.

McKeon was pleased. She said, "Fuck yeah."

"What?"

"The Lowries have a vanity plate, says ITSADOGE."

"What the hell does that mean?"

"Price says it's from that TV show, *Married with Children*, the dad was always making fun of his car, saying, it's a Dodge."

"Oh."

"Yeah, Price said he saw an interview with the guy, the actor, Ed somebody."

"O'Neill, he was a football player before."

"Right. Anyway, he was driving a Viper and when the interviewer said something, he put on that sitcom voice and said, it's a Dodge."

O'Brien said, "So, these Lowries, they're proud of their Dodge."

"Yeah, but whoever that is," McKeon said, pointing at the traffic-camera shot, "doesn't give a shit."

That's when O'Brien got it. She said, "It's a different car."

"Nobody wanted to kill the Lowries," McKeon said.

"So, who's driving that car?"

"Good question."

O'Brien said, "Holy shit, Mo, you're a real detective."

McKeon thought, yeah, maybe I am.

O'Brien walked around to her own desk and sat down, turning on her computer. She said, "You know, I had something about a car like that in my notes." She waited while her computer booted up, then called up a file, did a search for a Dodge 300 and said, "Holy shit."

McKeon stayed at her desk and said, what?

"Rebecca Almeida, killed herself in her Beetle down by Cherry Beach?"

"You wrote that up as suicide?"

"Going with the evidence. But in my notes here, the last person that we had on her nanny cam, one of her customers, Big Pete Zichello."

"Big Pete? We're looking at him for the Eddie Nollo hit."

"He's on the cam using the duct tape that was around the vacuum hose on her tailpipe."

"Sounds like one of David Letterman's routines, sounds dirty but it isn't."

"Oh, it's dirty," O'Brien said. "Everything about it's dirty. But we ran all the names and, of course, Big Pete came up. The task force's been following him, they had surveillance pictures, even some video."

"That night?"

O'Brien shook her head, said, no, said they were actually looking at someone else, wouldn't even say who, but they had Big Pete meeting with him. "But the thing was, there was a note in the file, he switched cars. Went from that Dodge," pointing to McKeon's monitor, "to a Lexus."

McKeon said, "Fuck me," and O'Brien said, watch what you say around here.

"So," McKeon said, "some asshole got the wrong car."

"Too bad, would be good to get rid of Big Pete."

"Would have been better for the Lowries, too. But who wants to kill Big Pete?"

O'Brien looked across the desks and said, "Who doesn't."

McKeon said, "Who'd you talk to on the task force?"

O'Brien said, "Barb Roxon, you know her," and McKeon said, we've met.

This time, though, McKeon decided not to meet her for a drink. She wanted one, though, wanted one bad.

So she called Price.

• • •

They'd spent the night at movie-star parties. Started at Bistro 990 on Bay, like everybody else, and then it was invitation-only — or more likely famous-enough-only, even though Richard didn't really recognize anybody. They'd passed the Schmoozefest in the parking lot of CITYTV on Queen West but Kristina said it was all desperate wannabes, kids taking their first step into selling out. "Getting on their knees," she'd said, "seeing how much money and fame it takes to lubricate the back door," and Richard knew it wouldn't take much, movie directors, actors, all the dealers and pimps and strippers and hookers he'd ever known were all starting to seem the same.

Back at her condo, Kristina asking again if he was thinking about buying his instead of renting and Richard saying, "Yeah, maybe," like he always did, and then she said, "Did you see Edmund trying to find out if Garry's single," and Richard said he thought he was trying to hire the guy.

Kristina said, "Hire, date, what's the difference, all relationships are business, right?"

Richard said, right, and she said, "And all business is relationships."

He said, yeah, and thought she was going to start talking about their relationship, neither of them had said anything about it, but she walked into the ensuite and he sat on the bed. He was thinking it was true, everything he had was because of his relationships and now, if that fucking Mountie was right, if Big Pete was really going to make his move, it would all come tumbling down.

Then he was thinking of the Stones, "Tumbling Dice," and Kristina came out of the bathroom naked and stood in the doorway, leaning against it, saying, "After all those young, skinny starlets, how do you feel about an old broad," and Richard said he felt good, but was thinking of Mick singing it, how all this low down bitching has got his feet itching.

She walked to the bed and pushed him back, climbed up on him, straddling him and unbuttoning his shirt. He did feel good. He wanted to feel better, he only needed to keep this together a few more days.

Kristina said, "What's this one?" tracing a tat on his chest, giving it little kisses, and he said, dreamcatcher, and she said, and this, and this, tracing her fingers over some more, barely touching his skin, just a little pressure, playful, but he knew where she was going. She traced the Saints tat, the skull with the devil horns and the flames, on his right arm, halfway between his shoulder and elbow, saying, "You were really young when you joined," touching the date there, 6-21-83.

Richard said, "Yeah, a kid," not telling her about the hangaround years, the prospect time before he got his patch and his tat.

She kept touching his arm, then moved back to his

259

chest, pushing him back on the bed, saying, "How long were you a member?"

Richard said, "How long?" and thought, she can't be serious, must be some game she's playing. Spend the night with her movie-star friends, all the phony tough guys, she wants to believe it's all phony. Richard thought about RoJo, quit in '89, told them all he was grown up, didn't need their shit, moved out to fucking Cornwall. Bought a truck, started long hauling, but he wouldn't cover up his tat or put a retirement date on it. All they asked, put the date on you left, but he wouldn't. Richard finally sending a couple of prospects out there with sharp knives, cut the fucking tat off RoJo's arm.

Now he was thinking Kristina must know that, she must know it's not something you just quit.

And then he wondered, did he know that?

She traced another tattoo on his chest, a diamond with "1%" in it, old and faded, and asked what it was.

"A club inside the club," he said. Back in the day, somebody said that only one per cent of all motorcycle club members were actually criminals. As big a joke as that was, it gave them something to call the long-standing members, the top guys, the One-Percenters.

Now she was moving down his body, kissing his stomach, unzipping his Hugo Boss pants and he was thinking, how much was he going to tell her? How much did she really want to know.

She kissed her way back up his to his chest, bit his nipple, then ran her tongue over it and said, "I thought you had to kill somebody to get this, the double D?"

Richard said, "Dirty Deeds," and didn't answer her question, thought, is she really asking?

She headed back down, pulling his pants all the way

off, saying, "So, you're like, really a bad guy," not looking up at him but he felt the pause, her whole body tensed up for second and he said, "Yeah, I'm the worst," and she laughed and bit the flesh around his belly button, saying, "You seem like such a teddy bear to me."

Made him think, yeah, that's the problem, I'm a teddy bear to everybody these days. And teddy bears don't last in this business.

Kristina had his pants and underwear down and she said, "You too tired?"

He looked down at her, sexy naked body, and he thought, she just want to distract me now? Or did she find out what she wanted to know and it doesn't bother her? Thinking, he should just ask her, just say, honey, do you really give a shit I killed a couple dozen sleazy drug dealers? Delivered a TV with a bomb in it to an apartment across de Maisonneuve Ave. from a police station, killed three guys who'd killed a dozen between them?

Thinking he must be getting old and soft like a teddy bear, he starts looking back on his life, all the guys he's taken out. Shit, never added them up, never wanted to know. Not like fucking Claude, adding a ring to the tat on his arm for every one, almost got around the fucking thing twice before some old Russian guy shot him at the airport. Fucking way to go out.

She climbed back up beside him, Richard thinking what smooth skin. That was something that changed in his years, he remembered in the beginning, the strippers and even worse, the hookers, bad skin, acne scars, a lot of just plain scars, crooked teeth. Now, though, all the chicks had good skin and not a single hair anywhere below their carefully plucked eyebrows and fake lashes, good makeup, the boob jobs so much better, hell they were even lining up

261

with the suburb girls to get nose jobs, going to the spas, getting worked over, spending their money as fast as they made it. And this Kristina, she grew up with money, Richard knew that. Daughter of Ronnie Northup, the Pot King, but that was back in the day, back when it was hippies and sticking it to the man, revolutionaries.

Lifetimes ago.

Richard said, "I'm not that tired," and she smiled at him but he could see it. She wanted out. The real thing was a little too real. He dropped his head back on the bed, felt her kiss her way her down and knew they wouldn't be fucking. She'd blow him, say she was tired, or the booze was finally giving her a headache. She'd found out what she'd wanted to know, what she'd known all along but didn't want to admit.

He felt her warm lips on him and he was thinking, when was *he* going to admit what he'd known all along?

Later, he got up and got dressed. He watched her sleep, thinking it was too bad, she would've had some fun in Costa Rica, but he knew she wasn't ready to retire, she liked the movie-star parties too much. Figured he'd call her before he left, set something up, she could come and visit. That would be good, it would make him feel like things were normal.

He only had to keep them normal for a few more days. He'd have to get rid of Big Pete himself, keep fucking Colucci from doing anything stupid, get down to Jaco, see Moctezuma, make it seem like everything was fine, just waiting on the scuba equipment. Plan where he was going, find a place in Panama maybe, or Belize, and then pick up the gold and go.

Leave Nugs and his fucking thugs standing around with their dicks in their hands, never met Moctezuma, he

262

wouldn't even talk to them, and Colucci still in charge, no one to come after Richard.

It could work.

He drove home, just about dawn, making a list of everything he'd need to do, thinking, yeah, it'll work.

Then he was thinking about that first trip to Costa Rica, coming in on the plane, mountains all around, like they were landing in a bowl cut into the top of one of them. He'd always thought the big city, the airport, would be on the water, but San José's inland. Back then the airport was so small the waiting rooms were actually outdoors, tents, and kids got dressed up in folk-dancing costumes to meet the planes. Tourism was new, early nineties.

Mon Oncle smiling the whole time, hell the guy was always smiling, asking Richard how come he always looked so serious, Richard thinking, oh I don't know, maybe because I have a million American dollars in my fucking carry-on bag and we're meeting a Colombian fucking drug lord. Maybe I want to know why you're so fucking relaxed? Mon Oncle'd never met the guy, just his assistant, and that was in Cuba, the real benefit of those direct flights from Montreal. That time it was a hundred thousand bucks, half up front. All the guys, Claude and Denis, Richard, Pierre — Mon Oncle convincing them all to put up ten grand apiece, said the guy would front them another hundred grand worth on consignment. They were so scared, what if the guy takes the money and fucks off, what if they get caught, what if the coke's too shitty to sell, what if, what if, what fucking if?

Turned out so good. Almost seemed too easy. Vito Costa's daughter, Sophia, gave them the name and phone number, Mon Oncle just called the guy, talked to him like they were old friends, the guy saying, yeah, I've heard of you, I saw that thing in the paper, meaning the massacre of the Hull chapter. Guy said he respected it, liked guys ran a clean house. So they flew to Havana.

Then, after they did a few deals that size the guy says, you want to try something bigger, so they moved up and moved up until they were meeting Moctezuma in Costa Rica.

Now Richard was thinking it was time to move up again, move up and out.

●　●　●

Get watched J.T. lift the two-four out of the trunk of the Avenger and said to him, "Blue?"

"All I know about beer," J.T. said, "is that there's ale and there's lager. This is lager, like most Canadian beers."

"What's ale?"

"Mostly British, Guinness, like that."

Get picked up the bottle of rum, the Cokes, and the bag of ice and said, "Guinness is Irish."

They walked to the boat, J.T. saying, what's the difference and Get saying, "English beer's the warm shit, you supposed to drink Guinness cold."

"I have to drink them all cold."

In the galley they gave the two hangarounds the beers and the rum and the Cokes and one of them, Dickie, said, "No munchies?"

Get thought J.T. would get pissed at the guy but he said, "Go to that store over on Barton, or call them, they'll send a kid. Shit."

Dickie and his buddy, could have been his brother they looked so much the same, complained about that store taking so long to bring over a pack of smokes and then J.T. said, "You don't have a TV in here?"

"Got the laptop."

"How can you watch porn on that?"

Dickie said, "You can," and J.T. said, okay, "Don't work too hard," and walked back out onto the deck.

Get, following him, said, "They good enough to guard this," and J.T. said, no, it doesn't look like it. They walked outside for a while, the little space between the pilothouse and the edge of the boat, Get looking down thinking it looked a lot further up from the water here than it did from the dock.

J.T. had a big ring of keys out when they got to the crew quarter doors but before he unlocked any he noticed one door was open a little and he said, "What the fuck," pushing it slowly and watching it open all the way.

Get said they had a party.

The bed was all messed up and the pillow was on the floor. J.T. stepped into the room and said, "Assholes." He picked up a red thong off the bed and tossed it on the floor, Get saying, "You think that's Dickie's or his brother's?"

J.T. said, "Slobs," and Get said, "Yeah, but they safe," looking at the used condoms in the little garbage can by the dresser.

Back in the hall J.T. said, you get what you pay for, I guess and Get said, "They paid for it all right."

J.T. unlocked the next door and said, "As long as they didn't go over to Hanrahan's, pick up strippers."

"Come on," Get said, "I bet the escorts deliver a lot faster than that kid brings the smokes."

"Okay," J.T. said. "Here we go."

There were half a dozen wooden crates lined up on the floor in front of the bed, the tops on them but not nailed

265

shut yet. J.T. lifted a lid and said, "Oh yeah." He took out the scuba tanks and then the specially fitted foam packing and then another piece of plywood that wasn't nailed in.

Then there was a row of gold bars.

Get said, "The real deal."

"Kilo bars, baby, twenty grand apiece, maybe twenty-five soon."

J.T. started lifting them out, handing them to Get, saying, "We'll put them in that other room, not the one stinks the boys used for their pussy party, the other one."

Carrying a couple bars at a time, Get said, "You never worry about your people?"

"What, that they'll fuck up? Every goddamned day."

"No," Get said, "what's that line the Navy fags use? Loose lips sink ships?"

"Need brains for that. You could hand those guys this gold, they'd have no idea what to do with it."

"No, I mean, they know it's here, they might tell somebody."

"Nobody stupid enough to steal from us."

When they'd moved the forty bars from the first case, J.T. put the lid back on and opened the next one.

Carrying the bars, Get said, "Not to steal, man, just to blab. This whole operation, cops like to find it." He was walking behind J.T. looking at his back, looking for some reaction, but he didn't get much.

J.T. said, "It's not worth it, man."

"Nobody ever gives it up?"

"No reason to, no leverage."

"Yeah? What if Dickie out there's looking at life in a room like this, but they don't deliver smokes and pussy?"

J.T. laughed and said, "Life? No man, we don't do life."

They carried more gold bars out of the scuba crates and into the empty bedroom and J.T. told Get that in Canada, federal time, you do one-sixth of your sentence.

Get said, "Holy shit."

"Oh yeah, man, that's it. And, pretrial time in the Don, that's a jail downtown Toronto, counts for double."

"Fuck."

J.T. said, oh yeah. "Look at fucking Spaz, couple of years ago he gets picked up for murder, killed a fucking bouncer in a strip club in Oshawa. Guy was smacking the chicks around, they couldn't work with the black eyes, bruises on their tits, shit like that." J.T. sat down on the edge of the messed-up bunk, wiped sweat from his face. "So Spaz takes care of the guy, beats him with a bike chain, strangles him."

Get said, "Shit," leaning against the door frame, using his T-shirt to wipe the sweat from his face.

"Yeah, and he gets picked up, some asshole narc cop was in the club, put Spaz at the scene, they had a lot of circumstantial shit. So they make him offers, you know, because they know he knows a lot of shit."

"Guy's what do you say," Get said, "full patch?"

"Yeah, why didn't he have a hangaround take care of it? 'Cause he's a fucking hothead, or 'cause he likes it, or he wants to show everybody he's still the big man, who knows?"

"Maybe he just wanted to warn the guy, scare him?"

J.T. laughed, said, that's what his fucking lawyer said. "The Crown, that's what we call the DA, try making him deals, but they got shit to offer."

Get said, "Murder, twenty-five years, no?"

"That's just it. You get picked up in the States, life is life. Or they give you five fucking life terms."

"Get that for dealing, too."

"Yeah, you know what Spaz tells them? He says let's go to fucking trial. That'll cost them a fucking million bucks, all the shit his lawyer'll throw at them. So, you know what he does, he pleads to manslaughter."

"You say he went out there to kill the man?"

"I watched him put on the leather gloves, pick out the chain. He pleads to man two, gets six years, but," J.T. said, "he's already spent six months in the Don."

"Counts as double."

"You're paying attention. So he's got to serve one-sixth."

"Which is one."

"Which his six months times two counts as."

"So he's out."

"Day he made his deal."

"He string them along for six months till he got it?"

"Wouldn't you rather do time counts as double, right in town where your wife can come visit? You can keep doing business."

Get said, fuck man, "Six months for planning to kill a guy and killing him. What do you have to do to get serious time in this country?"

J.T. stood up, opened another crate, pulled out the scuba equipment, and started lifting out more gold bars, saying, "No idea."

They carried more gold and J.T. told another story, told about how Nugs had a girlfriend for a while, hot chick used to lay out naked on the deck of his boat, and Get said this boat?

"No, a sailboat. Nice one. Anyway, turns out she was talking to a cop, giving her what she could. It was all small-time, bullshit stuff, but enough to tie Nugs up in pretrial for a while.

"Yeah, what happened?"

"They say she killed herself before she could give evidence."

"They say?"

J.T. said, "Well, she's dead, that's true enough," and Get thought, yeah, you mix that together with practically no jail time, who would inform on these guys?

Have to be as crazy as someone thinking about stealing from them.

When they had all the gold out of the crates and in the next bedroom J.T. said they'd have to get some lead, weight down the crates so they look right.

Get said, "So, I guess the French dude is out?"

"I guess," J.T. said. "These ship out tomorrow, then he's supposed to get on a plane."

"Gets where he's going, finds out his gold didn't make it?"

"I'd be shocked," J.T. said, "he ever gets on an airplane."

"You got some leather gloves, a motorcycle chain?"

J.T. locked the door and walked back towards the galley, saying, "We got all kinds of chains."

Walking off the boat, J.T. said, "We're still going to have to ship it down, we're still going to deal with Moctezuma, he's the Colombian, but we're making our own deal. Nugs might go himself, I might go with him."

"You the man now."

They got into J.T.'s car and he said, "I'm getting voted in, getting my patch."

"You got a sewing machine?"

"I asked them if they had iron-on." He winked at Get and said, "No, really, it's cool."

And Get thought, yeah it is.

269

• • •

The chick, Stacy, he was pretty sure that's what she called herself, said, "He's going to be here any minute, I should get dressed," and Richard said, "Take it easy, there's time," and she went back down on him.

Richard was on her bed, half sitting up with his back on the headboard, looking through the open bedroom door to the living room of the condo. She was all right, this Stacy, but she never used her hands at all.

The plan had some loose ends, sure, but he was making it up as he went, that's life, there's always loose ends. He knew he couldn't stay around any longer. Nugs and the boys would get rid of him soon enough.

When he'd shown up with the bright orange dog leash Stacy had said, "Oh, you wanna play like that," all flirty and he'd said, no, it's for later, and told her to call Big Pete, say she just had to see him. She'd put up a fuss, like Richard expected, but she made the call and it didn't even take that much to get Big Pete to say he'd be right over. Then, nothing to do but wait, Richard said let's go in the bedroom. She did a little lap dance for him, said it'd been a while and Richard didn't tell her he could see that. She undid his pants, pulled them down, and he said that was good, right there.

Now she kept stopping, looking up at the door and back at Richard and he was thinking maybe he wouldn't finish before Big Pete got there, wouldn't that be funny, standing there with his dick standing up, pants around his ankles. He said, "Honey, get to it," and she nodded and got back to it. Shit, she was slowing down, Richard figuring he finally realized it wasn't going to be a party, the men of her dreams all over her.

270

Like she was starting to figure out what it was going to be.

"Come on, relax," Richard said, "you've done this before," thinking, yeah, every day and usually trying to make it happen as fast as possible. Then he thought, no, most hookers he'd been with, they tried to drag it out a little, make a guy think he's a big stud, getting his money's worth. He said, "Yeah, like that." Finally she was really getting to it.

And Richard was thinking here he was, getting into it. He hadn't done anything like this himself in a long time, that was the thing about an organization like the Saints, you do the dirty work, you rise up to a level you don't have to anymore. Never thought about what *anymore* really meant, but if he was honest with himself he knew there was no such thing. He knew he'd never retire. Now he just needed to buy another couple of days.

Because he knew what would happen next. It was like Mon Oncle, started fucking younger and younger girls, looking for strippers with daughters. Richard thought about taking off then, retiring he called it, and talked to Sylvie about it. Of course he talked to Sylvie about it, he talked to her about everything. They started looking into Cuba, the Dominican, Venezuela — where they'd been a few times to meet Moctezuma and then he said let's meet in Costa Rica. Place was hopping, lot of online gambling set up there and prostitution was legal. It wasn't some third-world dive, either, it actually had a lot of things better run than Canada.

But then Sylvie went and got killed. Driving home from her mother's house, it wasn't even snowing that hard, Richard pissed she even went — like she did every goddamned Thursday night for years. Coming back on the 40, just this side of Trois-Rivières, fucking ten-car pile-up, Sylvie right in the middle, her Tahoe flipped about five times, no seat belt, what a mess. Richard went out to the accident scene, cops telling him not to look, him telling them to fuck off. One of them knew who he was, let him through. Goddamn. Richard sat down on the side of the highway, sat there in the snow for hours while the ambulances took away the survivors and the bodies, two other people killed besides Sylvie, and he sat there while the tow trucks moved the wrecks out of the way and the traffic started up again. The sun was coming up when he finally left, Denis driving him back home, Claude taking his car.

Then Richard spent a week with no fucking idea what he was doing. Nearly lost it on Sylvie's mother, old bitch wailing on the coffin, crying *"Mon bébé, mon bébé,"* looking at Richard like it was his fault, like he was the one drove her out of the house when she was thirteen, telling her she was stupid and fat. The rest of her family, her fucking brothers always with their hands out since he'd known them, lazy assholes, the funeral not being any different, wanting to know right away, who's paying for this. Richard taking them aside, saying who the fuck you think is paying for it? Who pays for everything?

Then that goddamned priest, going on about Sylvie making mistakes in her life, taking wrong turns, now being better off with the Holy Father, Richard thinking, right, you'd be singing a different fucking song if I'd coughed up another grand in your fucking funeral shake-down speech. Well fuck you.

It was driving home from that shitty church, biggest building in the shitty little town, Richard decided he wasn't going to roll over and die, like he thought. Alone in his car he had a talk with Sylvie, as if she was sitting there beside him like she always was, sitting sideways looking at him, saying, "What you going to do now? Nothing? Really? Nothing? Come on," smiling at him like she always did, "what do you want to do, Richard Tremblay?"

That was when he started to lighten up, started to say, what do you want me to do, like he always did. Laughing about that first time, they were kids, got together when that English broad he was seeing, Sharon, all of a sudden moved in with Pierre, and Sylvie came up to him, said he needed to get right back in the saddle. They were at Les Amazones, Sylvie was working, Richard was there by himself, out showing his face, daring someone to say something, looking to bust someone's head open, and Sylvie walked right up to him, said, "Yeah, that's right, you get dumped, you get right back up again."

273

Richard remembered thinking how no one was saying anything to him, everybody thought he was going to have to kill Pierre — which he did a couple years later, put a bomb in the fucker's Jeep, made it look like it was part of their war — but nobody said a word, the whole chapter, hangarounds and all in the bar, and now this Sylvie, standing there in a skimpy teddy, barely covered what little tits she had, looking him in the eye, saying, "Listen to me," and then she went up on the stage and that Aerosmith song started, "Back in the Saddle," Steven Tyler in top form.

And so was Sylvie, dancing for Richard like he was the only guy in the place, the only guy in the world, except everybody else in the place started seeing what was going on. They started to clap, Mon Oncle laughing his head off, the other dancers all cheering, Sylvie on her knees, her butt way high up, mouthing the words, "Back in the saddle again," patting her own ass, moving it all around and looking right at Richard.

By the time the song finished the whole place was up and cheering, clapping, chanting, "Richard, Richard, Richard," he was so fucking red in the face, but he just walked up on the stage, picked Sylvie up, took her into the dressing room and they fucked right there.

And fuck if it wasn't great.

They were finished and Richard said, "I guess I should listen to you," and Sylvie said, yeah, you should. It started as a joke but it worked.

So then, driving home from her funeral Richard could hear her saying, "You know what you want to do," and that's when he made his move, finished the takeover of Toronto and got rid of Mon Oncle. He thought maybe it was because he saw the guy pissing away everything they'd built, shit, they laid their fucking lives on the line every day for twenty years, they took on all comers, they made themselves into a coast-to-coast operation no one could touch, and Mon Oncle was going to get them all busted over teenage girls, shit. Richard thought he might just take off, do what he and Sylvie had been talking about but he couldn't do it without her.

For a while he didn't think he could do anything without her, so taking over this whole thing, becoming number one, that kept him going. And now, he felt like he could go, felt like he'd finished with this.

And, as he was thinking that, he finished with this Stacy and she stayed on him till he was completely finished. Still never used her hands, but didn't lose a drop. Richard could see where it was a specialty, maybe she learned to do it like that while her hands were tied, some guys liked that, but he could never get into it.

Now she was going into the bathroom and the phone beeped and she said, "That's him."

Richard said, buzz him in, and stood up, pulling up his pants.

Stacy stood there naked, like a deer in the fucking headlights, saying "I better get dressed," and Richard saying, it doesn't matter, just let him in. They walked into the living room, she picked up the phone, pretended to be thrilled he was here so fast and buzzed him in.

Richard stood beside the door and Stacy opened it, backing in, saying, I'm so glad you could make it.

Big Pete said, "Yeah, now that's the way to open the fucking door," and Stacy started to tell him how much she missed him, how much she wanted him and Richard stepped up behind him, wrapped the dog leash around his throat and pulled.

Stacy yelled and Richard said, "Shut the fuck up," and pulled and pulled. Big Pete struggled, thrashed around for a few minutes but Richard never let go until he was dead and then he lowered him to the ground.

"Fuck he's heavy."

Stacy was saying, oh my God, oh my God, oh my God and turning in little circles like a poodle that was going to piss on the carpet. Then she stopped and looked at Richard and said, "Holy fuck, you're going to blame this on me."

"As if anyone would believe you could do this."

She turned and ran.

Richard thought she'd run back into the apartment, lock herself in the bathroom, some shit like that, but she ran past him and out the door, into the hall.

He started after her, but as he stepped over Big Pete the

guy groaned, tried to grab his ankle. Didn't look like he'd get up, but it slowed Richard down, and when he got to the hall Stacy was gone and a couple of women were getting off the elevator, coming towards him. He looked at the door and realized if it closed it'd lock and he wouldn't be able to get back in, so he went inside.

Looking at Big Pete he said, "You stubborn mother-fucker," and dropped onto him, driving his knee into the guy's back. He got hold of the leash again and really finished Pete off.

Then, finally leaving the apartment, Richard was thinking, okay another fucking loose end. She had to be in the building somewhere, she couldn't have run naked into the fucking street. Must have a friend, probably another hooker. Maybe it wouldn't even matter, what was she going to do, go to the cops? Didn't matter.

276

Richard got to the parking lot behind the building, by then thinking okay, this Stacy doesn't matter, the point is Big Pete was shut up and that would calm everybody down, at least long enough for Richard to get out of town, get to Costa Rica and meet with Moctezuma. He unlocked the door, got in his Volvo, thinking maybe it was a nice enough day, take the top down, and he saw the door open on a Mercedes, silver SUV ML370, Michigan plates, a black guy getting out, coming towards him, looking familiar . . .

CHAPTER ELEVEN

PRICE AND MCKEON WERE DRIVING back into the city from Mississauga when Price got the call from Loewen, said to meet at a condo at Yonge and Sheppard so Price took the 427 north to the 401 and across to Yonge.

McKeon was saying that it was a good thing to sit the Lowrie kids down and tell them their parents didn't do anything wrong, they were innocent victims, caught in the crossfire of an underworld war and Price said, "One fucked-up war."

"Still," McKeon said. "Those kids have a ton of shit to deal with, it's good to get this part done." She was feeling a little better, feeling like a real detective for a change. When she'd figured out that Big Pete Zichello was the real target and called Price, he'd said, "You think that'll hold up in court," and she'd said, no, but it's good enough to tell the kids, the rest of the family, and he agreed with that. So she wrote up her notes and went home to her own family. Two days now without a drink, but it was supposed to be one at a time so that's all she thought about.

Getting off the elevator in the condo building Price said, "Holy shit," looking at all the cops and tech guys, and McKeon thought, yeah, this must be something.

Loewen was standing just inside the door and he said, "Hey," and looked at McKeon.

She said, what, and Loewen said, "It's fucked up."

"What is it?"

"Barb Roxon."

McKeon said, yeah, what, and looked at Price. They'd talked about how she was there when the car dealer died and she was the one who had the surveillance stuff on Big Pete — but she didn't say who he was meeting with. McKeon had called her, tried to talk to her but just kept leaving messages.

Loewen was saying, "We moved on the bikers this morning," and Price said he saw it on TV, they used a battering ram to bust a hole in the front wall of the clubhouse.

"Brought ETF guys from all over the province."

McKeon said, "Barb was on that?" They'd walked through the condo's small living room and down a hall.

Loewen stopped by the door and said, "Not really, she was on the Italians, but it's all getting mixed up now."

Price said, "How come the only multiculturalism that works in this city is the criminal kind?"

"They've got no politicians, don't have to have committee meetings."

"Guy doesn't agree with the policies, they deal with him."

McKeon looked through the door to the bedroom and said, "Shit."

Barb Roxon was on the bed, dressed in jeans and a T-shirt, covered in blood, half her head splattered on the wall behind her, gun in her hand.

Loewen said, "She left a note on her computer. Well, a lot of notes, files, all kinds of shit. Did you know what she went through after Mike died?"

McKeon was still staring at the corpse, not enough of her face left to really tell if she'd put on makeup, and said, "I didn't really know her."

Loewen said, neither did I, really. "We were on the task force together, the joint forces, but she spent a lot of time with Monette, that Mountie they brought in to run it. Shit, it looks like there's a lot in her notes about him. Anyway, she was pretty depressed, no family." He looked at McKeon and said, "She thought you were getting close."

"What?"

"That car salesman, it's all over her notes. Looks like he came to her as an informant, had stuff on the Italians and the bikers, worked for both of them, or he was trying to switch sides or something. Anyway, it looked like he was ready to step up, give us all kinds names and dates and numbers, wear a wire all over town, even testify."

Price said, "Holy shit," and Loewen said, yeah, I know.

McKeon said, "Been looking a long time for someone like that."

"So Roxon says she got the order from Monette to get rid of him, she wrote it down, I guess." He motioned to the laptop beside her on the bed. "She emailed it to the whole task force this morning, it's how come we're here."

McKeon said, "Fuck."

"Monette's the guy they brought in to fix the thing up," Price said, "after the last fuck-up."

"Looks like he came in dirty."

"Guess we better look pretty close at who takes over next."

Loewen said, "You know how far this sets us back?"

"At least the raid this morning will take most of the headlines."

They walked back down the hall to the condo's small living room, Price saying, "Where's Wong?" Wong was the deputy chief of police.

"The PR department's coming in, they've got a lot of shit to spin."

"Again."

Loewen shrugged. "Life in the big city."

Levine came in the condo then, saying, "The big bad city." He saw McKeon and said, "I'm sorry, Maureen," and she said, yeah.

O'Brien came in behind Levine and said, "What a cluster fuck."

Levine said to Price, "Looks like your women's intuition was right, Andre, that hooker in the Beetle down at Cherry Beach? Looks like Big Pete Zichello killed her."

"And," O'Brien said, "it looks like her friend, Stacy somebody, killed *him*."

"And," Levine said, "get this. Then she killed the king of the Saints, Richard Tremblay."

Loewen said, "What the fuck?"

"I know, what a day," Levine said. "I'm just glad I'm not on the task force, have to straighten out this shit."

Loewen said, thanks, buddy, and Levine said, "Don't mention it."

McKeon was looking around the condo, barely a thousand square feet in an anonymous building in the middle of nowhere, and thinking she was so glad she wasn't going to end up like this. She looked at Price and said, "Come on, we should go," and he was out the door, saying, see you all later.

They drove back to 40 College mostly quiet. In the parking lot McKeon got into her car and Price asked if she was driving straight home and she said, yes, Andre, and he said, will you get pissed off if I follow, and she said, "If you're as bad at it now as you were in vice," but he did anyway, all the way to East York.

She parked in her driveway and waved as Price drove on, then walked into the house, the two-bedroom starter she and MoGib were going to fix up and sell so they could move into Riverdale and have another baby.

One day at a time, it seemed a long way off.

* * *

Get watched Sunitha put books into a cardboard box she got at the liquor store and he said, "You proud of your heritage."

She said, "I haven't read this yet, that's all." *Brick Lane*, the writer's name something Ali. Sunitha said, "How many boxes you say I could bring?" Tossing in more books, *The Kite Runner*, *Black Bird* by a guy with a French name but the book was English.

"A couple." There were two brand-new backpacks bought that morning at the Mountain Equipment Co-op on King sitting by the door, stuffed with Sunitha's clothes. "We can meet up with Tommy, put some in his truck."

"You really think we'll get hassled at the border? You have Michigan plates, you're an American citizen, right, you're not an immigrant?"

Get said, yeah, he was a citizen, but, "My family didn't come through Ellis Island, we didn't get welcomed to the country, you know? Borders make me nervous."

Sunitha walked into the kitchen, one open room really,

kitchen and living room, saying, "I have a Canadian pass-
port, that be okay?"

Get was sitting on the couch. He said, "Maybe we
should say we're both American."

"Or maybe," she said, coming back to the living room,
"I could hide under the bed in Tommy's sleeper." She was
enjoying it, her dream come true. "I'm not taking anything
else, I don't need this crap. I can just buy new, right?"

"Live in the hotel."

"What a great idea. Spend the rest of my life living in
the hotel, being served. Thailand has great hotels."

"I've heard," Get said. "But I've never been."

Sunitha packed up all the stuff in her bathroom, practically filled one of the backpacks with shit, Get didn't
know what most of it was. She showed him the strip of
maybe five condoms she had left, said maybe they should
get some more before they hit the road, maybe go to the
Condom Shack on Queen, get the rainbow ones, ribbed,
maybe the flavoured ones.

Get said, "I bet they have all kinds in Thailand," thinking it was fun to watch her, her plan coming together. She'd
been right about it, millions of dollars worth of untraceable
gold bars, her old friend Russell Akbarali running the
MoneyChangers could take it off her hands, turn it into
cash — digital cash, he said, put it in the bank anywhere in
the world. Get watched her close up the backpacks and he
wondered when she planned to dump him. They were
going to drive out to Hamilton, steal the gold off the boat
and drive back to Toronto, give it to Russell and then drive
down the 401 to Detroit. Sunitha had no problem at all,
she said, with Get spending a couple of days doing business, getting them new IDs, and then they were going to
drive to Chicago, fly to L.A. and then to Thailand.

He had a feeling, once the gold went to Russell, that her plans wouldn't include him anymore. Too bad, he was thinking, he liked her, might even like to read some of the books she packed, talk to her about them . . .

She came over and sat on him, straddled his legs and looked him right the eyes and said, "This is so fucking great."

"You don't think you'll get bored?"

"What?"

"Sitting on a beach."

"Not for years."

"What then?"

She was moving a little on him, grinding into his lap, smiling as his dick got hard, saying, "Get you some little blue pills."

"Maybe with you, I won't even need them."

"Maybe not." She kissed him on the mouth, licking his lips, sucking them, saying, "We have time?" and Get said, sure, we the boss now, and they did it right there on the couch.

After, in the shower together, Get was thinking maybe she wasn't planning to dump him after all and then he thought, shit man, get that out of your head.

But he didn't think he'd ever meet another woman like her.

Later, driving out of Toronto on the Gardiner, heading towards Hamilton and Niagara Falls, her tiny bare feet up on the dash of Get's Mercedes, Sunitha told him, you go the other way it's five hundred kilometres to Montreal, "Call it the Hindi 500, so many going back and forth."

Get said, "You not going to miss this place?"

She was looking in the rear-view and said, "Are you kidding? I'm so glad I'm never going to see that big concrete dick again."

283

Get said he thought everybody in Toronto was proud of that tower and Sunitha said, yeah, we love it.

Then they were on the QEW, another big divided expressway, and he asked her if she ever thought about having kids and she said, never. But then she said, "Never when I was there, you know, fucked up in Canada. Why, you?"

The way she was looking at him, he kept looking back, almost hit the Hyundai he was coming up behind before he changed lanes. He couldn't tell if she was just stringing him along, talk about anything he wanted till she got that gold, but he said, "You know, someday maybe."

"Live in the expat community in Thailand."

"What if I wanted to come back to America."

"Get back in business?" She was turned sideways now, looking right at him.

"Maybe not my old business."

"Go legit?"

He said, yeah, knowing how many times he'd heard that bullshit in his life, heard his mom say to the girls working for her, yeah honey, you go legit, you work for ten bucks an hour, ride the bus two hours a day, wear the same pair of shoes everywhere, you like that a lot more than this.

Sunitha said, it can be done, though. "Takes one, maybe two generations."

Get said, "That's all?"

She said, "Sure. It's what we're doing in Canada, why my father dragged us here, it's what Russell's doing, it's the history here."

They were out of downtown, now they were passing houses and malls. Get said, "What do you mean?"

"Look, back in the Depression, you had prohibition, right, no alcohol?"

284

Get said, not legal alcohol, no.

"Right. Well, Canada didn't have prohibition, at least not the whole country and not for as long. Booze was still legal all over the place, they could make as much whiskey and gin and beer as they wanted, so they did, and shipped it all down to you."

"Just like," Get said, "the dope they shipping now. It's practically legal here."

"Yeah, not quite, they just don't have the billion dollars for the war on drugs you have."

"Not enough guys finding a way to skim off that war, had to find a new one."

"Yeah well, whatever. What I'm saying, the smugglers, the bootleggers in Canada, they all made tons of money. And when prohibition ended in the U.S. they already had all the distilleries and breweries up and running, they were legit. Now they have hospitals named after them, their sons and sons of sons run the biggest companies in the world."

Get said, right, "And you think that'll happen with dope, too? It'll get all legalized and J.T. and the boys already have grow ops set up all over?"

"No, I think when it gets legal the tobacco companies will run that show, or maybe it'll never get legal, I don't know, but what I do know, it doesn't matter where you get your money, once it gets into the system, once it gets laundered, like they say, it's nice and clean and no one asks you where it came from."

Get knew that was true, almost. The amount of shit he bought, his Mercedes, his clothes, three-thousand-dollar watch, everything he ever laid down cash for, not once did anybody ever ask him where he got the money. But it was always hanging out there as a possibility, somebody wanted to, they could trip him up. He said, "Never?"

"Well, you know," Sunitha said, "they got Al Capone for tax evasion, so you have to be careful."

"Find the right business."

"Yeah. Russell's already practically out," Sunitha said. "You saw, his legit businesses are making money, the cheque cashing, the money exchange, the restaurant, shit, I never thought he'd make a dime with a restaurant."

Get said, "He's talking about franchising."

"Last year I would've said he was crazy, franchising fast food, Indian-style food, Kentucky fucking tandoori chicken, all over the country? But now I don't know."

"He's got a better name, I forget what it is. Look at the Chinese, calling the fucking thing Ho Lee Chow. Back in the day Italian food must have been wild and crazy, now, I never seen a city with so many pizza places."

Sunitha took a cigarette out of her pack and said, "So, it's possible, you want to do that. What's your legit business going to be?"

And Get thought, yeah, no one he knew ever thought that far ahead, everybody just trying to make it through the day alive, through the week. You get a good couple years, anything else is gravy, living on borrowed time, waiting on some more desperate punk-ass kid looking to make his fortune or some cop get so lucky he actually picks you up.

Then he looked at Sunitha, cracking the window an inch and blowing out smoke, and he thought, the fuck am I doing? Talking to this chick like it might really happen, but thinking, shit she's getting to me.

He said, "Maybe books," and she said, what?

"My mom, she thought she'd write a book. You ever heard of Vickie Stringer? Urban lit?"

"Like chick lit?"

"Lot of chicks, but not just," Get said. "Stringer, she's also from Detroit, Eastside, Miller Middle School, Cass Tech and all, but she ended up in Ohio running whores and dope, got busted, went to prison."

Sunitha took a drag on the smoke and let it out slow, saying, prison, shit.

"Yeah, and while she's there she writes a book. I don't know, maybe she saw somebody on Oprah, you know?"

"All that, look how much I've been fucked over," Sunitha said. "What a survivor I am."

Get said, yeah, thinking again how much he liked this Sunitha. Shit, he could talk to her, she was straight up, her own life, the world, she saw it for what it was. He said, "But nobody would publish it, big surprise. But she gets out of jail, publishes it herself. Starts her own publishing company. And she sells it same way she sold dope, on the street, nail shops, hair salons, sells thousands of copies to all the chicks."

"Right," Sunitha said, "because no one else is writing books that deal with the black urban female situation."

Get laughed, said, yeah. "At least, not up front, honest." He looked at Sunitha, watched her smoke, not say anything, like she was thinking about it, understanding it. "So, you know where it's going, she writes another book, sells that, then she starts getting books from other people — usually chicks in prison, not always. My mom always said she was going to write one, all her experiences, shit," he shook his head, "she's never finished reading one."

"That doesn't stop everyone," Sunitha said. "Sometimes, people read too many, make all their stories about other books."

Get said, yeah, and he could see her thinking about that. He thought she'd probably tried to write something, she might even try again, and he thought it might be cool, he'd like to see what she come up with. He thought about asking her, but said, "So now it's a movement, all the publishers getting in on it. The new Motown, Detroit strikes again."

"So that's it," Sunitha said, looking at him, "you want to be a publisher?"

He thought, shit, he might publish her book, but then he had to get that out of his head.

They'd passed the turnoff for Niagara Falls, kept on the way to Hamilton, but now they passed the exit and kept going.

Sunitha said, "Aren't we supposed to be over there," and Get said, yeah, that was the plan.

"But," he said, "that's not going to work."

She said, no? Looking right at him, sitting up in the seat, taking her feet off the dash, getting as far away from him as she could in a car going seventy-five miles an hour. "What's the new plan?"

He looked at her, knowing he'd never meet another woman like her.

● ● ●

J.T.'s head was pounding, his eyeballs hurt. He was standing in the sun by the pool house watching the party, so hungover, but damn he was satisfied. He'd been making fun of it in his head, this bullshit vote, this Boy Scout ceremony making him a full patch, but when it happened, motherfucker, it felt good. All the big boys there, Nugs, Danny Mac, Ozzie, Spaz, OJ — J.T. thinking when he walked in, the gang's all here, and smiling, yeah, the gang. He was worried he'd laugh, wouldn't be able to take it seriously, or start to think it didn't mean shit, like the initiation in the Army, but when it started — it was real.

Now, at the barbecue in OJ's backyard — back forty they called it because it was a few acres in an old farming town west of Toronto called Norval, the whole area getting paved over for housing developments and big-box stores spreading out from Georgetown and Brampton — J.T. felt good. Driving in he'd thought it was funny, a brand-new Jehovah's Witness Kingdom Hall on one side and a huge mosque on the other, OJ telling everybody, "The farmer who sold me the property could live with my blackness, once he found out I wasn't Catholic."

OJ's wife, Tanya, laughed and said, "There so many people moving in for these old-timers to be scared of, we starting to look good."

J.T. was thinking, yeah, we're looking good.

The prospects, Boner and Mitch and a whole bunch J.T. didn't know, were cooking thick steaks on barbecues that were oil drums cut in half, filled with charcoal, their girlfriends serving drinks and cleaning up as they went.

Everybody having a good time.

Gayle came up to J.T. and asked him if he wanted any aspirins and he said no, said the sangria was doing the trick.

She looked around the yard, the big fence, the in-ground pool, kids going off the diving board and down the twisting slide, must have been fifty people at least, and she said to J.T., "You wear your hoods, they all spank you?"

"I'm not going to be able to sit down for a week."

"Sacrificed some chickens?"

"Blood everywhere."

"Seriously, they really piss all over your colours?" His *originals* they called them, his leather jacket, the sleeves torn off and the patch on the back — most of the patch, he wouldn't get the bottom rocker, the word "Saints," for another year.

J.T. said, "You're dying to know what really happens, aren't you?"

"Right, like I can't imagine."

"No," J.T. said, "you can't," winking at her and watching her shake her head and smirk. Really though, he knew she could imagine what it meant, what stepping up to this level was all about. These guys, they say they have your back, they really do. Hell, he'd killed a lot more guys in Afghan, dozens of them, mowing them down, tossing grenades into caves, burying them alive, but it wasn't the same, nobody gave a shit. These guys, looking around at the barbecue, Spaz standing in the pool with his daughter on his shoulders, chasing his son, his wife Sherry blasting him with a water pistol from the diving board, J.T. knew it was more than talk here. Once you're in you're in. This is for life.

"It's different now," Gayle said. "For us."

J.T. was looking at her and she didn't seem unhappy, seemed like she was going with it just fine. She smiled at him and then looked away and he followed her look, seeing Nugs standing by the barbecues, beer in his hand, laughing at something Danny Mac was saying. J.T. said, "It's different for everybody."

Then Gayle winked at him and said, "We'll get used to it," and walked back to the chairs beside the pool, the wives sunning themselves.

J.T. saw a hangaround walk by and said, hey kid, "What am I supposed to do with this empty glass?" and the kid looked around, like he was looking for a garbage can or something and then looked back, quick, and said, "Sorry, you want another one?" and J.T. said, that'd be good, yeah, and started walking towards the barbecue, see if the kid could find him.

Nugs was saying, it was going to be a great run, "Haven't been on a run in too long."

"We go up through Ottawa?"

Danny Mac said, no, "We'll go through Montreal," and J.T. was picturing it, a thousand Harleys roaring through the city, right down Ste. Catherine Street, going on up to Mont-Tremblant, taking over the whole resort, guys from across the country. Hell, they'd be coming in from New York, California, all over the States, from England, Sweden, Germany, everybody coming to see how these fucking Canadians took over the whole thing.

Nugs said it would probably be the last one, "Then we put away the bikes and leathers, it's a new era."

Danny said, yeah, our era.

Nugs said to J.T., "Too bad we couldn't have your party at the clubhouse, woulda been a nice send-off for the place."

"You see that shit on TV?" OJ was laughing.

"Fucking cops looking like they won something, carrying that shit out like it was the Stanley fucking Cup."

J.T. said, yeah, well, too bad, but it was great anyway. They'd spent a little time moving out their important stuff, all the computers and most of the guns and money, left just enough to make it look like something, Nugs saying that was the deal he'd made and no one complaining.

Cops, the whole fucking task force, came in at dawn, used a battering ram to bust out the bricks of the front wall, right beside the steel door, J.T. said they called it a mousehole in the army. Don't want to go in through the door, everybody knows where the door is, hit a wall, take them by surprise.

Danny Mac said, "Hey Boner, when they busted that wall and came in, what did you say?"

Boner flipped a steak and looked up, getting ready to tell the story again, like the fiftieth time that day. "Fucking cops, they bust open the wall, come crawling in like fucking rats, wearing that armour, shit. I wait till they stand up, look around, and I say to them, hey asshole, the doorbell's working, you know."

And for the fiftieth time that day he got a laugh.

Nugs said, "No, they did good, they got the press out, that's what we wanted." Nugs's plan. They'd bought the rest of the buildings on the block — an abandoned old three-storey hotel, half a dozen broken-down houses and an auto-parts store, and they were going to redevelop the whole thing — put up a twenty-five-storey condo building. When they'd first started talking about it the real estate agent, some chick Nugs was seeing, Roxanne, said the main thing holding the neighbourhood back was its image as biker territory. Nugs said she'd told him people would need to believe that they were completely gone and a press release just wouldn't do it, so he and Danny Mac came up with this idea of a police raid, get it all over the TV, newspapers, everywhere. Look like the whole place was being cleaned up, make it a lot easier to sell their condos.

OJ'd said, "We calling it Hog Heaven?"

They were going to have to buy the building back at auction, the cops' Proceeds of Crime division wanting to get it on the market right away, but like Roxanne said, who's going to bid against you, you own the whole block.

Boner said, "Rare's ready," and Danny Mac said,

292

that's me, baby, "I want that fucking cow to scream when I cut into it."

Nugs said to J.T., "The steaks are a gift from Angelo Colucci."

J.T. said, cool.

Nugs said, truth is, "I don't really give a shit which wop we deal with. Now that the Frog and the fat guy are out of the picture, Angelo knows the deal's with us, that's all that matters."

J.T. said, "Good. It's a good deal. We get everything we want."

Nugs said, yeah, we do, and J.T. was thinking it looked good on Nugs.

Then OJ said, so, "J.T., what the fuck's up with you and women?" and J.T. froze, stood like there like a fucking statue looking at Nugs and Danny Mac and OJ looking back at him, thinking, this it? This where they tell him they know about him and Gayle, and take him further into the back forty?

"She was always hot," Nugs said, "but she had some attitude. Thought she was going to fuck off with our gold," and they all laughed.

J.T. said, "Shit," laughing to himself, but feeling a rush. "Yeah, some attitude." J.T. saying Sergeant McGetty's taking care of her, never be seen again.

OJ said, good. "Too bad he couldn't stick around one more day, party with us."

"Yeah, too bad," J.T. said. "Had to get back to the motor city. He's got some shit to work out, stuff with his mom."

Nugs said, "Family."

The hangaround came up with J.T.'s sangria saying he didn't know where he'd gone, had to look all over for him

293

and J.T. said, well, "You're here now, that's good," taking the glass and thinking it was true, they get so many guys want to join, they can just keep getting bigger. Now he was a full patch, like he told Get, it was like being a made guy, he didn't need to get his hands dirty anymore, he just collected, made decisions.

He said to Nugs, "Yeah. Family."

• • •

Nothing but trucks in line at customs on the Ambassador Bridge, Get thinking again how much faster it would have been if he'd taken the tunnel.

Sunitha said, "You know it would have worked."

And again he said, "I know."

He could see the Detroit skyline on the other side of the river, the Ren Centre so much taller than everything else.

She said, "You sure about this?"

Get looked at Sunitha and thought the only thing he was sure of, he wanted to spend more time with her. They were driving past Hamilton, plan was, he was supposed to get rid of her, pull into the woods somewhere and do it, but instead he pulled up at the McDonald's outside of Woodstock and his cousin Tommy said, "This the love of your life?"

Maybe.

And she was all right about it, she called him some names, sure, but she knew the score. Get told her J.T. and the boys would even calm down about it, think it was a joke someday. They could go down to Costa Rica, check out this resort Richard had, she could get some time on the beach like she wanted. Get said to her, "But you could never live in some third world country, people packed in so tight, always looking over your shoulder."

Now it was their turn at customs and the black woman, looked to be in her fifties, smiled at Get and asked him what was his citizenship. He opened his wallet, his driver's licence on one side, his U.S. Army ID card on the other, and said, "I'm about five miles from where I was born."

The woman looked across to Sunitha, sitting up now, shoes on, and said, "Did you purchase anything on this trip?"

"Spent all our money in restaurants," Sunitha said. "Toronto's expensive."

The woman said, it can be, you don't know where to shop. "You didn't buy anything at the discount mall, they have Jones New York, and Sunitha said what discount mall?

Get said, "Just the other side of Windsor there, we passed it," and Sunitha said, "I didn't see that," and the customs lady laughed, said to Get, "Welcome home, sergeant, hope you had a good trip," winked and waved him through.

Get thought, yeah, pretty good.